PANDEMIC

PANDEMIC

Yvonne Ventresca

Sky Pony Press
New York

First Edition

This is a work of fiction. Names, characters, places, and incidents are
from the author's imagination or used fictitiously.

Sky Pony Press books may be purchased in bulk at special discounts for
sales promotion, corporate gifts, fund-raising, or educational purposes.
Special editions can also be created to specifications. For details, contact the Special Sales Department, Sky Pony Press, 307 West 36th Street,
11th Floor, New York, NY 10018 or info@skyhorsepublishing.com.

Sky Pony® is a registered trademark of Skyhorse Publishing, Inc.®, a
Delaware corporation.

Visit our website at www.skyponypress.com.

10 9 8 7 6 5 4 3 2 1

Library of Congress Cataloging-in-Publication Data

Ventresca, Yvonne.
  Pandemic / Yvonne Ventresca. -- First edition.
     pages cm
  Summary: "Lil is left home alone when a deadly pandemic hits her
small town in New Jersey. Will Lil survive the flu and brave her darkest
fears?"-- Provided by publisher.
  Includes bibliographical references.
  ISBN 978-1-62873-609-0 (hardback)
  [1. Epidemics--Fiction. 2. Influenza--Fiction. 3. Sexual abuse--Fiction.] I.
Title.
  PZ7.V564Pan 2014
  [Fic]--dc23
                                    2013037354

Printed in the United States of America

To my encouraging mother and father,
and to my loving husband and children.

PANDEMIC

CHAPTER 1

*As with many serious contagious illnesses, it wasn't
immediately apparent what we were dealing with.*
—Blue Flu interview, anonymous US government official

I stood on the smoking corner behind school reveling in my aloneness. Not many smokers had the same schedule, which made the corner the perfect place for solitude. We always stayed a foot off the high school property, near the big oak tree, and since we were allowed to leave during last period study hall, we weren't technically breaking any rules.

As if rules mattered.

"Hey, got a light?" Jay Martinez asked, interrupting the quiet. In the fall, he'd moved from Arizona to live with his aunt down the block from my house.

I handed him my half-smoked cigarette. Cupping the burning ember, he used it to light his own. He didn't fit in with the other smokers, but then neither did I. My black clothes, basic ponytail, and minimal makeup placed me in my own category. Maybe Lazy Goth. But the nice thing about smokers was that they didn't exclude anyone.

"Thanks." Jay passed my cigarette back to me. "Is New Jersey always this cold in April?"

Being the new guy at school made Jay the flavor of the month with the other sophomore girls. They craved him in a nauseating kind of way. He was dark, tall, and lanky, and tended to over-communicate. Totally not my type. Now he ruined my aloneness with weather chatter. I shrugged so he'd get the idea that I wasn't in a talking mood.

"Ethan was hoping to run into you," he said.

Another shrug. I'd managed to avoid my ex for months. No reason to change the pattern now.

"So . . . do you have Robertson for bio?" he asked.

I nodded. Jay definitely wasn't taking the hint.

"What are you doing your report on?"

"Emerging diseases," I said, finally giving up on staying silent.

"Cheerful stuff."

The school projects I chose did favor the dark this semester. American history report? The decision to drop the bomb. English book talk? A collection of Edgar Allan Poe's stories. Thematically, Ebola hemorrhagic fever fit right in.

"What are you writing about?" I flicked the accumulated ashes. "Lung cancer?"

He smiled. "The biology of taste. I write restaurant reviews on my blog and that was the closest topic I could think of. Do you like eating at restaurants?"

Leaning slightly forward, he held eye contact a little too long for me. Was he flirting? Nervous, I pulled my sweater tighter around me and crossed my arms. A flirtatious guy was the absolute last thing I needed in my life. No boyfriends, no coy conversations for me. Not anymore.

Jay's unanswered question stayed suspended in the air along with the smoke ring I blew.

"Dinner? I don't get out much," I said, stubbing my cigarette into a sand-filled can another smoker had left behind. "I have to go."

"See you around."

Maybe I read too much into the conversation, but his eyes seemed to question: You need to leave so soon?

It was all I could do to keep myself from breaking into a run.

ᴗ

I entered our house through the garage, surprised to see my mother's Hybrid parked inside. She wasn't usually home this early on a Thursday.

I spritzed perfume to cover the cigarette smell and popped a mint into my mouth for good measure.

In the kitchen, I washed my hands before grabbing a glass. Shutting the cabinet quietly, I hoped Mom wouldn't notice. She was in her bedroom directly above me, noisily opening and closing drawers.

"Lily, is that you?" she called.

Damn. "Yeah."

She came down the stairs, soft little steps combined with the jingle of jewelry. "How was your day?"

"It wasn't bad." I grabbed the organic milk from the fridge. "You're home early."

"I'm packing for Hong Kong. There are some new developments in the lead poisoning fiasco, so GREEN needs to have a presence there."

Mom worked for the Great Reclaiming of Everyone's Earth Now—GREEN—an environmental watchdog group.

"When do you leave?"

"Tomorrow morning," she said. "You can invite Megs to stay over while I'm gone. Or Kayla. We haven't seen her lately."

Mom and Dad were so clueless. I hadn't spoken to Kayla in months, since our big fight.

"I'll be fine alone." I poured the milk and then grabbed some oatmeal raisin cookies, ready to hole up in my room until any lingering smoke faded from my clothes.

I snacked in bed while trying to read my history homework. The last social studies test hadn't gone well, which wasn't exactly a surprise. It should have been English that I hated, with the foreshadowing, antagonists, and metaphors that Mr. B had taught us. But somehow my brain couldn't process history: the past, the many policies, and all the political maneuvering. My eyes glazed over in twenty seconds as I attempted to read about the Marshall Plan.

After my failed attempts to finish the chapter, I took a break from history to read an article about how people in the Middle Ages carried herbs in their pockets and wore sachets around their necks to try to prevent illness. The new English teacher had approved my poetry analysis topic, an investigation into whether the nursery rhyme "Ring Around the Rosy" was really written about the bubonic plague. It was way more fascinating than the Cold War.

My phone pinged with a text.

> Megs: R u doing hw?
> Me: No, I'm texting u.
> Megs: Ha! Pls open ur history notes. U know u need 2.

Me: They r open.
Megs: U can't fool me. Focus!

I was tempted to lie, but Megs knew me too well. And she was right. It was only a matter of time before my parents checked the online grade book and then I was screwed. Most of my As had dropped to Bs and US history had plummeted to a D. The lower grades would be a red flag for Mom and Dad, and we'd probably spend hours analyzing what Mom would label "the unhealthy drop in my academic performance" before they confined me to the house forever.

Me: OK. I'll study.
Megs: Promise?
Me: Ur annoying but yes.
Megs: Good! If u get grounded my life will b
          ovr. TTYL.

I kept my word, reading through my notes until something crashed in the hallway, followed by Mom's screech.

Oh no. I jumped out of bed. The crashing sound could only mean one thing.

She'd discovered my emergency supplies.

On my way down the hall, I paused to rescue some rolling cans of black beans. Sure enough, my mother stood in front of the closet, an avalanche of nonperishable food at her feet. I should have known she'd need her suitcase. I could have offered to be helpful, gotten it out for her, so she wouldn't have seen. But now—

"What in the world is all this?" she asked. "Is your father storing extra food in here?"

It would be convenient to blame Dad. Since he worked as the senior editor for *Infectious Diseases* magazine, I could probably convince her that he'd have at least the minimum emergency provisions suggested by the Red Cross stashed in the house. But as much as I'd mastered small lies lately, the skill to tell a big one was as elusive as scientists' cure for the common cold.

Mom took one look at my face and knew the truth. Her curious expression hardened into her own special brand of parental worry.

"I can explain," I said, hoping to head off the tirade.

She pointed at the large stockpile of food, feminine products, and, my personal favorite, the emergency hand crank radio that could also serve as a phone charger. "Hurricane season is over."

"We should always be ready for a crisis," I said. "It doesn't matter what time of year it is. Even the government says so."

"Right. Have you spoken to Dr. Gwen about this?" She waved her hand at "this," diminishing my months of saving, planning, purchasing. "When you see her next time maybe we should check about you going more frequently. Maybe—"

"No, no. She said after . . . well, she said this is normal."

Mom gave me the look, the one that zings into your soul and drags the truth out.

"Well, Dr. Gwen didn't call it normal, exactly," I said, rebuilding a tower of cans on the floor of the closet. "After emotional stress, there are all kinds of coping mechanisms, things people do to feel secure. She said 'behaviors which instill an increased sense of safety' are OK, or some crap like that."

"Lily." My mother closed her eyes and did some secret Mom-trick to calm herself. When she opened them again only the slightest hint of worry remained on her face. "I'm trying to empathize."

I glanced at her suitcase. "Getting ready for your trip?"

"Yes, but don't change the subject. Does Dad know about your stockpiling?"

I rolled my eyes. "It's basic stuff, nothing extreme," I said, which was my way of hedging until I could tell him.

She surveyed the shelves, gesturing at the beans, the chicken broth, the boxed pasta. "You're planning on surviving on chili and linguini? Not cooked together, I hope."

I smiled, guessing that meant she wouldn't call

my therapist. "There's soup and canned vegetables, too."

"Well—" Her ringing cell phone interrupted us. "Hi, honey," she answered.

Dad rarely called from work, so I hoped she wouldn't have time to mention our discussion. I used the chance to escape to my room so I could push the bottled water farther under my bed.

They didn't understand. But I needed to be prepared for anything.

⌣

To avoid Mom, I stayed in my room until dinner. The kitchen smelled awful, which meant she had attempted to cook again. The best thing about her trips was that Dad and I could order takeout.

As the three of us sat around the table, I fended off the usual "How was your day?" questions. Being an only child meant serving as the sole focus of my parents' concerns. I needed to steer the conversation away from myself before Mom mentioned my emergency supplies and had me returning to frequent therapy. These were the times when having a sibling to fight with would have come in handy.

"How long will you be gone?" I asked Mom.

"Two weeks or so. I wish I didn't have to leave now. I thought we could shop for your Spring

Formal dress this weekend. Maybe something blue to bring out your eyes?"

I wasn't going to the school dance, but I nodded anyway. There was plenty of time to break that bit of news to her.

Mom rambled on about having to cancel some local meetings because of her trip. "And I'm missing the bird-banding demonstrations at the Great Swamp this weekend," she continued. "I thought we could have gone together, as a family."

The bird banding would draw lots of Mom's environmental friends and I would have gladly done extra homework to avoid it. She was famous in our town for her causes, especially pioneering the "Idling is Evil" campaign, which encouraged parents to turn off their car engines while they waited to pick up kids at school. I had to admit it was a good concept, because who wanted to breathe in smelly car fumes while you were waiting for a ride? But it still irritated me to be with her and too many earth-friendly people at the same time. They treated her like a goddess instead of my regular mom.

"Sorry you have to miss it," I said, trying to keep my voice sincere. I took a second roll from the basket and used it to push her concoction around, covering the pink roses that bordered the plate's rim. It seemed to be chicken with a mushroom and ketchup sauce, but I didn't want to hurt her feelings and ask. Mom was sensitive about her cooking. The bread was good, though. Apparently it was hard to screw up twist-and-bake crescents.

"There's plenty of food for while I'm gone," she said. "I left a tray of lasagna in the freezer. Take the plastic wrap off before you heat it. And I can save some of this chicken, too."

I caught Dad's eye. We were both thinking take-out.

"We'll be fine." He took another bite of crescent roll, turning to me. "Would you feel better sleeping at a friend's house next weekend? I'll be away, too, covering a conference in Delaware. I won't be long. One or two nights."

I had gone through a period where I always wanted someone home with me. Dr. Gwen advised my parents to ease me into being alone again. First they'd go for short walks within earshot. Next they'd stay out longer, running an errand, then seeing a movie, then spending a long evening out with friends, until I seemed more like my old self. It had taken months for me to perfect my brave front each time they left.

"I'm OK staying here. What's the conference about?"

Dad loved his job at *Infectious Diseases*. When I started pumping him for information about antibiotic resistance, the return of measles, and bioterrorism attacks, Mom had warned him to stop discussing anxiety-inducing scenarios in front of me. But he enjoyed talking about his work for the magazine, so it was easy to get him going.

"The conference focuses on emerging infections," he said. "There's been a lot of buzz about an influenza antigenic shift. Viruses change gradually all the time through antigenic drift. But a major change, a shift, creates a new flu sub-type and—"

"Keith." Mom narrowed her eyes into the "shut up and stop indulging her" look.

"Uh, pass the rolls, please," he said.

"Is this a new conference?" I asked. Meaning: Should I add the flu to my worry list, along with lead poisoning?

"No, Lily, they hold it annually, but they change the topics each year." He looked like he wanted to say more, but didn't. Instead, he changed the subject. "What time do you leave for the airport tomorrow?" he asked Mom.

While they discussed Mom's schedule, I dumped the rest of my meal in the trash, covering it with a paper towel. Then Dad mumbled something about conference prep and left the kitchen.

"What are your plans for tonight?" Mom asked.

I put my plate in the dishwasher. "Studying." Megs's mom had arranged a movie night for the two of them, so I didn't have much choice but to stay in my room and do homework.

"I need to leave early, so I won't see you in the morning," she said.

I was almost out of the room when I glanced at her, storing the uneaten food in a reusable container. Dad had been busy with work lately, and she looked so lost for a moment, so small and alone. I turned back, gave her a quick hug, then retreated.

In my room, I checked updates on my phone. I had alerts set for a variety of phrases, including "terrorist attack," "emerging infectious diseases," and "mysterious illness." The latest news was worrisome, as always. Police foiled a bombing attempt on a train in Chicago. Four people were sick from an unidentified illness in Maryland. A listeria outbreak caused the recall of cantaloupes from Guatemala. Based on today's news and our dinner conversation, I added "lead poisoning," "influenza," and "food recall" to my alert list.

I snuck downstairs after my parents were in bed. Our organic cantaloupe was from California, but I threw it out anyway. I pitched the honeydew melon, too, just in case.

Portico, New Jersey, was still safe. Snuggled under my quilt, I tried to sleep wrapped in the comfort of that illusion.

CHAPTER 2

We assumed the virus would start overseas, most likely in
Asia, and that Americans would have time to prepare.
We were wrong.
—Blue Flu interview, New Jersey public health officer

A chill settled in the air on Friday, so I detoured to the lost-and-found table near the main office before leaving school. I needed to find my favorite black sweater, the long one with flowy sleeves. I wasn't as good about details as I used to be and must have left it in one of my classrooms again. Teachers were quick to dump forgotten items onto the heap.

Principal Fryman's voice boomed over the loudspeaker. "Happy Weekend! Our food drive begins Monday, so be generous with your donations. Please lend a helping hand and bring in nonperishable food. Remember, charity begins at home, or in this case, at Portico High."

Another food drive. I shuddered, more from my

memories than the cold. Initially, I had been honored
when the most popular teacher, Mr. B, had recruited
me to help organize the donations last semester.

It had seemed natural that he'd asked me, giv-
en my involvement in community service projects
over the years. There was the coat drive, the pen pal
program I'd started between local senior citizens
and third graders, and the Penny Power collection
"where small donations add up to big results." I
had believed that as a teacher, Mr. B wanted to mo-
tivate students to help others, to create some greater
good. But like a trick-or-treater in an elaborate Hal-
loween costume, he wasn't what he seemed.

So my community service days had come to a
halt. Sighing, I mentally slammed that door and
focused on my sweater search. A pair of sneakers
and a single Ugg boot threatened to teeter off the
pile. *Wouldn't you notice if you lost your shoes?* I sift-
ed through other people's forgotten stuff, wishing I
wore rubber gloves. When someone put a hand on
my shoulder, I jumped.

"It's just me," Ethan said. In the four months
since our breakup, his bangs had grown longer, but
the easy smile and puppy dog eyes were still the
same.

"You startled me."

"Sorry. Want me to sort through the pile with
you?"

"That's OK," I said.

"You don't want me to help?" he asked, and I knew we'd shifted from finding my sweater to something deeper.

"Well, dumping me didn't help much." My tone was sassy. Sometimes pissing someone off was the quickest method to push him away.

"It was mutual, Lil."

"You said the words."

"After you stopped acting like my girlfriend."

"Whatever." I stared Ethan down, daring him to continue the argument.

"You're so different now." He softened his voice. "Remember when you'd rush to find me, to sneak a kiss between classes?"

A memory flashed of the last afternoon I'd met Ethan at his locker. "Have I told you that you look great today?" he'd said.

I'd twirled for him in my floral skirt. "Not since lunch."

A fast glance for teachers before he'd pulled me toward him. "We're all set for next weekend, right?" he'd asked when we stopped for air, his arms lingering around my waist. "I planned the best day to celebrate our year together."

"Yes," I'd said, breathless and eager.

But we broke up before I ever found out what he'd arranged. Leaning on the lost-and-found table now, I shook my head as if I could dislodge the memories and toss them away. Our relationship seemed forever ago.

Ethan swiped his bangs to the side like he always did when he was nervous. It was one of his endearing quirks. "Will you ever tell me what was really going on when we ended it?"

I avoided his eyes. I thought this conversation was over months ago, that his big question—Why?—could be ignored permanently.

"What if I could guess?" he asked.

My insides tightened into the size of a matchbook. Mr. B had taken an extended leave for "personal reasons" after I told the police what happened. News of a cheating scandal in the math department occurred around the same time. Luckily, that overshadowed the gossip about his absence from school.

Ethan couldn't possibly know the truth. Could he? Needing something to do with my hands, I folded a clean-looking sweatshirt and placed it carefully back on the table.

"I don't know what you mean," I said, grabbing a gray T-shirt to fold next.

He crossed his arms. "OK, I'll wait for you to tell me. Because one day things were great, we were on the verge of our anniversary, and then you pulled away."

"I'm sorry." I thought about how good it would

feel to be honest, to finally be free of the weight. But what would he do with the truth? Pity me? Judge me? Feed the rumor mill at school?

His friend Derek walked over, with Jay not far behind. "Yo, Eth, ready to go?" Derek asked. "We've been waiting."

Jay looked with concern from me to Ethan, then back to me again.

"Yeah, I'm done here." Ethan turned away. "Totally done."

Fighting the urge to crawl into the discarded clothes and weep, I threw the T-shirt down and headed outside. Sometimes I missed him, the innocence of how he'd hold my hand, the late night talks, the daisies in my locker. I even missed the way he would text me too much. But there was no going back now. With a cigarette between my lips, I leaned against the big oak, sweaterless and shivering.

⌒

I read another article about people getting sick in Avian, Maryland. Avian was a seaside town, only one hundred and fifty miles from Washington, DC. Officials speculated about everything from tainted water to a bioterrist attack. Dinner with Dad was the perfect time to dig for more information.

"What's going on in Avian?" I asked over our

non-organic fried chicken. "Is it something contagious?"

"It's too soon to tell." Then he changed the subject to cantaloupe, and soon we were discussing the difficulty of recalls and the importance of public health communication. I tried to steer the conversation back to the mysterious illness, but Dad wasn't going along with it.

After we cleaned the dishes, he dropped me at Megs's house. Her kitchen was cozy and smelled like butter. I felt safe there, sitting on a comfy stool at the counter next to a large pantry with etched glass doors. Megs's friendship always kept the outside world at bay for a little while.

"What's new?" Megs pushed a big plastic bowl of popcorn in my direction.

I took a handful. "Ethan talked to me after school."

She raised her eyebrows in concern. "Are you reconciling with your shallow, over-texting, but oh-so-sweet ex?" She'd never been an Ethan fan.

"No. The opposite of reconciling. He said I've changed."

"Well, he's right for once."

I gave her the stink eye.

"Don't narrow your eyes at me like that, Lil. Ever since . . . well, suddenly black is your new favorite color and—"

"It's fashionable."

She made an exasperated sound, something between a sigh and a groan. "How many classes did you cut this week?"

"I didn't—"

She stared me down.

"OK," I admitted. "Three. Well, four if you count health, which I don't." Sometimes on my way to class the urge to exercise my free will became so great that I couldn't continue down the hall, find my seat, and absorb the required information. I had to leave.

"It's a matter of time before you get caught."

Confident, I shook my head. My elaborate system of passes involved the library, the school nurse, and the main office. No teacher had unraveled my scheme yet.

"You know I'm right about changing. You skip class, quit your favorite clubs, and keep to yourself, like a hedgehog curled in a ball for protection."

"So now I'm a hedgehog? Thanks," I said, feigning annoyance.

"A pessimistic hedgehog. But come on, you know I love you."

I would have been mad at anyone else for being honest. But we'd known each other since kindergarten, back when there were three other girls with her name, until my classmate Megan Salerno had become Meg S., then my best friend Megs.

Still, I could only take so much self-analysis.

"Homework?" I asked, nodding toward her open laptop on the counter. It wasn't unusual for her to get a start on assignments, even on a Friday night.

"Actually," she said, "I met this guy online."

"Online? That's not good."

"Oh stop. We're only chatting."

"Really? So your mom's at work then."

"Yeah. She won't find out," Megs said. "I always erase my history. Besides, she's being unreasonable about the whole chat thing." Megs's mom was a town police officer. Not exactly someone who would allow her daughter to have a cyber-relationship.

I'd learned that, statistically, most sexual assault victims knew their abusers. But that didn't mean strangers were safe to hang out with, either. "You're sure this isn't dangerous?"

She nodded. "It's through Morris County, for teens only. No adults. And he seems like a nice guy. We've been asking each other questions. Favorite color, that kind of thing."

"Does he go to our school?"

"Lil, do I look like an idiot? I didn't tell him what school I go to. What if he's a stalker?"

The eye roll was so tempting. But I stopped myself midway, as if her ceiling was suddenly interesting.

"He wants to know if there are other kids in my family," she said.

"Yes, seven protective older brothers. All black belts."

"Ha ha. My lack of siblings isn't exactly classified."

Megs was an only child like me. That was what drew our mothers together years ago. One play date led to another and they became close friends at the same time Megs and I did.

"He has a brother and two sisters," she said.

"It would be pretty ironic if he did go to our school. Lots of guys we know have families like that."

"Name one," she said, calling my bluff.

"Hmm. How about Derek? Maybe you're chatting with him and don't even know it. Has your mystery guy typed 'Yo' yet?"

"No. But he asked me what my favorite picture book was. He babysits a lot. Isn't that sweet?"

Yeah right. "I heard Derek loves to babysit."

"Shut up. I need a picture book. I can only think of *Where the Wild Things Are*, but he might think it's a hint that *I'm* wild. So I need a different story."

"Hmm. There are the classics, like *Goodnight Moon* or *The Cat in the Hat*."

"OK." She typed as I munched on popcorn.

"You didn't tell him your name, right?" I peered over her shoulder at the screen.

"No. His username is 2009. I'm AG872."

"What does that stand for?"

"Nothing. It's totally random. Aren't you proud of me? I didn't use my name, my house number, my birthday—"

"I'm glad you have some common sense." I swung my feet back and forth. "Is it almost movie time?"

"Why don't you type for a few minutes? Pretend you're me. I'll get the movie queued up."

"I don't want—"

"It's fun. Ask him a question."

The whole scenario made me fidgety. I did not trust some unknown guy potentially pretending to be something he wasn't. That's exactly what Mr. B had done; he'd perfected his caring teacher act, fooling the principal, the other teachers, and, most of all, me.

I could explain my reluctance to Megs. She would listen. Or I could make a simple excuse. "I might repeat something you already asked," I said.

"Scroll back and read through our conversation. It'll be fine."

Sometimes it was easier to give in to her than to fight. I glanced at what they'd discussed. Then, with a sigh, I started typing.

> AG872: What school do u go 2?
>
> 2009: Can't give that info out. What if ur a 50 yr old man?

I couldn't help smirking. Maybe I wasn't the only worried one.

> AG872: How old r u? 52?
> 2009:　16. u?
> AG872: Same.
> 2009:　Fav class?

I hesitated for a second. But it wouldn't hurt to tell the truth.

> AG872: Bio. u?
> 2009:　Family Consumer Science. You prob call it Home Ec.
> AG872: We have FCS too. Unusual fav for a guy. Ur a guy, right?
> 2009:　Ha ha. Yes, male. And I like FCS for the desserts.

I hoped for Megs's sake that he wasn't morbidly overweight.

> 2009:　What r u doing tonite?
> AG872: Watching movie w/friend.
> 2009:　Anything good?

"Megs, what movie are we watching?" I called to her in the family room.

"Some drama about the end of the world."

"Really?" Of course Megs knew about my paranoid streak.

"Oops," she said. "I guess I didn't think that through. Want me to pick a different one?"

"No, it's OK."

> 2009: U still there?
>
> AG872: Yeah. Movie is end of world drama.
>
> 2009: So what's it like as only child?

I paused. It felt weirdly easy to tell the truth online, like telling secrets to the wind.

> AG872: Pressure. No other kids to distract them. If I do anything wrong they focus their laser-beam parenting on me.
>
> 2009: What have u done wrong?

Megs walked back into the kitchen. "Ready?"

"You came just in time. I was about to turn you into a troublemaker."

She laughed, reading the screen.

"Did I do OK?"

"Except for biology as my favorite subject. Blech." She started typing.

> AG872: Sorry. g2g. Same time tomorrow?
>
> 2009: Can't wait.

After she logged off, we huddled on her couch and watched the movie. It was horrible. Disease, death, and disaster. I peeked through my fingers, practically hyperventilating at the end.

"Sorry," Megs said. "Bad movie choice, huh?"

"I definitely need to buy more supplies."

CHAPTER 3

"Survival of the fittest" doesn't necessarily
apply during a novel flu virus.
—Blue Flu interview, emerging infectious disease specialist

On Saturday I arrived at ShopWell early for my four-hour shift stocking the shelves. After the Mr. B incident, I'd quit my job at the church office, where I had to be polite all the time. Despite the dust, lining up canned goods was quietly satisfying and gave me a much-needed employee discount.

Having extra food in the house calmed me. I'd noticed this—an odd inner peace—before Christmas, when I'd run a grocery errand for Mom and had bought more than she'd indicated on her neatly itemized list. I didn't need to eat the food; it was simply comforting enough knowing it was there.

I started small, buying a few extra items whenever I could. After several months, the cans, boxes, and bottles secretly expanded from my own closet to the one in the hallway that my parents rarely used. The extra towels, sheets, and suitcases concealed the food behind them. Unless, of course, Mom packed for an unexpected work trip.

I straightened bottles of salad dressing. Gloves helped with the ick factor, especially when the shelves were slimy. While I worked, I mentally ran through my existing supplies. Usually the trick was to buy items that fit into my backpack, like canned vegetables or boxes of dried soup mix. But today was the perfect time to buy bulky stuff with Mom away and Dad distracted with his conference. When my shift ended, I did some toilet paper shopping, grabbing as much as I could carry home.

My elderly neighbor, Reggie, was my favorite cashier. He didn't have the shortest line, but I waited in it anyway because he was always cheerful. I studied him like an exotic animal at the zoo. In the months since I first met him, I'd never once seen him grumpy.

"Hi Reggie. How are you?"

"I'm mighty fine, Miss Lil. Mighty fine. That'll be $20.32." He helped me cram the TP into Mom's reusable shopping bags, then hummed softly as I dug the cash out of my jeans pocket. The song sounded like "Zip-A-Dee Doo-Dah."

I counted my money, but only had four crumpled fives. Not enough.

"Um," I stammered, "I'll have to put one back." I started to unload a four-pack, but Reggie shook his head.

"Don't worry." He took my fives and plunked some coins into the register, humming away. "You can pay me back next time."

"Are you sure?" I didn't mind asking favors from close friends, but kindness from other people made me vaguely anxious. Before I could protest further, Reggie happily greeted the next customer.

I stepped outside into the spring warmth. The weather was perfect and I breathed in the scent of blooming flowers, relaxing the tension in my shoulders. The bright sunshine and chirping robins seemed to give the meteorological finger to Old Man Winter.

Cars crowded the parking lot. ShopWell anchored a row of stores, including a pharmacy, a coffee shop, a bookstore, and a bank. Based on the traffic, today seemed like a popular day to be out running errands. A red convertible with the top down paused to let me cross in front of it. I lifted my hand to wave thanks to the driver but froze midair.

It was Mr. B.

Emotions washed over me. Fear. Anger. Hatred. Like a giant wave, the feelings threatened to pull me under, to drown me. Since he stopped teaching, it never occurred to me that I would see him again unexpectedly. I wasn't prepared.

Did he notice me? Sunglasses hid his eyes and his expression remained the same. A guy sat in the passenger seat, a younger version of Mr. B, wearing an orange Portico Pharmacy T-shirt. He said something and Mr. B nodded, his elbow resting on the open car window. Other people would see a guy in his mid-thirties with wavy brown hair and intelligent brown eyes. Just an ordinary man casually pausing for a pedestrian.

Right.

Hurrying past, I walked on autopilot, the bags of toilet paper banging against my leg. I kept my eyes down, as if that made me invisible, as if Mr. B couldn't possibly recognize me.

I never let my mind replay the whole movie of what happened. After telling the necessary people—my parents, the police, a therapist, the principal, Megs, and Kayla—I was done talking about it. Completely finished. But sometimes images broke through, like when I flicked TV channels and caught a snippet of a horror film before quickly changing the station.

Fragments of memories flooded my brain now: Mr. B standing too close. His faint smell of aftershave and sweat. The inkling of fear before I even realized why I was afraid.

"You want to spend time with your favorite teacher, right?" he'd said, his voice husky. "So many beautiful girls. And I chose you."

Trying to focus on the present, on staying safe, I checked for his car. The convertible turned left, moving away from me. Up ahead, a guy paused to light a cigarette, his hand cupped to block the breeze. *Jay*.

I rushed to catch up to him, grateful that I wouldn't have to walk alone.

"Hey," he said, slinging a plastic bag of groceries over his shoulder. "Heading home?"

I nodded.

"Want one?" He held out the pack.

Smoking on the street corner behind school seemed different than walking brazenly through town with a cigarette in my mouth, but at the moment I didn't care. I slid one out of the pack, hoping he wouldn't notice my shaky hands.

"Here," he said, lighting it for me.

I inhaled deeply.

"Big plans for the weekend?" he asked.

While we smoked and walked, I glanced around discreetly, but didn't see Mr. B. "No, I'm babysitting tonight."

"Me too. I was supposed to see that pirate movie with Derek and Ethan, but my little brother's sick." He held open his yellow shopping bag to show me children's pain reliever, a coloring book, crayons.

For once, I welcomed Jay's chattiness. It gave my heart rate a chance to slow to normal.

"Strep throat," he continued. "My aunt planned to go to a fundraising dinner dance, so big brother to the rescue, you know?"

"Not really. I'm an only child."

"Oh." He glanced at my bags, rolls of TP poking out of each one. "I thought maybe you had a huge family."

I envisioned my cheeks flushing from pink to red. At least today wasn't a tampon-shopping day.

"Big sale," I said. "And I like to have extra stuff around. Have you ever been in a store right before a hurricane? The shelves empty in hours. In a disaster, batteries, flashlights, and even everyday things are hard to come by. And I saw this freaky movie last night about the end of the world. What if our food supply was disrupted? You can never be too prepared."

He glanced over at me, but I couldn't quite read his expression. He could either be fascinated by my unique perspective or doubtful of my emotional stability. I wasn't sure which.

"So, you think the world's going to end?" he asked. "And you'll need extra toilet paper to see you through?"

I almost smacked him in the head with a pack of UltraStrong. Why didn't I stick to my usual un-conversational ways? But it was too late. I paused, choosing my next words carefully.

"It's not that the world's going to end, exactly. But the future is too uncertain. I don't think we can guarantee that life will continue the way we expect."

There was more, of course, that I didn't explain. Like how I used to care about being Good with a capital G: the hard-working student, the model daughter, the loving girlfriend who didn't go too far. In exchange for my Goodness, all I expected from the universe was safety. It seemed fair enough, in the ways of karma, religion, fate.

But life wasn't fair. Or very safe.

So all deals with the universe were off. Only worrying, preparing, and planning for any possible disaster made me feel better. That, and the searing warmth in my lungs when I inhaled, the welcome rush from the nicotine.

We reached the stoplight and waited for it to turn green. I glanced around again. Still no sign of Mr. B.

"Shit happens," I concluded.

"True." He took a drag of his cigarette, looking away.

"You agree?" I expected a debate.

"My mother . . . she died within months of finding out about the cancer. So one day life is great. The next, you don't know."

"I'm sorry," I said, for lack of anything original.

"Pancreatic cancer is a nasty disease. The survival rates totally suck." He didn't make eye contact, but he kept talking, as if now that he started, he felt driven to explain. His voice sounded hollow with grief. "After we stayed with my grandparents in Phoenix for a few years, we moved here to live with my aunt."

His aunt worked as the nurse at the high school. I'd been to her office plenty of times as part of my class-cutting this semester.

"My brother doesn't remember Mom as much as I do," he said. "I'm not sure if that's good or bad."

Where was his dad? It wasn't something I could politely ask. I slowed my pace, wondering how I could survive without either of my parents, wondering how Jay held it together.

Sometimes I envisioned getting the phone call that my parents had died. I played the scenario out in meticulous detail: answering the phone on the second ring, the solemn male voice breaking the news. In my warped imagination, they were killed in a car accident like Megs's dad. But while she still had her mom, in my case, the funeral arrangements, the grief, the day-to-day survival all became something for me to handle alone. It was a morbid fantasy, but Dr. Gwen explained that it wasn't uncommon. After one trauma, the mind might vividly imagine others as a way to feel prepared.

Did Jay ever imagine someone else in his family dying? He seemed so stable and responsible, but maybe it was only sadness in disguise.

"I didn't mean to be all serious." He flicked his cigarette away as we neared our street. "So, when did you start smoking? It's a disgusting habit."

"A few months ago."

"Is that when your shit happened?"

And just like that, a jolt of fear short-circuited my other thoughts. Mr. B flashed through my mind again, his breath in my ear, the unwanted kiss. Afterward, Dr. Gwen had said it was a choice whether to view myself as a victim or a survivor. As if I really had an option. The decision never felt like it was mine to make.

I shuddered but tried to cover it with a shrug. I couldn't fake an answer, couldn't carefully compose one. "There are some things I'd rather not discuss."

"Fair enough," Jay said. "If you ever want to talk, I'm a pretty good listener."

I nodded as if considering it. But this wasn't a topic I'd change my mind about. Jay's listening skills would never be enough to drag my secret into the open.

CHAPTER 4

Prior to the Blue Flu, the most deadly pandemic in the United States was the Spanish Flu in 1918. It claimed the lives of over half a million Americans. The projected totals for the Blue Flu are expected to easily surpass that.
—Blue Flu interview, government official

Babysitting someone new was always awkward, but Cam and I broke the ice after playing five games of Pretty Pretty Princess. Then I gave her a manicure, alternating Cotton Candy with Fuchsia Fiesta on every other nail. That sealed the deal.

"You are the Best. Babysitter. Ever." She beamed at me, a big smile that revealed a few missing baby teeth.

Mom had gotten me the babysitting gig for Ms. Schiffer, a single mom who waitressed after her nine-to-five job. It was Mom's way of encouraging me to be independent, to continue some of the activities I'd done before the incident. Not having brothers or sisters to annoy me at home, I always liked caring for other people's kids. At least temporarily.

"We have an hour until bed time. What's next?" I asked.

"Can we play another game?" Cam opened a cabinet in the den to reveal princess versions of both Memory and Chutes and Ladders.

Uh oh. Princess overload. But I knew all about being an only child and the excitement of having someone over to play with.

"How about one more game, some fruit, then educational television?" I asked, half-joking.

"How about two games, ice cream sundaes, then my favorite dance show saved on the DVR?"

"All right. You've got a deal."

Cam had great recall for a six-year-old and I lost both games of Princess Memory.

"Did you let me win?" she asked as I scooped vanilla ice cream into a bowl.

"Sadly, no. You beat me fair and square."

Cam drowned her ice cream in strawberry syrup and rainbow sprinkles. "Let's eat while we watch TV," she said. "Mom always lets me have snacks in the den."

The couch was a pristine cream color. I doubted Cam ate messy food on it, ever. "Why don't we eat in the kitchen while you tell me about the photos?" Snapshots of Cam covered the refrigerator door, held in place by various insect magnets: butterflies, ladybugs, dragonflies.

"OK." In between spoonfuls, she explained each

picture. "That's me at the Turtleback Zoo. The monkeys are my favorite," she said. "The hayride was at the pumpkin farm. We picked our own pumpkins. Mom carved a jack-o-lantern for outside, but then the squirrels chewed it. I was sad, but she said squirrels need to eat, too."

"Who's that?" I pointed to a picture of her sitting on a man's shoulders.

"That's Uncle Robbie, Mom's older brother. Sometimes he comes with us on our weekend adventures. Mom said since I don't have a real dad, it's good for me to spend time with him. But when he burps super loud, Mom gets annoyed. She said he has bad manners and did he want his only niece belching like that?"

"What did he say?"

"He said burping was natural. So was passing gas."

I laughed. "Your uncle sounds funny."

"Yeah, I love him a lot. Mom says since we have a small family, the love is extra strong."

Next to the snapshot with her uncle, there were birthday pictures and holiday ones, too. She pointed to a formal photo of her in a short black-and-white dress with a top hat. "That's from my dance recital. I take classes at Miss Lauren's School of Dance."

"I like your costume. You look pretty." I cleaned up our empty bowls.

"And I'm talented, too," she said.

We sat on the couch and watched her favorite dance reality show, cozy under a homemade afghan. Cam had a lot of opinions about whether the judges were right. When the program ended, she hopped onto the coffee table.

"Want to see my talent show number, Lil?"

"Sure. You can dance on the way to bed."

Cam wiggled, shook, and twirled down the hall of their one-story house. She had a cheerful bedroom, with a fluffy pink throw rug and a comforter with big bright flowers. The walls were decorated with her artwork, hung in plastic frames.

"Now it's your turn," she said once I tucked her in.

"How about a sleepy dance?" I turned off the overhead light and switched on her butterfly night-light. I remembered being six, thinking that the little glow would keep all kinds of troubles away.

"Come on, Lil."

I shook off the gloomy feeling. Not wanting to lose my Best Babysitter status so quickly, I did a short version of the robot.

"Wait!" Cam said. "Milkshake missed it!"

"Milkshake?"

She pulled a worn-looking brown-and-white stuffed cow from under her covers. "Do it again so he can see."

"OK, but then it's lights out." I danced again, while Cam made Milkshake bounce up and down.

"This is his cow dance," she said. "I taught him everything he knows."

"He's got some cool moves. Now goodnight, Cam. Goodnight, Milkshake."

"Goodnight, Lil. I hope you babysit me again soon so I can give you some dance lessons."

"I hope so, too."

With Cam finally asleep, I checked my phone. My heart jumped a little when I saw a text from Ethan. After our conversation yesterday, I didn't think we'd talk again anytime soon. I was instantly sucked back into the reality of being sixteen again instead of a carefree six-year-old. Talking with Cam was straightforward. With Ethan, I had to interpret what he wrote and what he really meant.

Ethan: Did u find what you were looking for?

Clever. Kind of a loaded question in disguise. Either that or he really cared about my lost-and-found search, which I doubted.

Me: Nope.

I could ask him how the pirate movie was, but then I'd have to explain about walking home with Jay, which would be easy to misinterpret. Jay seemed closer to Derek than to Ethan, but he was still part of that friend group. I didn't think they had much in common, but guy friendships seemed to form a lot easier than girl ones.

He answered a few minutes later.

Ethan: It was nice 2 c u. Talk again soon?

That made me pause. Yesterday was more of a veiled fight than a pleasant chat. He did get one thing right during that conversation, though: I had drifted away on purpose, causing the breakup by default. After the situation with Mr. B, being with Ethan overwhelmed me, his every touch sending me into a panic. Since I didn't trust him enough to tell him what happened, our time together became colored by little lies. What started as a solid relationship began to crack and chip. The end was inevitable.

Yet he hinted that maybe he knew the truth. Well, he certainly didn't learn it from me.

Where was he going with this? Since we'd broken up, he'd only had a five-week relationship with a vapid girl named Cassandra. It had been weird to see him with another girl, to watch as they walked down the hall with his arm slung over her shoulder. It was like a mixed up out-of-body experience, watching him with someone that should have been me. Right when I got used to it, their relationship ended. Some people gossiped about her dumping

him, while others said it was his choice. I didn't
know which story was true and it didn't really matter much. What mattered was that he had dated
someone else, created new memories with Cassandra while I stayed stuck in the past.

Was he trying to reconcile with me now? Was I
ready for that? It wasn't like I could say, *No, I don't
think we should talk ever again*. And part of me wanted to get back to living, to move forward. I thought
about how Ethan would gently push the hair from
my eyes when I used to wear it loose and flowy.

Did I want to talk again soon? Yes, I could handle conversation. I could try.

Me: Sure.
Ethan: Great.

And that was that.

Besides his texts, there was a less exciting email
from Mom, explaining the time difference, offering
souvenirs, ensuring that I was OK. So I went from
the future possibilities with Ethan to the grounded
details of my mother. It was actually easier to send
her a message than to talk.

Mom,

Glad you had a safe trip. I don't really need a
souvenir but if you see anything small I could
put on my desk that would be good.

Dad and I have been eating fine. I'm babysitting for Ms. Schiffer's daughter now. She's
sweet. No problems.

Miss you.

Love, Lily

The email felt only slightly fake, like I was trying too hard. But it would make Mom happy if I
sent more than eight words. I clicked send before
changing my mind.

The rest of the weekend was dull, filled with my
lame attempt to catch up on all the homework I'd
been ignoring. My assignments had somehow multiplied in my backpack, like mold in a damp, dark
place.

Monday would have been more of the same, except for the headlines. I didn't need a special alert
about diseases anymore. The situation in Maryland
had hit the mainstream news.

CHAPTER 5

*The US government recommends keeping at least a three-day
supply of food and water on hand for emergency situations.
How many Americans have done even that much?*
—Blue Flu interview, survivalist blogger

My mouth dropped open in horror as I read the
news after school. At least a hundred people
in Maryland had fallen ill with flu-like symptoms.
Apparently, a married thirty-something couple had
died from a respiratory illness in coastal Virginia
last week, but had been buried before the disease
became big news, so no tests were done. A few in-
stances of flu had been reported in Delaware, too,
as if the illness had quietly snuck up the coast in a
secret invasion. The article closed with a reminder
for people to practice healthy hygiene by washing
their hands frequently and covering their coughs,
which didn't feel quite lifesaving enough.

I called Dad. He wasn't at his desk, so I tried to
leave a casual message. "Hi, it's Lily. Call me when

you get a chance." I ended with a cheerful lilt to my voice, then paced around the house until the phone rang a half hour later.

"I have to work late tonight," Dad said. "Can you make yourself something for dinner?"

"Sure. Don't worry about me." I waited to see if he would mention the illness on his own. Mom had coached him not to alarm me, and anyway, I'd get more information if he thought it was his idea to discuss it.

"Um, good. That's good," he said.

"Is everything all right?" I could hear the tap-tap of typing in the background. "You sound distracted."

"A little. Angela's out sick when I need her the most."

I always liked his assistant. When I was younger and school was closed on a workday, I'd go to Dad's office. Angela would let me write on the conference room whiteboard with colored markers or photocopy my hands and feet. She'd drawn the line at the butt copy. Her baby was due next month and I could tell she'd be a good mom.

"You're busy getting ready for the conference?"

"Yes, that, and following this illness in Maryland. It's unusual."

"What's going on?" I asked, trying to keep my voice light.

But Dad must have heard the panic because he reined it in. "It's OK, Lily. The CDC is investigating all unusual respiratory ailments in the region."

He cleared his throat nervously, as if realizing his mistake a moment too late. Any mention of the Centers for Disease Control and Prevention was worrisome for me. Very worrisome.

"Why would they be involved?" I asked.

"This disease is similar to seasonal flu, only worse."

"What makes it worse?"

He paused. "It's more deadly. And given Avian's proximity to Washington there's some paranoia about bioterrorism."

I knew all about paranoia. "On a scale of one to ten, how concerned should I be?"

"I'd prefer that you concentrate on school. I checked the online gradebook. Not good."

Ugh. I'd hoped my grades would go unnoticed for a few more weeks. And now there was no way to continue the conversation about the flu.

"Could you hold off telling Mom about school? You know how she worries. And I spent a lot of time on homework over the weekend."

"Hmm," he said. "I guess I can wait until she gets back from her trip."

"Thanks, Dad. I'll study extra tonight."

I did try. But my mind kept drifting to various disaster scenarios. Dad's distracted attitude didn't help. My grades would normally require a thirty-minute discussion, so this disease was definitely on his mind. I rechecked the news about Maryland several times throughout the evening, but there wasn't much new information, only a re-hash of what I'd already read.

At least the local news was uneventful. The town news site, *Portico Press*, profiled the bird-banding extravaganza Mom had missed, complete with a photo. In the group shot, I recognized a few of Mom's environmental friends and Dad's assistant, Angela. I emailed Mom the article link and reassured her that Dad and I were not malnourished.

Giving up on academics, I texted Megs.

Me:	Want 2 meet 4 din?
Megs:	U come here? Pizza & homework?
Me:	Nerd. C u soon.

I gathered my books and left. Two blocks from Megs's house, a girl with long black hair crossed the street in front of me. My stomach lurched. It was Kayla. Before turning the corner, she glanced over and registered my presence. Then she looked away, as if I were a stranger. She and Megs were the trusted allies who knew what happened in the fall, the two friends I had painfully confided in.

Only Megs had believed me.

The night before my dreaded return to school, Megs and Kayla visited me, both squishing onto the end of the bed.

"You look like crap," Kayla said. "But I'm glad to see you."

"Thanks, I think." Nervous, I tried to smile, but my mouth felt stiff.

"Not contagious anymore?" Megs asked. Mononucleosis was my cover story for missing school after Mr. B.

"No." When I wasn't pretending to be sick, there were secret meetings with the principal, the school superintendent, my guidance counselor, and a therapist. Dr. Gwen had encouraged me to be honest about what happened, whenever it felt safe. It had been harder to lie to my friends than to Ethan. It was time to let them know.

"I was never really contagious," I said. "The mono-thing was, um, not exactly true."

"It's something really bad, isn't it?" Kayla asked.

I nodded.

"Oh my God. A terminal illness?" Megs grabbed my hand. "You don't have something life-threatening, do you?"

I wanted to laugh and cry at the same time. The whole situation was so absurd, yet incredibly painful.

"No, it's not medical." I took a deep breath, try-

ing to summon my courage. "Something . . . something happened after school last Friday."

They waited through my long pause.

"With Mr. B."

Kayla sucked in her breath.

I told them, in halting words, what he had done,
what he had tried to do, skipping most of the physical details. Numbness settled over me as I spoke,
as if it had happened to someone else, to another
trusting girl.

Megs squeezed my hand. "That's horrible."

"You two are the only friends who know. You
can't tell anyone. I'd die."

"You reported it to the police?" Megs asked.

I nodded. "I didn't talk to your mom, though."

"How come this isn't all over the local news?"
Kayla sounded upset that she hadn't known about
it sooner.

"I don't know the details exactly, but my dad
said it is being kept out of the press while they investigate. To protect me, I guess, or maybe to protect Mr. B until they figure out if they have enough
proof to arrest him. It's kind of my word against his,
so he's on some type of leave while the police try to
gather evidence. But at least he's not teaching."

Kayla finally spoke. "That's awful."

"I know. I'm doing better, though."

"No, I mean, he's such a talented teacher."

I narrowed my eyes at her. "He's a total creeper."

"Everyone knows he's hot. If you didn't want to be with him, all you had to do was say no."

Her words stunned me. She couldn't be serious.

"I would have said no if he had bothered to *ask* instead of . . . instead of groping me. There wasn't a lot of conversation going on, Kayla, before he shoved his hand up my skirt."

She stood. "Well, maybe he misinterpreted, thought you were interested—"

I stood, too, straightening out my pj top, smoothing the wrinkles with great care, as if that would stop the anger from consuming me. "Then he could have asked me on a date and I could have stopped it right there. Why are you interrogating me?"

"I think—" Megs started.

"I'm not interrogating you," Kayla said. "I just have trouble seeing it play out like that. I've been in meetings with him, been alone with him for a whole year. He's never tried anything." She flipped her long hair.

I had been prepared for questions, sympathy, and hugs from my two best friends. Of all the possible reactions, disbelief was not one I had anticipated. Kayla doubted me, choosing to side with our teacher instead.

How could she? How dare she? My face flushed. "Are you calling me a liar?"

"No, I don't think you're lying exactly—"

The shock of betrayal surged through me. That's when I slapped her. I'd only seen it in movies, but it felt damn good.

Megs gasped.

Kayla raised her hand to the cheek where I'd hit her. She grabbed her bag and left without another word.

⌒

Megs was typing on her computer when I arrived. I could tell by her grin that she wasn't doing math homework.

She looked up and must have caught the expression on my face. "What's the matter?"

"I saw Kayla on the way over here."

"And?"

"She pretended not to know me."

Megs frowned in sympathy, motioning for me to take the stool next to her.

"Something's been bothering me," I said.

"The fact that our former BFF lacks a brain?"

"Seriously. Do you think I could have somehow, unintentionally, brought on the whole situation with Mr. B—given him the wrong idea?"

"No way."

I must not have looked convinced.

"Did you like him like that?" Megs asked gently.

"No."

"Did you ever think, 'if only I was older'?"

"Never."

"You can't blame yourself. And what he did was wrong—illegal—no matter how you analyze it."

"But . . . why do you think Mr. B . . . I mean, why did he pick me?" I weaved my fingers together, forced them to rest quietly on my lap. I watched them carefully as if my hands held the answers. "Kayla thought he walked on water. There were prettier girls and certainly more willing ones. . . . I don't understand why. Maybe if I knew that, understood what I could've done to prevent it, I could let the whole thing go."

She reached over and squeezed my shoulder. "It wasn't your fault," she said softly. "I don't think there was anything you could have done. It was a bad situation, but not something you could have seen coming."

"But do you think I seemed weak or something? Like an easy target?"

She shook her head.

"My parents won't talk much about the investigation, but I know it's taking longer than they thought. That can't be good. If no one else comes forward and he starts teaching again—"

"Don't think about it."

"Well, I never want to be the victim of any

more bad situations. If that means keeping an emotional distance and stocking up on canned food, so be it."

"We'll never understand what he was thinking. But you're one of the strongest people I know."

I met her eyes, checked for judgment. But there was only support. "Strong? I can't even open the pickle jar," I said, trying to lighten the mood.

"You have inner strength. Remember when I broke my wrist? And the bone was pushing out of my skin?"

"I told you the plank wobbled too much to make a good balance beam."

"You didn't even panic. You wrapped my arm in your sweatshirt and brought me to my mom," she said. "Give yourself a break, Lil. You're strong and good-hearted and giving. Maybe he wanted to corrupt that somehow."

I breathed deeply, considering what Megs said. "Do you think I can ever walk around like a normal person without having flashbacks? The memories ambush me out of nowhere."

She swiveled her stool back and forth. "I don't know. Maybe the feelings take time to fade, like grief. You still have the sadness with you, but it recedes into the background more. You never forget, but you function. At least that's the way it was with my dad dying."

Megs's dad had been a great guy, the kind who made up games to play with us in the backyard. Her swing set could turn into a spaceship or the Amazon jungle when he was around. It was when he died unexpectedly that I first tried to negotiate with the universe: my Goodness in exchange for my family's safety.

But I hadn't counted on Mr. B.

"You'll be OK," Megs said.

I wasn't so sure. Could I be physically comfortable with someone again? Maybe with someone familiar, like Ethan?

I made an effort to smile, then gestured to the computer, needing a change of subject. "Are you chatting again?"

"Yeah. He seems amazing. Smart, funny."

"He's the most perfect guy you've never met."

"It feels like I *do* know him. We've covered favorite novel, worst subjects in school, and bad habits. He smokes, which I'm not crazy about."

"What did you say your bad habit was? Flirting with online disaster?"

"Puh-lease."

I wanted to support her, wanted Megs to find love, but I wanted it to be with someone safe. Not a stranger, someone unknown, possibly dangerous. "OK. But I'm an unwilling accomplice."

"I know." She paused. "I was trying to think

of a flaw. Nothing that would turn him off, maybe something intriguing."

"You're going to make one up? Why not tell him something true?"

"I want him to like me!"

"Right. Because it really matters what stranger-boy thinks."

"Are you going to help me make up a good bad habit or not?"

"Fine." Megs was my best friend. Actually, my only real friend. I wanted her to be happy. "Maybe you could smoke, too."

"I'm not an idiot with a death wish." She scowled in disapproval.

"Right," I said. "Drinking problem?"

"No. That's too serious."

"Perfectionist?"

"Too phony."

"Straight A student?" I asked.

"That's not a fault! But it's too geeky. He might not like that."

"Don't be such a pessimist. Maybe he likes smart chicks."

"Ahh, that's it! I'll tell him I'm a pessimist." She started typing. "You're a genius. Then I can say something flirtatious, like, 'The pessimist in me fears our relationship can't go much further.'"

"Yeah, then what?"

"He'll offer to meet me."

"Megs, you can't. I know you're having fun with this, but meeting a stranger is insane. And unsafe. And other cynical stuff."

That's the thing about Megs. Whenever we played truth or dare, she was a dare-girl all the way. While I preferred truth, she was a fearless risk-taker.

"Don't worry," she said. "I have a plan."

CHAPTER 6

Worrying about influenza is as stupid and time
wasting as worrying about global warming.
—Blue Flu interview, news commentator

During the week, I carefully followed the Maryland virus in the news. The authorities had performed a biosecurity check of nearby labs and had conducted other investigations deemed too secret to publicize, so most reporters concluded the link between the illness and bioterrorism was ludicrous. A few continued to argue for a conspiracy theory. Whichever it was, the flu-like disease wasn't waiting for anyone's verdict. It continued to spread at an alarming rate.

But I didn't need a news feed to tell me that the situation worsened. I could tell by looking at Dad. When I stumbled into the kitchen for breakfast on Friday, he was making coffee. Dark circles underlined his eyes and his posture drooped.

"What's the matter?" I asked.

"Huh? Nothing, really. I'm fine. Preoccupied. Things have been busy."

"You must be getting ready for your trip tomorrow."

"Yes."

"And following the spread of the flu?" I handed him sugar for his coffee.

"Yes, that too. It's hard when something hits this close to home."

"Close to home?"

He swallowed, hesitating. "There were fatalities in Maryland, hospitalizations in Delaware, and now eight people in New Jersey have been reported sick."

My heart raced, but I made an effort to remain perfectly still. If I panicked, Dad would clam up. "New Jersey?" I asked with only the slightest tremor in my voice. "I didn't know that. Near here?"

He stirred his coffee for what seemed like forever.

"Dad?"

"I suppose it's better if you hear it from me. It struck Morris County. Five people from Portico are ill, plus a young couple from Madison and a man from Florham Park. It will be in today's paper."

"What is *it* exactly?"

"The CDC is working on a definitive diagnosis. They're trying to determine if the people knew each other, or if these are isolated incidents. The victims had similar symptoms."

Fear crept up my back on light spidery legs. "What are the symptoms?"

"Typical flu stuff, like fever, cough, fatigue, but they come on fast and fluid builds in the lungs." He paused.

"Tell me, Dad."

He sighed. "They're starting to call it the Blue Flu."

"Like when the police call in sick instead of striking?" Megs's mom had explained that to us years ago.

"No. It's called the Blue Flu because sometimes the lack of oxygen . . . well, in advanced cases, it causes the victims' skin to change color."

"Maybe I should stay home from school today."

He tried to give his reassuring Dad smile. "It's nothing to worry about, yet," he said.

Yeah right. Dad just didn't want me to become an emotional wreck with Mom away. I skipped breakfast and forced myself to get ready for school.

⌒

"Don't forget," Principal Fryman reminded us during the Friday morning announcements. "Tomorrow is the annual Portico Career Fair. April showers bring May flowers, so get your feet wet this weekend and help support Portico's 'Doorway to Learning.' Remember, it's our biggest fundraiser of the year. Also, the food drive is still going on. Collection boxes are located in the main lobby. It's better to give than receive! And, we're pleased to announce a poster contest sponsored by the Morris County Health Department promoting proper illness etiquette. Sneeze into your sleeve, wash your hands, that kind of thing. Rules and requirements are available at the office. Remember, you have to be in it to win it!"

He ended his announcement with a noisy cough that made me shudder.

I dropped off a box of pasta and three cans of peas for the food drive while on alert for other sounds of illness. I went through the whole morning hyper-aware of any possible germs around me. Each sneeze and every sniffle registered in the paranoid part of my brain. By lunchtime, I drooped with exhaustion. Megs and I ate across from each other at our usual table. The cafeteria noises washed over me and I stopped trying to distinguish the individual sounds.

"Are you all right?" Megs asked.

"Tired, I guess. Feeling anxious, too. What's up with the illness poster contest?"

"I don't know. It sounds dumb."

"Don't you find it worrisome? Why are they

running it now, unless they're concerned about this flu spreading?"

"You're spiraling again. Downward descent."

She was right, of course. But before I could respond, Jay walked by, saying hi to me as he passed on the way to Derek and Ethan's table. Megs almost knocked over her iced tea. "What was that all about?" she asked. "I didn't know you guys were buddies."

"He lives on my street, remember? And we've talked at the smoking corner."

"Hmm. I can see you with someone like him."

"He's nice, but not BF material."

"Why not?" she asked.

"He's got that cool, popular vibe going on."

"Exactly. He's cute. Dark hair, dark eyes—"

"Girls drool over him. Not my type."

"What's not to like?" Megs asked. "I heard he was at a party a few weeks ago. He's reviewing restaurants for his blog and a bunch of girls offered to go out to eat with him. Kayla practically threw herself at him and he still left the party alone."

"Blech. My point exactly. Too much drama."

"But he's picky. That shows integrity."

"Maybe I should introduce you if he's so great."

"No, thanks. I've got my online friend to occupy me for now. But you've got to date again sometime." She spoke quietly. "I know you're healing and all that, but sooner or later you'll have another boyfriend. Someone better than Ethan."

"Later," I said. "Much later. I have other things to worry about."

I tried to imagine Jay and Kayla as a couple. She didn't seem his type. Not that I knew what his type was, exactly. So it was only out of curiosity that I searched for his restaurant reviews after school. Dad suggested Chinese or Japanese for dinner and Jay's blog had its own section on our town website.

Portico Press
New Kid in Town
by Jay Martinez

Phantom Sushi on Main Street offers good food despite the weird name. (I kept worrying the food might disappear. Our kimono-wearing waitress assured me it would not.) I recommend the April Blossom roll if you like sushi, or yaki udon (thick rice noodles) with chicken if you're not a fish fan. The mochi dessert comes in mango, vanilla, or green tea. Mango is good; green tea tastes like a bad jelly bean flavor. This is a nice place for a date if you're comfortable using chopsticks.

Reservations preferred but not required; takeout orders can be picked up.

Jay had a pretty good sense of humor. I doubt he ate at the restaurant alone. Not that I cared. Anyway, no picking up food tonight. Dad would prefer delivery so I stuck with our usual place.

I glanced through my school email account. My guidance counselor had sent a message that she needed to meet with me. That couldn't be good. Had one of my teachers realized I was skipping class? It didn't feel like a problem I should deal with tonight.

Next, I checked for updated flu news, but it mirrored what Dad had already told me. I planned to pump him for more information about the virus during dinner. But right as we sat down to eat, the phone rang. Dad moved away from the table, murmuring in the next room. After he hung up, he came to the kitchen, his skin pale, forehead creased, mouth drooped. Bad news.

My guidance counselor wouldn't call my parents yet, would she? I put my fork down perfectly straight on the folded white napkin. "What's the matter?"

"Angela . . . she's at Morristown General. They had to do an emergency C-section."

"Is she all right? And the baby, too?"

"The baby's doing well so far. A boy. But Angela . . . she's in a medically-induced coma." Dad took off his glasses to clean them on the corner of his shirt, first the left side, then the right. After putting them back on, he blinked a few times, as if trying to make something clearer. "The doctors don't know exactly what happened. They're running tests."

"Is it that illness?"

"It looks like it. There've been more cases today."

Fear heightened my senses. Everything around me became clearer: the ticking of the kitchen clock, the worry lines on Dad's face, the smell of our uneaten lo mein. The invisible horror had slithered into our everyday lives. Even though it had been what I was expecting, even imagining, the reality was more paralyzing than I thought.

Then something worse occurred to me. I stood, then hugged Dad hard. "You've been exposed," I whispered.

"No, honey, Angela worked from home last week. I haven't seen her. But there's been at least one death in New Jersey."

I swallowed.

"It seems scary, I know. It's a horrible time for me to leave you. I tried to cancel. I really tried. But since the conference focuses on emerging infections, with this new flu activity, it's transforming into a major event."

"Could I come with you?" Desperation crept into my voice.

"I considered that, but I'm sharing a room with

the social media editor from California. I checked into available rooms, but with other conventions booked at the hotel, there aren't any," he said. "I'm only a train ride away to Delaware if you need me. And Mom called. She's finishing up her business and trying to take an earlier flight back. She might even beat me home."

"But—"

"It's the weekend. You could stay in the house the whole time if you want. It's probably a good idea to avoid crowded places right now."

I blinked, willing myself not to cry.

"I'm sorry, Lily. I know this is tough. Do you think you'll be all right for a few days?"

"Yes," I said, because it's what he wanted to hear.

We both pushed the food around our plates, no longer hungry. After dinner, back in my room, I picked at my nail polish until the garbage can was littered with black flecks. The panic kept bubbling up, threatening to spill over, and no amount of picking or pacing seemed to help.

Sitting on the floor with my legs crossed, I practiced deep breathing the way Dr. Gwen had taught me. Breathe in, two, three, four. Breathe out, two, three, four. Finally, the panic subsided enough for me to try to separate facts from my heightened emotions.

Dad had written a lot of infectious disease articles and one thing I knew for sure: experts had said another pandemic would occur. They knew it for certain. What they didn't know was when.

Was it now?

I tried calling Mom, but with the time difference, her voice mail kicked in. I hung up, rehearsed a normal-sounding message, then called again.

"Hi, Mom. Glad you'll be home soon. It would be great if you would call. Love you." My voice only cracked the slightest bit.

To keep busy, I checked my email. There was one message from school about Career Day:

Instant Alert from Portico High School

Just a reminder that Career Day begins at 11 a.m. Saturday morning. We're pulling out all the stops to make this a banner event! Get a leg up on learning about the profession of your choice and support Portico High. Admission at the door is $6.00. A $1.00 discount is given with a nonperishable food donation to our spring food drive. Bring some bills and some beans and learn about the career of your dreams!

Students, don't forget that your volunteer participation counts as extra credit for the subject of your choice. Sign in at the door to receive credit.

With the flu in our county, Career Day was no longer an option, giving me a lot of time to fill this weekend. To start, Dad gave me his credit card to order flowers for Angela. That killed twenty minutes. Straightening my already tidy closet took a few more. Opening each desk and dresser drawer, I surveyed the contents as if for the first time. Did I really need last year's science notes? Or plans for community service projects I would never pursue? I tossed and purged, leaving a neat pile of photos and some current school papers. I even made my bed, carefully tucking in the pale green sheets and folding back the cheerful quilt I'd had for years. It didn't matter that it was almost time for bed. I kept moving, straightening pillows, refolding clothes, taking out the trash.

When Dad closed the door to his office to make some calls, I hovered outside, straining to listen. His conversation didn't seem flu-related, though, so I checked on my emergency stash, lined up the cans, made neat stacks of the boxes. Finally, the tight band of fear around my stomach loosened a little.

I remembered how freaked out people were during the H1N1 outbreak several years ago. The first round of vaccine ran out in a few hours and people in our town practically rioted. Dad mentioned once that if a new flu ever emerged, it would take at least five months to develop an updated vaccine.

The important thing was to survive until then.

CHAPTER 7

As a result of this illness, career opportunities are expected to increase for emerging infectious disease specialists over the next several years.
—Blue Flu interview, author of the annual "US Job Predictions" report

Dad stood at the door ready to leave. "I'll be home on Monday," he said, giving me a big hug.

I clung to him a moment, but he expected me to be brave. Then he was gone.

Megs called to make plans. "What time are we leaving?"

"I'm not going."

"What are you talking about?" she said. "Everyone goes to Career Day."

"That's the problem. The school will be too crowded. People in Portico have already gotten sick from the virus that's going around. It's too risky."

"Come with me for a little while. Long enough to get the extra credit. You need to pull up your social studies grade, right?"

"My dad just left. I want to stay holed up in my room with a big bottle of antibacterial soap."

"I know. But you could check in, volunteer for a while, then leave. No one will know if you cut your shift short. Come on, Lil."

"I don't know. . . ." But the combination of boredom, Megs's begging, and my D in history finally convinced me. Dad had seen my grades, and with Mom on her way home, the academic clock was ticking. After breakfast, Megs and I walked to school together.

"Are you nervous?" she asked.

"A little anxious. Have you been following the news?"

"No. Most of my computer time has been spent with you-know-who. I really like him."

"Do you even know his name?" I asked.

"The site rules were not to give names."

"Since when do you follow the rules? Come on, Megs. You can't truly know someone from chatting online."

"You're right. That's why I'm going to meet him tonight."

I halted immediately. "No way. He could be a murderer. Your mom's a cop. You know the horror stories about these situations better than I do."

"I have it all figured out," she said. "We're meeting at the coffee shop at six-thirty. It's crowded then. I checked it out yesterday. He said he'd be carrying a certain book, that I'd know him when I saw it. He doesn't know what I look like, so if it doesn't feel right or if he seems like a creeper, I can walk out. No harm done." She pulled at my arm to get me walking again. "Come on. We'll be late."

I moved reluctantly, not wanting to let the subject drop. "What if he's ugly?"

She faked a punch to my arm. "His personality is totally hot. Maybe I can ask him to the Spring Formal."

"Maybe," I said, unconvinced. "But I think it's a dumb idea. Do you want me to come with you?"

"That's sweet," she said. "But I'd rather go alone."

We arrived at school and checked in at the volunteer table. By then, I was more worried about Megs than the flu. How could I persuade her not to meet this stranger? But we didn't get to discuss it once we arrived. Megs was working refreshments and I'd been assigned as a wandering guide, handing out maps and giving directions.

I decided to give it fifteen minutes before I bailed. After grabbing a pile of handouts, I waited in the gym doorway where I was supposed to meet the previous shift. Inside the stuffy room, kids crushed together as they went from table to table. Principal Fryman wandered among the groups, most likely sharing his cliché-filled greetings.

I spotted Kayla talking to Jay. His back was to

me, but she was all smiles and straight posture. I had witnessed her flirting enough to know that she was good at it. She seemed to strike the perfect balance of needy and independent that left guys defenseless.

She strolled away from him, moving in my direction. "Would you like a map?" she asked the girl in front of me.

It was the first time we'd been within speaking distance since that day in my room. I knew all about the high road and how I should have taken it instead of slapping her. I'd rehashed the situation a hundred times afterward. Deep down, I never felt entirely apologetic. I was mostly confused, hurt, and pissed off that my supposed friend would doubt me about something so serious. But sometimes remorse snuck in, like a sour candy mixed with a batch of sweet ones.

"Would you like a . . . oh, it's you," she said, noticing me.

"I'm the next shift."

She handed me the remainder of her stack. "Good. I've got better places to be."

"Kayla—"

She sauntered away.

I took a step after her, then stopped. Forget it. We hadn't spoken in months. Now wasn't the time to reconcile.

I needed to focus on getting through a few minutes of this sucky event. Once I was safely at home, I could analyze the Kayla situation while alphabetizing the disease-related books in Dad's office. News stations were available 24/7 for my worrying pleasure. Or I could watch a movie, something stupid and light, wallowing in my solitude.

A tall guy standing next to me sneezed. I stood on the threshold to the gym, observing the throng, hearing the coughs, thinking about germs.

I couldn't do it.

Who was I kidding? If there was some type of flu going around, I couldn't immerse myself in a crowd of potentially contagious people, not even for fifteen minutes. My legs trembled as I scurried from the school with my head down. Sitting outside on the front bench, I took a few deep breaths, feeling better. Leaving was the safest course of action. I had abandoned the maps and was rushing across the parking lot to the smoking corner when Ethan intercepted me.

"Hey, Lil."

He fell into step next to me.

"Hi." I had an unlit cigarette ready in my hand and I couldn't help twirling it nervously.

"I guess you don't need the extra credit?"

"Um, I was keeping Megs company for awhile. I don't really feel like staying."

"It's still hard for me to believe you smoke now."

"Things change, right?"

"Maybe," he said. "But not everything has to be different."

We reached the oak tree and I lit up, exhaling loudly in protest.

"I'm glad I ran into you," he said.

"Yeah?"

"I've wanted to talk to you. I think that I . . . " He pushed his bangs across his forehead. "I still miss the way things used to be. With us. Remember the park? That was one of the best times ever."

Of course I remembered that day. We'd had an old-fashioned picnic by the pond, then took turns feeding each other a hot fudge sundae we'd gotten from the ice cream truck. We'd kissed for the rest of the afternoon, lying on the grass in the sun.

"I could spend forever like this," he'd said, holding me close.

If I shut my eyes, I could almost feel his arms around me, his lips pressing on mine.

No. That was before. Now he stood across from me, watching me smoke, catching me off guard with this conversation. I tried to imagine what it would feel like to be together again. Familiar in a good way? Or awkward now that my secret had created an invisible wall between us?

"Look, I'm not saying we have to start going out again. But what if you came over? We could hang out, watch a movie. Maybe that mash-up of all the fairy tales. That's it. No commitment." He took a step closer, narrowing the space between us.

Please don't kiss me. I froze while he brushed a strand of hair gently away from my face, the way he'd done a million times before.

With that motion, the familiar gesture, my resolve weakened. "All right," I whispered.

"Tonight then? Seven-ish?" he asked.

"Oh." That was sooner than I expected. "Um, OK."

"See you then."

I wasn't sure what I'd gotten myself into, but I didn't see us living happily ever after.

~

I washed my hands as soon as I got home.

It was a quiet afternoon. Dad called to check on me, and I answered an email from Mom, telling her about stupid stuff like Career Day, but leaving out my plans with Ethan. After heating her gross lasagna for dinner, I changed into a nicer black shirt, one with lace sleeves.

I dreaded checking the local news, but felt compelled to know what was happening. One article online summed it up.

Portico Press
Mysterious Illness Strikes Local Residents
by Jenny Silverman

Seasonal flu in New Jersey usually peaks in February. But that's not the case this year in Morris County, where fifteen people have been hospitalized with a flu-like illness, dubbed the "Blue Flu." In at least one case, the disease proved to be fatal. Elizabeth McKinley, 32, of Portico, New Jersey, died at Overlook Hospital in Summit yesterday. Dr. Brodey told reporters, "Ms. McKinley was in good health until late Tuesday. The illness struck suddenly, and despite our best efforts, we were unable to save her. Our thoughts are with her family at this time of tragic loss."

Symptoms include: high fever, headache, aches and pains, fatigue, weakness, cough. Extreme exhaustion may occur with the onset of these symptoms. Seek medical attention if necessary. Known cases of the Blue Flu have occurred in Maryland, Delaware, and New Jersey to date. Scientists from the Centers for Disease Control and Prevention (CDC) continue to work with local health departments to investigate this illness.

I thought about the stranger from town who died. Did she have a big family, lots of friends, maybe a boyfriend who would miss her? I imagined a whole existence for her that ended unexpectedly.

The news reinforced my desire to stay home, away from all possible germs. But cancelling with Ethan would be awkward. I wasn't sure if I looked forward to seeing him or not. It was hard to imagine snuggling with him on the couch the way we used to. Just the thought of physical contact made me fidget, so it took me twice as long to polish my nails with Licorice Heaven to match my clothes. They were reasonably dry when I got a text.

Megs: Come over! Fashion emergency!
Me: B there in 15.

I found Megs surrounded by a dozen shirts heaped on her bedroom floor.

"What should I wear?" she asked. "I need something to go with my favorite jeans." She plopped on her bed, face flushed.

I hesitated, torn between worrying about her safety and wanting to support her romantic longings. "You're sure you want to go through with this?"

She nodded.

"Then don't worry, we'll find something. You have great clothes." I glanced at her alarm clock. It was 6:15.

She followed my eyes. "I'll be fashionably late."

I pulled out a turquoise blouse that had fabric cutouts in the back.

"I need to look good from the front, not when I leave," she said.

"Right." I told her about Ethan while I searched her closet for something better.

"Are you sure you want to start with him again?" she asked.

"I don't know. He made it sound like, how could I not give us one more chance?" My phone pinged. "Ugh."

"What's the matter?"

"Ethan's already texting me." I sighed. "He's looking forward to tonight."

"Ah, it's nice to see he hasn't lost that stalker-ish quality."

I glared at her.

"Lil, you know I'm right. If your heart's not in it, don't go."

"I miss my old life before . . . everything." I kept flipping through her closet.

"But dating Ethan again won't magically turn back time. It won't make the other stuff vanish."

"I guess you're right," I said.

"Hmm . . . at least we both have dates tonight."

"It's not a date. I'm going over to his house."

"I'm sure we'll have a lot to talk about tomorrow," she said. "I can't believe I'm finally meeting him."

Near the back of the closet, a black top with three-quarter sleeves was lodged between two camis. I didn't even take it all the way out before Megs shook her head. Her face was shiny and I realized she was sweating. "Are you nervous?"

"A little. I'm not feeling great. I think it's all the excitement."

"You shouldn't go if you don't feel well."

She scowled at me. "I have to go. I can't explain it. It feels like part of something bigger, like destiny."

I pursed my lips together to keep from spouting my opinion. After pulling out a pale blue shirt, I held it against her. "This will look good with— "

My fingers brushed against her arm. She was burning hot. I put the back of my hand against her forehead the way Mom always did to me. "You feel feverish."

"I'm fine." She swayed as she tried to stand.

"Megs, you're sick." Fear made my voice quiver. "You can't go. This is crazy."

"It's too late to cancel." She sank onto her bed, coughing. "Can you get me a glass of water while I change?"

"Sure." I hurried to the kitchen. Mrs. Salerno sat at the counter, a newspaper spread in front of her.

I had to tell her about Megs. She'd forgive me for missing her date, eventually. "Mrs. Salerno, I . . ."

She looked at me, waiting.

Then we both heard it: the crashing sound from Megs's room.

We raced up the stairs. Megs lay sprawled on the floor next to her toppled bedside table.

"I felt dizzy, and then . . ."

Mrs. Salerno scooped her up and laid her on the bed. "Let me get the thermometer."

After her mom left the room, Megs looked at me, pleading. "I need you to do me a favor."

I knew what she was about to ask. "No way."

"Please? You don't have to talk to him. It'll be crowded, so he won't notice you. Look for the guy carrying a book, something that would have meaning to me. Then I'll tell him later how sick I was, that I couldn't make it."

"I'm supposed to meet Ethan soon. And a crowded shop mean germs."

"Could you tell him you're running late? It wouldn't take much time. If you walked in and out, it's like two minutes of exposure." She widened her eyes, pleading.

This was important to her, no matter how much I disapproved. I considered it. For my best friend, I could probably handle a few moments in a public place.

Megs sensed me cave. "And if you could sneak a photo—"

"I'm not taking a photo of some creep who'll follow me home and dismember me!"

"But you'll go? Please?"

I sighed. "No speaking to him, right?"

Her squeal of joy ended in a coughing fit. "You're the best."

"If I don't make it home alive, be sure to send out a search party."

She snuggled under the covers. "I'll be having blissful dreams about him until you report back."

Mrs. Salerno returned. "You should leave, Lily. It's probably too late, but if she's contagious . . . "

Contagious. Could she have the flu? No, not Megs. She was fine earlier today. I ticked off the symptoms. Fever, cough, sudden onset of illness. I couldn't deny the possibility. "Will you take her to the hospital?"

"The hospital!" Megs shrieked.

Mrs. Salerno's eyes reflected my worry. "I'll take care of her. You should go."

"OK. I'll talk to you later."

I scrubbed my hands in their kitchen sink before heading to the coffee shop. If I spotted her guy, great. If not, I'd go right to Ethan's. That was it. But why did I feel so nervous?

Maybe it wasn't about meeting a stranger.

Maybe the anxiety came from my BFF getting sick. But Mrs. Salerno was with her. She'd die before she'd let anything happen to Megs.

What about me? Could I have just been exposed to a deadly virus? I imagined the tiny germs floating around in her room, an invisible menace, my every inhale putting me at risk. Even as I walked to the coffee shop they could be multiplying in my lungs and—

Get a grip. I had to stop making myself crazy. I couldn't exactly give up breathing as a preventative measure. Yes, Megs was sick, but that didn't mean she had the flu, or that it lurked inside my body, waiting to assault me.

I glanced at the time. I'd be about ten minutes late for her date. Maybe the mystery guy would already be gone. I texted Ethan, letting him know I was running behind. He sent back a frowny face.

Inside the coffee shop, I checked out the other customers while I waited my turn to order. At least everyone looked healthy. Two moms chatted with toddlers on their laps. A heavy-set guy about our age talked on his cell phone at a table by the window. Hmm. Could he be Megs's friend?

Then I spotted who I'd imagined her talking to: an old man who needed a bath, hunched in the corner in his torn raincoat. I didn't see a book on his table, only a newspaper. "Illness Invades Suburban

New Jersey" the headline screamed. The large, bold type scared me, and so did the guy reading it.

She's been chatting with a creeper. I knew it.

Shivering, I ordered a decaf caramel latte with skim milk to go. While a long-haired guy made my drink, I glanced at the rest of the customers. There was a group of girls, maybe college-aged. No other boys.

That was it. I had done my good deed. After getting my coffee, I turned to hurry out and crashed right into Jay, knocking his book to the floor.

"I'm such a klutz." I picked up the paperback and handed it to him. Miraculously, the plastic lid contained my drink.

"I'm sorry I'm late." His cheeks reddened.

"What?" I held the door handle, ready to go.

He stared at the paperback a moment before slowly handing it to me.

I took it, confused. *"The Anti-Optimist's Guide to the Universe?"*

"I kept hoping it was you," Jay said.

CHAPTER 8

*One troubling aspect of the flu in 1918 was the number of
healthy young adults who died. There is concern
that the Blue Flu may follow the same unusual
and deadly pattern of fatalities.*
—Blue Flu interview, emerging infectious disease specialist

Clutching the book, I could almost hear the *click, click, click* of my brain slowing as I stood in the coffee shop facing Jay.

"All those times online," he said. "Did you know it was me? It took me awhile to figure out it was you."

Perplexed, I stalled for time. "What made you think it was me?"

"When we walked home from the grocery store that day, you mentioned the end-of-the-world movie and being an only child, like we talked about online."

"Oh," was all I could manage before sinking into the nearest chair. Megs had been chatting with Jay, and he thought he was chatting with me. Wow.

"Wait here. I'll get my coffee and be right back," he said.

I nodded, then rested my chin between my palms. I glanced at the book. He'd told Megs she would know it was him based on the title. *The Anti-Optimist's Guide to the Universe*. I thought back to her inventing a flaw, saying that she was a pessimist. How was I ever going to explain this to him? Or to her?

Jay sat across from me. He smiled, a shyer smile than I was used to seeing at the smoker's corner. "You're more reserved in person. But when we were typing, I felt connected, you know? And when you suggested meeting, I thought you figured out who I was."

"Well . . . you see . . ." I took a deep breath, decided to plunge in, like starting with question number one on a test I hadn't studied for. No skipping around. "This is going to be confusing, but you weren't chatting with me. It was Megs Salerno."

"But you mentioned the movie and—"

"That one time it was me. But the others—"

My phone rang. "It's Megs," I told him.

She spoke so low I could barely hear her. "I'm on my way to the hospital."

"It's good to see a doctor, to be safe. Which hospital? Morristown General?"

"Yeah."

Hospitals meant more sick people. But I'd worry

about that later. Our friendship had to trump my fear. "I'll meet you there." I tried to think of people I could ask to drive me. Maybe a taxi would be faster?

"No. My mom said . . . if I'm contagious . . . "

"I should be there with you. If you're contagious I've already been exposed."

The coffee shop got quiet. People stared in accusing silence. Apparently I wasn't the only one worried about the mysterious disease.

"Sorry," I mouthed to Jay before going outside.

"Lil, are you there?"

"Yes, I'm here." I leaned against the brick wall, away from the door.

"I'm going to hang up and send a text, OK?" she said.

"Sure."

Megs:	don't want Mom 2 hear.
Me:	got it.
Megs:	i feel awful. and scared.
Me:	wish i was there.
Megs:	me 2. i've never felt this sick b4.
Me:	doctors will help u.

Please. Please let the doctors be able to help. If Dad's assistant had gone into a coma . . . but she was pregnant. This was different. This had to be different.

| Megs: | if something happens 2 me |

Me:	shut up!
Megs:	i mean it. if something happens ur the best bff. 4 the record i'm pissed 2 die a virgin.
Me:	ur not dying. or i will kill u!!!
Megs:	lol. seriously, u can have my necklace. the 1 with blue pearl dad gave me.

Oh God, oh God, Megs please don't be that sick.

Me:	ur scaring me. u will be fine.
Megs:	where r u?
Me:	@ coffee shop. with ur mystery guy.
Megs:	!!! we r @ hospital. have 2 go. I <3 u.

Please let Megs be OK. Please.

I forgot about everything else, absorbed in a walking-home prayer for Megs. I was considering more effective bargains I could make with the universe when Jay caught up to me, flustered and annoyed.

"You didn't say good-bye."

"Megs is sick. Like, hospitalization-sick." The words sounded robotic, detached. *This cannot be happening.*

"Oh." The annoyance faded from his face. "Mind if I walk with you?"

I shrugged. He held out a cigarette and I took it. We paused for a second to light them. The simple act calmed me a little.

My phone pinged with a text. "Ugh," I mumbled. "It's Ethan." I was going to be even later than I thought. But I couldn't deal with texting him now.

"I thought the two of you were over," Jay said. "Or I wouldn't have met you tonight."

"We are over, sort of, I guess, but Ethan isn't the point. It's Megs. She really likes you. I chatted with you that one night, when we were about to watch the movie. And she joked about pessimism being a weakness, since it's clearly mine. But otherwise, your relationship was with her." I inhaled, then exhaled, watching the smoke drift into the air and disappear. "I'm sorry if we misled you. When Megs got sick, she begged me to come to the coffee shop to see who would show. She's at the emergency room now."

"You must be worried."

"She's been my best friend since we were five." My voice hitched in my throat and I willed myself not to cry. We walked in silence for a couple of blocks. I was grateful for the quiet.

"Maybe you should text her," I said, "and make plans for another day? It might cheer her up."

He shook his head. "It's you I've been thinking about."

My head spun. Megs was being treated at Morristown General for a potentially fatal disease, to which I may have been exposed. Her dream guy was crushing on me like a scene from a bad romantic comedy. Ethan would have a fit when I canceled tonight. And all I wanted was to go back in time, to be walking to school this morning with my happy, healthy best friend.

I dropped my cigarette butt, smushing it with my foot. "I don't think . . . look, you're a nice guy, but you don't know me that well. I'm not really girlfriend material."

"What does that mean, 'not girlfriend material'?"

I needed to stop this whole disaster before it got worse. "It means I don't want someone texting me and touching me and invading my emotional life. Besides, Megs likes you. You should get to know her better."

I expected an argument. Ethan would have argued. Like a starved pit bull with a bone, he wouldn't have let it drop.

"Fine," Jay said softly. "I'll see you around."

Once inside the house, I found myself stomping around, even though Jay had been perfectly gracious. When did everything get so complicated?

Sinking into the couch, I checked my phone. Ethan had sent eleven texts, wondering why I didn't show.

He answered on the first ring. "Where have you been?"

"I'm sorry. The whole night got messed up and I lost track of time. Megs is sick."

"You're at her house?"

"No, her mom made me leave in case she's contagious. They went to the hospital."

"Oh. It's still not too late to come over. I have everything planned. Waiting home alone isn't going to do you any good—"

"I . . . I don't think I should." I realized the truth I'd shared with Jay applied to Ethan, too. I didn't want to be his girlfriend again. It wasn't going to work any better now than it had the last time.

"I'm not asking for a commitment—"

"I know. But I'm exhausted, and confused, and this probably isn't the best time to see each other."

"Fine," he said before hanging up on me. At least he would stop texting for a while.

I changed into comfy pjs and spent most of the evening waiting for word about Megs. I checked online multiple times, expecting to find new information about the flu. Finally, an updated article was posted. More than two hundred cases had been reported in Portico, with twelve fatalities.

I read through the dozen names, catching my breath at the one I recognized.

Angela.

I sank back into the chair. The *Portico Press* had a whole article about her, but I couldn't bear to read the details. I made a mental list of the differences between Dad's assistant and Megs. Angela was pregnant; Angela was older; Angela might not have used antibacterial soap.

After an eternity, Mrs. Salerno called.

"We're still at the hospital," she said. "Megs is in serious shape."

No, no, no.

"Can I come see her?"

"She can't have visitors, Lily. I'm sorry."

Her voice sounded strained, as if she'd been crying. Mrs. Salerno never cried.

Fear made my hands tremble. I clutched the phone harder. "She's going to be OK, right?"

"Her lungs have been affected. The doctors . . . they don't know. I'll call you if there's any news. You should let your parents know if . . . if you start to feel ill."

I sat there dazed for a long time after we said good-bye. How could this happen so fast? It was in her lungs. Megs had perfectly healthy lungs. She didn't even smoke.

Finally moving, I took the cigarettes from my backpack and flushed them down the toilet. Megs would be proud. Then I tried to reach Mom and Dad, leaving the same message for both of them: Come home.

Chapter 9

Quarantines will not reduce the spread of influenza unless they create total isolation. In most cases, absolute segregation is nearly impossible.
—Blue Flu interview, contagious diseases expert

In my dream, Megs and I sat on the swings at the park. The rain had just stopped, and the air had that fresh, spring smell to it that we both loved. We swung back and forth in unison, chatting about nothing, about everything.

"You're going to find love when you least expect it," she said.

"What are you? A fortune cookie?"

She laughed, a cheerful, bubbly sound. "Let's go higher," she said.

We pumped faster, until it looked like we could kick the sun.

"We don't have much time," she told me. "I'm going to jump. Love ya!"

"Megs, wait!"

It was too late. The swing next to me creaked back and forth, empty.

~

I woke up with a yelp to the sound of the phone on Sunday morning, feeling around until I found it.

"Hello?" My voice was raspy and tired.

"Lily, it's Dad. Are you all right?"

"Yeah, I just woke up. Where are you?"

"I'm in Delaware packing up. I'll be home as soon as I can, by dinner at the latest."

"You got my message about Megs last night? Mrs. Salerno said I can't visit her. It seems so unfair."

"She'll be isolated, honey, until they determine exactly what's wrong. This illness is spreading fast. The public health department may contact you and the people she's been around—"

"Yesterday was Career Day."

"Oh my God."

He'd participated last year, talking to students about journalism, so he knew how hundreds of people attended from all over Morris County. It would be impossible to track who Megs had been in contact with.

"I'm glad you stayed home," he said.

I squeezed the phone. I couldn't tell him I'd been there, not even for a little while.

"Do you think Megs will recover?" I asked.

"I'm sure she's getting good care," he said. "Do you have any symptoms? Fever, achiness, coughing?"

"No, I'm fine. Do you think Megs has the same flu that Angela . . ."

"I don't know. I hope not," he said. "Look, I need you to remain inside the house, at least until I get there. Don't go out at all."

"Like a quarantine?" Fear gripped my stomach and squeezed tight.

"A voluntary home isolation, honey. Don't even answer the door."

"For how long?"

"We'll talk about it when I get back," he said. "You should rest and drink lots of water. You're sure you feel healthy?"

Actually, I had a monster headache, but that was probably from the tension of worrying. "I feel fine."

"Any word from Mom?"

"No. Why? Has the flu reached Asia?"

"It's only a matter of time," he said. "But I'm sure she's OK. Maybe her call isn't going through. It took me several tries. Everyone's probably checking on family, overloading the phone system."

"Yeah, you're right." I hoped it wasn't anything more than that.

"I'll call in a few hours when I have my travel plans worked out. I'll text if I can't get through. We should have her flight information by then, too."

I kept my voice calm, trying to think rationally. "I thought I'd buy more supplies. Mom might have told you about the extra food stored in the closet?"

"She mentioned it." His tone implied it had actually been a lengthy conversation.

"If we have to be isolated for a long time, it won't be enough. We'll need even more."

"You can't leave the house—"

"I can order online, Dad. I have your credit card from when I bought flowers . . ." *For Angela. Before she died.*

I didn't finish my sentence aloud. I didn't have to.

"Go ahead and use my card to buy what you think we'll need," he said. "I'll see you soon. Call me if anything changes."

I searched the kitchen for comfort food, finally settling on macaroni and cheese for breakfast. After eating, I took my temperature. It registered normal all three times.

From the isolated safety of Dad's office, I logged onto the computer and browsed the virtual aisles of the online grocery store. After filling my shopping cart with mostly nonperishable items, I selected delivery for tomorrow. Then I went to a drug store site and made a bunch of purchases there. The thought of the supplies should have calmed me, but my hands shook a little and I felt fidgety. Did that mean oncoming flu or just nicotine withdrawal? It didn't seem like I'd been smoking much, but I'd kind of lost track.

I really wanted a cigarette. I tried chewing gum instead.

There was still no word from Mrs. Salerno. Each time I called the hospital, the phone line was busy, and she didn't answer her cell. I paced around the house in frustration, not able to get through to Mom, either.

After ten tries, and many deep, calming breaths, I finally sent Mom a text telling her that Megs was sick, that Dad was on his way home, that I was fine. It was easy to hide the worry when she couldn't hear my voice.

I needed to do something constructive to pass the time. Using a yellow pad of lined paper, I wrote out the days of the week down the side, with columns across the top: me, Mom, Dad. Starting with the perishables, then factoring in my stockpile and groceries on order, I filled out each box with three meals and one snack a day. My supplies would provide enough food for about four weeks.

On a fresh sheet of paper, I listed activities to pass the time alone, starting with the useful (reorganize my history binder) and ending with the silly (download the new drawing game I wanted to try). If I didn't get sick, I had enough resources to avoid the rest of the world for a long time.

I tacked the grid to the inside of our pantry. I had a plan, a solid one. Now I just needed Megs to recover and my parents to arrive home safely. When Dad finally called back, I lunged for the phone.

"I need you to stay calm," he said.

Fear surged through me like an electrical shock.

"What's wrong? Are you sick?"

"I'm healthy, but they've quarantined my hotel. It's impossible for me to come home."

I leaned on the kitchen counter for support. But it wasn't enough to steady me. Clutching the phone, I slid to the floor in a terrified heap.

CHAPTER 10

Lily? Are you still there?" Dad asked.

Huddled on the kitchen floor, I gripped the telephone. "Why would they quarantine your hotel? How long until you can leave?"

"The CDC made some progress identifying the exact illness. They've determined that it's a novel H5N1 that's causing the flu," Dad said. "The virus has mutated. Traditional H5N1 would bind to the respiratory cells deep in the lungs. It was deadly, but didn't spread. This strain is binding in the upper respiratory track as well."

"In English, Dad."

"It's bird flu. It's deadly and highly contagious. They've traced the source to migrating waterfowl, like the ones they banded last weekend at the swamp."

I gasped. "Mom almost dragged us to that!"

"I know. And Angela was there, along with several other people who've become sick."

"You said you didn't have any contact with Angela. So why are you quarantined?"

"Bad luck, really. There's a national bird banding convention at my hotel."

"You're stuck with tons of potentially sick people?"

"We're confined to our hotel rooms."

"Have you spoken to Mom?"

"Yes. She's trying to leave Hong Kong, but they've cancelled most of the flights to the East Coast. There are rumors Newark Airport will shut down soon."

I took the phone into my room and climbed into bed. Dad was quarantined. Mom was stuck in a foreign country. My best friend was sick. I was home alone after possibly being exposed to a fatal illness. The panic made it hard to breathe. I focused on each inhale, every exhale, as if my body might forget how to breathe properly.

Dad cleared his throat. "I know this is difficult. I called my stepbrother—"

"Uncle Jim? I've met him like twice in my whole life."

"I know. And he can't come anyway. But I'm trying, honey."

I pulled the covers up to my chin, realizing how isolated and alone I was. "Dad, if I start to feel sick—"

"Are you ill now?"

"No, but just in case, who would I call? You're away, Mom's away, Mrs. Salerno is at the hospital. . . ."

He was quiet a moment. "What about Reggie? He's right down the street."

My neighbor and happy ShopWell cashier. I would have preferred a motherly-type, but I guess he would do.

"He's trustworthy, Lily, and . . ."

"And what?"

Dad sighed. "He's statistically in a good age bracket for survival."

"I thought old people were most at risk from the flu?"

"Not in this case. It's too soon to tell definitively, but based on the fatalities so far, it seems to be less deadly to the younger and the older."

"How young?" I asked.

He paused.

"Dad, I can hear it from you or the news."

"They're predicting that kids fourteen and younger will have a higher survival rate. So will adults over age fifty."

Could this get any worse? "Then at sixteen, I'm

screwed. And you and Mom are in the deadly zone, too."

"I know it seems bad. I'll keep checking on you. Texting is probably easiest. Let's send messages every few hours. Do you want me to call Reggie, tell him your situation?"

"No," I said, unconvincingly.

"I'll contact him. And there's one other thing I need you to do." He lowered his voice. "I have some medicine hidden in the safe. It's an antiviral. I want you to take it."

"Will it work with this strain of flu?"

"I don't know. But it could offer some protection if you've been exposed and may lessen the symptoms if you do get sick. Of course, there's no guarantee now that the virus has mutated, but it's better than nothing. The first two numbers of the combination are written in pencil inside the laundry room door. The last number is 88."

"Got it. But what about you?"

"I'm guessing they'll treat us here. You should start taking the medicine, once a day for ten days, as a precaution. If you show any signs of the actual flu, take it twice a day. And don't tell anyone about it."

"OK." I had gotten good at keeping secrets.

After we hung up, I concentrated on breathing for a long time. Then my phone beeped with a message.

The Board of Education will be meeting with the Morris County Health Department tomorrow to discuss whether to close Portico schools. You will be kept in the loop and updated accordingly. In the meantime, please do not send your child to school on Monday if he or she is exhibiting flu-like symptoms, or is otherwise not fit as a fiddle. Check the school website to learn more about the common cold versus the flu. In a nutshell, your child should be fever-free for twenty-four hours before returning to school after an illness.

The Morris County Health Office has asked us to remind students to practice respiratory hygiene (cough into your sleeve, not your hand) and to encourage frequent hand-washing. Keep them as clean as a whistle! Please note: the poster contest judging has been delayed, but we will save all submitted entries until a later date.

Because of health and safety concerns, we will consider a masking policy if school remains open. Each student would be given one surgical mask. Although the flu virus may be able to penetrate the woven material, the mask may prevent large respiratory droplets (due to coughing or sneezing) from being transmitted to others.

Thank you for your cooperation.

The school sent a second message not long after.

Instant Alert from Portico High School

We have received a number of inquiries about masks colors. They are only available in sky blue. Patience is a virtue, so hold tight. Further details will be provided soon.

The emails distracted me a little. If people were well enough to worry about how fashionable the masks were, then not everyone was falling over ill. That was a good sign, I hoped.

I dragged myself out of bed to open the safe, which was hidden on the closet floor in the laundry room. Dad said most burglars wouldn't look for it there. It took a few tries before I figured out that the combination started with a counter-clockwise turn. Finally, the door clicked open.

Whoa.

While I had been stockpiling food, Dad had been accumulating quite a collection of medicines. There were cipro pills for anthrax, potassium iodide tablets for radiation, and a bunch of prescriptions I didn't recognize. They were all grouped in sets of three. Dad was definitely prepared. Did Mom realize I wasn't the only worrier in the family?

I took out the box of medicine he mentioned and

closed the safe. A swallowed pill later, I didn't feel any better.

When the phone rang, I said a silent prayer for good news. Dad could be released, or Megs could be better. Maybe Mom's flight had landed and she was minutes away. I didn't recognize the number on caller ID.

"Hello?" I answered with crossed fingers.

"Lilianna?" Mr. B asked.

Hope left my body along with my breath.

CHAPTER 11

We've known since 1972 that waterfowl host just about every influenza virus there is. But no mutated virus could be passed from human to human. Until now.
—Blue Flu interview, anonymous researcher

At the sound of Mr. B's voice, the memories came crashing back.

"Lilianna, I need to discuss something with you," he continued.

"I . . . I . . ." My ability to speak was gone.

I didn't slam down the phone or hurl it across the room. No drama. The drama had already occurred at his house. Instead, I pushed the "End call" button. Then I found the website for the phone company and blocked all future calls from his number and any unidentified callers as well.

What could he possibly want to speak to me about? It was crazy that he would call the house. If my parents had answered, they would have contacted the police, made a formal complaint. He must have known that. And did he really think I would just have a nice chat with him on the phone?

I needed to get rid of the angst, to find a way to release the fear. Finally, I went into the basement, closed the door, and screamed until my throat felt raw. At first I worried that the neighbors would call the police, but the yelling felt good. No one came to check on me.

It was a long sleepless night. I must have dozed off at some point because I woke up to a rainy grayness that matched my mood. Leaving the house wasn't safe. Now that Mr. B had called, staying inside didn't feel so secure either. I spent a lot of time pacing.

At noon on Monday, the church rang its bells. On a calm day, the sound carried to our street. Today their tone seemed sad, mournful.

I shook off the feeling. Of course the bells today were the same as any other day. Usually I only heard them on the weekend, when school was out. For a moment, I relished the fact that history class was taking place without me. Mrs. Nubrik would be droning on and on right that very minute.

This consolation didn't last. I still couldn't get through to Megs or Mrs. Salerno, or Mom or Dad. Hours of worry stretched ahead of me like a desolate road I had to travel alone.

Going to church suddenly seemed appealing. It was an odd longing, because I stopped attending mass regularly after Mr. B. I tried once or twice, but restlessness replaced the peace I used to feel when the light shone through the stained glass windows. Soon a few skipped weeks stretched into months. Dad was pretty much agnostic and Mom eventually stopped asking me to come with her on Sunday mornings.

But church was off limits now. There was no way I could go during my self-imposed quarantine. I convinced myself that any prayer counted, whether I was seated in a pew or not. I focused my silent entreaty on Megs and her health.

I wasn't particularly hungry, but forced myself to eat some corn flakes with bananas. I had just finished when the doorbell rang.

"Leave the groceries out there please," I said through the closed door.

"Lilianna Snyder?"

I peeked through the side window.

"I'm Officer Raitt. I need to speak to your parents."

"They're not here. I've been exposed to the flu so I'm not supposed to open the door."

"It's all right. It's police business."

"Just a minute." I found one of Mom's old sweaters in the coat closet and pulled it on over my pjs. Cracking the door the tiniest bit, I recognized Officer Raitt even with a pale blue mask across his mouth and nose. He had stopped Dad for speeding once on Noe Avenue, but let my father go with just a warning.

"How are you today?" he asked.

I stepped outside with a nervous stomach. Police at the door couldn't be a good thing. But even my pessimistic attitude couldn't imagine what would cause a cop to come to our house in person. Maybe someone called the police about last night's meltdown after all? How could I explain my crazy screaming?

"Fine, thank you."

"Are you symptomatic at all?"

"No." Maybe that's why he was here, to take me away and lock me up somewhere if I had the flu. Thinking about it made my throat compulsively tickle. A small cough escaped against my will.

Officer Raitt seemed preoccupied and didn't react. "Sorry to stop by unannounced. Um, Detective Salerno asked me to come."

Oh, that explained it. Megs's mom must be worried that I caught the flu. Mom and Mrs. Salerno were thoughtful like that, looking out for each other's daughters. Sometimes it could be annoying, as if having one overprotective mother wasn't enough. Today, it warmed me like hot chocolate with marshmallows on a blustery day.

"You can tell her I'm doing all right. It's nice of her to ask you to check on me."

Officer Raitt looked away, toward the neighbors' house. He studied their property for a long time. I followed his gaze, seeing damp shrubs, a neat lawn, an ordinary home. Nothing to hold his interest for so long.

Finally, he spoke. "There's no easy way to break this to you." He sighed, a heavy, unhappy sound. "Megan passed away yesterday."

"Megan?" I tried to process the information but my brain clouded over. "You mean Megs?"

He nodded. "Detective Salerno asked as a favor if I'd talk to you, break the news in person."

"Megs is . . . dead?" I asked, not comprehending the words.

"Yes. I'm sorry."

"But the hospital . . . the doctors were taking care of her. She was admitted Saturday night. And she's been studying for her AP test next month. Megs takes school very seriously."

"I know this is difficult for you."

"We were picking out clothes for her date. Her mom drove to the emergency room right away. Mrs. Salerno doesn't like to take chances." I shook my head. "You know them, personally, right? There must be a mistake."

"I wish it was a big misunderstanding," Officer Raitt said. "Because of the widespread illness, the funeral arrangements for Megan have been postponed. We'll try to keep you informed."

"The funeral . . ." I stood there, eyes wide, heart empty. "I need to call someone. My parents. I have to tell them."

"Yes, you should let them know. It's probably better if you can be with your family right now. I'm sorry I can't wait for them to return. I have too many next-of-kin notifications to make."

"Next of kin? How many people have died?"

"I can't give you an exact figure. But off the record, staying home is probably a good idea," he said. "Here's my number in case you need anything."

I tucked his contact info into a pocket and watched him stride toward his patrol car, toward a day filled with delivering bad news. I fought the urge to beg him to stay, not to leave me alone with the sadness.

After he left, I didn't want to go inside to the photos of me and Megs on my desk, to the black shirt I borrowed from her and never returned, to the kitchen counter she'd sat on a thousand times after school. I went through the back gate and kneeled in the wet grass in my pjs. The air had that just-rained magical smell from my last dream about her.

Mindlessly, I pulled out blades of grass one by one until I made a large empty patch, losing track of time. Piling the grass in my palms, I let the breeze scatter the pieces. The world seemed so vibrant: the bright sky, picture-perfect clouds, a mourning dove cooing nearby. But Megs wasn't a part of it any longer. How could that be?

Yet part of me had known it in my heart since the dream. Megs was gone.

In a way, she had said a final good-bye to me in that dream. She would have known I needed the last conversation, the closure. I hated loose ends, and Megs understood me better than anyone.

Megs was a part of my everyday life: the drama, the boredom, the survival. After the Mr. B incident, Mom and Dad had an unspoken rule not to talk about it unless I brought it up, which I never did. But somehow discussing it with Megs was different, less intimidating. Unlike my family, she wasn't analyzing the long-term emotional implications to my mental health. She just listened.

Only Megs believed I could study anything I wanted in college, even major in history if I put my mind to it. To her, the future was a blank page with no lines. Anything was possible.

Once we made chocolate chip cookies in the middle of the night then ate them straight from the baking sheet while we discussed our ideal careers. In between giggles and bites of gooey sweetness, we ruled out nutrition-related fields that would discourage midnight snacks.

Megs and I spent one sleepover planning our weddings in detail. We found pictures online of our perfect white dresses and elegant bouquets: roses for her, lilies for me. She wanted to have her ceremony outside under an ivy-covered cabana on a beautiful spring afternoon.

A day just like today.

The phone rang. What if it was Mr. B? I hesitated. What if it wasn't?

I moved like a sleepwalker back inside the house. It was Mom. Finally, the tears came.

CHAPTER 12

Portico has become a hotbed of flu-like activity with more than 200 cases reported among its 10,000 townspeople. This has resulted in a record number of departures. "I'm not sure leaving Portico is the answer," Mayor Hein said. But residents seem to disagree and cars jam all major roads exiting Portico. When a policeman asked one mother where she was taking her three children, their beagle, and their parakeet, she replied, "Anywhere but here."
—Various Blue Flu interviews

Mom was stuck in Hong Kong, Dad in Delaware. I was in voluntary quarantine hell, monitoring my temperature every hour, waiting for the flu to descend upon me. If I sat perfectly still as the minutes ticked by, maybe I could sense the illness shift in my body, feel the cells mutate, and mandate them to stop.

The groceries came. That was the highlight of Monday. After putting the perishable stuff in the fridge, I spent most of the day sleeping between bouts of nausea. Whether it was the antiviral medicine or the grief, I couldn't say.

Dad kept his word, texting me every few hours to check in. He insisted on ignoring text language and spelled out every word.

> Dad: I tried to get a journalist's exemption from the quarantine. They told me there is no such thing. I'm attempting to invent one.
>
> Dad: On a serious note, Mom told me about Megs. Not something that is easy to text about. You OK?

It took me a long time to type the five words, to condense the overwhelming sadness into alphabetical characters.

> Me: Not really. Come home soon.

Later:

> Dad: There is no official word on how long the quarantine will last. They've got people in masks cleaning the rooms. Probably too late for that. Are you still healthy?
>
> Me: Yes.
>
> Me: Hurts 2 think about Megs.

When I wasn't checking for his messages, I didn't know what to do with myself. I couldn't send flowers, visit her grave, or do any of the normal grieving things. Hours passed as I gazed outside, staring at the clouds. Remembering all the good times she and I had together made my chest ache.

On Tuesday, I texted her.

> Me: I miss u.
>
> Me: U will never believe who the mystery guy was.
>
> Me: J! Isn't that weird.
>
> Me: How can u b gone?
>
> Me: I really miss u.

The phone rang in the kitchen and for a crazy second I thought it was Megs. I let it ring and ring, crying, unable to answer it. The machine clicked on and the caller hung up.

I did not want to think about Mr. B calling again.

I turned on the TV as a distraction and realized I wasn't the only one in hell. Apparently, the flu had gotten stronger as it moved up the coast, with each state struck harder than the one before. New York and Connecticut prepared for the worst and various cases were being reported across the United States.

The camera panned over a group of somber gray tents. "The governor of New Jersey has declared a state of emergency," a reporter wearing a pale blue mask narrated. "Tents like those behind me are being erected outside many Jersey hospitals to deal with overwhelming demand. Retired nurses and doctors are asked to help wherever possible. While schools, churches, and 'nonessential' businesses decide whether to remain open, the governor encourages them to keep the greater good of the public's health in mind. 'Loss of business income and school days can be recovered,' he said in a press conference earlier today. 'Loss of life cannot.'"

I stared at the tents. Megs and I had camped out in her backyard once. Or at least tried to. We made it until about midnight before we dragged our sleeping bags inside, grateful for the sturdy walls and ceiling to protect us from the outside world.

The next news segment pulled me out of my thoughts. A doctor described the mechanics of the virus and how it affected the lungs. "The lack of oxygen," she explained, "causes cyanosis, a blue discoloration of the skin." A photo of an unidentified victim filled the screen, the face mostly obscured for privacy. But the ears were navy-colored as if they were covered with dark blue ink. I stood in the family room afraid to move, transfixed by the horror of it all.

The next reporter also wore a mask. "I'm on location at the biggest ice arena in Morris County," he said.

I recognized the building. We skated there once—me, Megs, and Kayla. Kayla skated with a fluid grace while Megs and I slid around the rink, clutching each other and giggling.

"Because of the large number of deaths here and in the surrounding counties, the ice skating rink behind me is being used to handle the overflow of bodies."

I turned the TV off, not wanting to imagine Megs as part of an overflow, another dead person stacked in the cold ice arena. She deserved so much more than that.

I needed to talk about her before the sadness crushed me with its weight. I texted Mom and Dad with no responses. When the phone rang again, I checked the caller ID before answering. It was Jay.

"Hey, I'm home from school today, too," he said. "I wanted to see how you were doing."

I managed to tell him about Megs's death.

"I'm sorry," he said. "It's never a good time to lose your best friend. I won't say anything lame about God's will or how it was meant to be."

"Thanks."

"I don't know if this will make you feel better or worse, but she's not the only one. Some other kids from school have died, too."

"Who?" I asked, dreading the answer. Not that I would miss anyone more than Megs. But locking myself inside our house hadn't stopped the march of death through our town.

"Jennifer Williams."

From my bio class.

"Teddy Rhodes."

My former cigarette supplier.

"And Jose Rodriguez."

The class vice president.

"Those are the kids I've heard about," Jay said.

"Well, I didn't think it was possible to feel even more miserable."

"I know. It's surreal. I was thinking about starting a student memorial page through my blog. I could list the . . . fatalities, keep it updated for our town. I talked to Jenny Silverman at *Portico Press* and she thought it would be a good way for people to share info, a place to check in. Especially if they close the school," he said. "My aunt says even if they don't close it, I'm not going this week. My two older sisters are at Arizona State. She's forbidden them to attend classes, too."

"I didn't realize you had sisters. I thought it was only you and your little brother."

"I mentioned it when we chatted online. Maybe that was to Megs? Anyway, only my brother and I moved here. My sisters didn't want to leave. So my aunt tries to boss them around from a distance."

"I've been staying home under a Dad-imposed quarantine, too, since he found out Megs was sick. But it's been almost three days."

"Do you have any symptoms?" he asked.

"Not yet."

I told him about my parents. "It's hard not to

have them here during a crisis. Normally, Mrs. Salerno would be here for me. But she's probably trying to cope with everything."

He was quiet for a moment.

"What's the matter?" I asked.

"I didn't want to be the one to tell you. But Mrs. Salerno . . . she didn't make it. They wrote a tribute to her on *Portico Press*."

"Oh." Sadness overwhelmed me yet again. Angela, Megs, Mrs. Salerno. The other kids from school. I curled up on the couch, tugging the blanket around me.

"Are you OK?" Jay asked.

"OK is relative these days."

I wasn't really all right, but telling the truth was too hard. I couldn't admit that my world felt like a lone island battered by a tsunami. Everything washed away, but the real damage hadn't been realized yet.

And the forecast called for more disaster. A cynical voice whispered in my head, *it's only the beginning.*

Jay interrupted my brooding. "Do you think they'll list our assignments online? Maybe they'll send us another cliché-filled alert. Something like: you might think we can't teach an old dog new tricks, but as luck would have it, we've convinced our teachers to communicate lessons online. It's all in a day's work."

Any other time I would have laughed. But not today.

"They have to cancel classes," I said. "If they can close an airport, how much more bureaucratic do you think it would be to cancel high school?"

"True," he said. "I wonder if they'll add back the lost days in June."

"I guess it depends how long we're out. I think if it's a state of emergency, we don't have to make them up."

"Yeah, that's what Kayla thought, too," he said.

"Kayla?"

"We've texted a few times."

"Oh." I should have realized that if she liked him, she'd take the initiative. She always did. But it made talking to him suddenly feel uncomfortable. "Well, I should go." As if I had such a busy schedule for the day.

"Sure," he said. "You can always stop by if you get stir-crazy."

"Thanks." But my plan for surviving the pandemic meant avoiding potentially-infected people, which basically meant everyone. Especially guys who liked Kayla.

Bored, I checked my phone. Bonus! I found texts from Dad *and* Mom.

Dad: Two people from our conference have

fallen ill. They're trying to separate the
healthy from the sick. I'm taking pages
of notes for my article. But I wish I was
home. Let me know that you are still
well.

Me: I'm OK. More kids from school have
       died.

Dad: Hang in there and DO NOT attend
       school.

Me: You don't have to convince me.

Mom was still getting the hang of the texting
thing.

Mom: hi lily

Mom: it's mom

Mom: miss you lots

Mom: stuck in airport

Mom: with hundreds of other americans

Mom: desperate to get home

Mom: if i could steal a plane i would

Mom: at least we are still healthy

Mom: i've been thinking about megs

Mom: and how hard it must be on you

Mom: when aunt caryn died i took lots of walks

Mom: movement helped

Mom: don't stay in bed too much

Mom: text me soon

Mom: bye sweeter

Mom: that was supposed to be sweetie

Mom: what is up with spelling on this thing
Mom: love you

After letting Mom know I was all right, I took her advice and moved through the numbness, doing stupid things, like dusting. As if the dust mattered. But it did feel good to be busy. The laundry was next. Then I unpacked the rest of the groceries that had been delivered, along with the stuff from the drug store site, too. They wouldn't fit upstairs, so I reorganized the kitchen pantry, carrying supplies down from both my bedroom closet and the hall closet until the kitchen was full. The neat rows of cans gave me a satisfied feeling. So far, the once-a-day antiviral dose seemed to be working. I had taken it three nights in a row.

I wondered if they had given Megs the antiviral. They must have. At least I wanted to believe they'd tried everything. But then that begged the question: Why didn't it help her? And what if it didn't help me?

✦

Wednesday morning it was official. School was closed indefinitely.

Instant Alert from Portico High School

On the advice of the mayor, the Portico Police, and the Department of Health, ALL SCHOOLS AND OFFICES in the Portico School District will be closed until further notice. All athletic and extracurricular activities are also cancelled. It's better to be safe than sorry.

Teachers will be asked to update their school websites with assignments to be completed by healthy students. When this crisis has passed, we look forward to getting back into the swing of things. Thank you for your support and cooperation.

When the phone rang, I was half expecting it to be Jay again, pointing out the clichés in the alert.

"Hello, Miss Lil."

"Oh, hi, Reggie."

"How are you holding up on your own?"

It was nice to know that someone was looking out for me. "I've been fine. Symptom-free. Did my dad tell you to call?"

"He said I should check that you're not hosting any parties."

"Ha. I think the whole town is completely party-free. How've you been?"

"All's well here. I'm heading to work soon. Not that there's any food, but they want a few employees in there to dissuade potential looters."

I envisioned aisle after aisle of empty shelves. "There's nothing to eat? In the whole store?"

"Some leftover items, here and there, but it's slim pickings. We were supposed to receive shipments soon, but the flu has impacted the delivery people, too. I guess they can't find enough old people who are still capable drivers."

"That's not good."

I wanted to ask if he had enough to eat. What if Reggie were starving? But the selfish, survivalist part of my brain insisted I shouldn't share. Depending on how long the crisis lasted, every bit of food could become critical.

Squeezing the phone, I tried to decide. "Do they know when the next trucks will arrive?"

"No one can tell. But I have extra food if you need some," he said, as if sharing were as easy as breathing. "I'll eat supper at the Senior Center. A bunch of us have been meeting for meals, combining supplies. No one seems desperate yet. Do you want me to bring you some dinner?"

I choked back tears. What was happening to me? How could I have become so self-centered? "I'm OK. Thanks for checking on me."

"If you need anything, give a holler."

Feeling despicable, I paced around the house. I'd been reluctant to split my food with an old man who only wanted to look after me. What kind of human being was I to hesitate like that? I dialed Megs to tell her what an awful person I was, then remembered she wasn't there. The grief crashed into me all over again.

When the sobs faded to a whimper, I found my sneakers. Walking through the neighborhood wouldn't be a magical cure for my grief, but maybe Mom was right. Maybe it would help. I would try anything to make the aching stop.

I tried to focus on the practical, like the fact that today was garbage day. When I wheeled our trash to the curb, the clatter seemed so loud that I lifted the can and carried it the rest of the way.

As I walked down the street, all the normal spring noises were missing. No lawn mowers buzzed. No cars passed me. No neighbors walked their dogs. Nature still prevailed: sparrows twittered, squirrels chattered, and breezes fluttered through the trees. But without the usual human sounds, Portico transformed into a ghost town.

A few other people had put their trash out, too, but not many. As I passed each home near mine, I couldn't help wondering which families were healthy, which were ill, and which had fled town in hopes of avoiding the flu. Would Megs still be alive if the Salernos had left? What if I had convinced Megs to skip Career Day? Would she still be here?

Four houses away from mine, the Goodwins' baby cried loudly, interrupting the silence and ending my what-if spiral. It wasn't a normal cry, but a continuous high-pitched wail. Mrs. Goodwin and my mom were do-you-have-a-cup-of-sugar neighbors, but I didn't know her well.

I continued passed the house, not seeing a single soul. Was it safe to be out alone? It was daylight but I couldn't help thinking that if someone wanted to hurt me, there would be no one around to help. That realization was as worrisome as the flu. Freaked out, I turned around a few blocks from home and hurried back.

The baby still cried as I passed by the Goodwins' house. The glass storm door was closed, but the wooden one behind it was wide open. I crept to the front and peeked inside. Most of the lights were off, giving the entranceway a gloomy air. I doubted anyone would hear the doorbell over the baby, but I rang it anyway, then jiggled the door handle. It was unlocked. A striped tabby cat ran to the door, staring at me with yellow-green eyes. Its plaintive meows combined with the baby's bawling.

Something was wrong. But if the flu had infected the Goodwins, I didn't want to risk being exposed. Using my cell phone, I called information for their number, then listened as it rang inside the house. The answering machine kicked in. "We can't take your call right now . . ."

At the sound of the voice, the baby quieted for a moment. Then the sobbing began again, louder and more distressed.

Standing by the front door, I shifted my weight from one foot to the other. I considered dialing 911. But what would I report? A cranky baby?

"Mrs. Goodwin?" I called.

Still no answer. I turned, then took a few steps away from the house. *This is none of my business.* The wailing rang in my ears. *It is not my problem.* I counted to thirty, willing the frantic cries to stop. They didn't.

Taking a deep breath, I returned to the door, opening it slowly. A flash of tabby stripes ran out past me, making me jump.

"Mrs. Goodwin?" I called. "Mr. Goodwin?"

The kitchen was empty. I waited for someone to come out, to ask me what I was doing. No one did.

I moved stealthily down the hallway, feeling like an intruder. But I couldn't leave the baby now. The howling guided me into a bedroom on the right. The baby stood in the crib, his face mottled and red, his jumper damp. Behind his crib hung a sign with animal-shaped letters that spelled out his name: Tobias Kutchner.

"Hi, Tobias Kutchner. I sure hope you're not sick. The flu doesn't affect many babies, right?" I didn't want to hold him, to come into contact with him, but I couldn't exactly leave him alone again.

"We have to find your mommy. This room smells like you need a diaper change." Summoning my nerve, I put my hands under his arms to lift him. Something squished under my fingers as I reached his back.

Poop. And lots of it.

Disgusted by the grossness, I put him back down. His screams reached a new decibel.

"It's OK, it's OK," I said, more to myself than the baby. Grabbing a blanket from the crib, I created a barrier between his dirty body and my own. "We need to find a bathroom to clean you up, TK. Do you mind if I call you TK, little buddy?"

I started to carry him out. Two steps toward the door, I stopped babbling and froze.

Oh dear God.

In the corner of the room, Mrs. Goodwin sat slumped over in a rocking chair.

CHAPTER 13

*Our emergency plans can handle an unexpected absenteeism
rate of roughly 40–50% in critical sectors. We're currently at 75%.*
—Blue Flu interview, senior manager of the
NJ Water Association

I stared at TK's mother. The angle of her head and the bluish tinge of her ears told me she wasn't napping in the rocking chair.

"Mrs. Goodwin?"

I thought about touching her wrist, checking her pulse, but even if I were willing to risk the germs, my hands were covered in poop. Unnerved, I backed out of the bedroom, then spotted the bathroom. Thankfully, there were diapers and other supplies away from the body. I laid TK on top of the blanket on the changing pad.

Mrs. Goodwin was dead.

I fought the urge to run, concentrating on the snaps holding his terrycloth outfit closed.

Dead across the hall.

I opened the box of wipes.

Dead like Megs. From the killer flu.

The stench soon obliterated any other thoughts. It took the whole box of baby wipes and a large bath towel to finish the job. I bundled the entire mess in the towel and dropped everything into the garbage. In all my hours of babysitting the Sullivan twins last summer, I'd never seen such a mess.

TK's skin looked pink and irritated so I quickly slathered diaper ointment on it. A spare outfit was folded neatly next to the sink. While I dressed him, he started to cry again and the sound unnerved me. I couldn't ask his mother for help.

Think, Lil, think.

He was clean but still miserable. Probably hungry.

After washing my hands for as long as he would let me, I carried him into the kitchen where a bowl of creamy soup congealed on the counter. That could have been today's lunch or dinner from last night. How long had TK been stranded in the crib with Mrs. Goodwin sick? Inside the fridge, three filled baby bottles were lined up in a row next to a can of cat food covered in tin foil. I took a bottle out intending to warm it, but TK wailed as soon as he spotted his meal.

"All right, don't get a stomach ache."

He slurped loudly while he drank in my arms. I sat on the edge of a kitchen chair, ready to jump up if . . . if what? I wasn't sure, but after seeing Mrs. Goodwin, I didn't want to get too cozy. We needed a plan, one that included getting away from the dead body as soon as possible.

A stroller leaned near the front door. After a few tries I was able to unfold it while holding TK. He cried for a minute while I readjusted him and the bottle, but soon he was strapped in and ready to go.

I had the door open with TK in the stroller when my planning mind kicked in. *Take supplies*, it said. *Leave contact information.*

Right. I scribbled a quick note so Mr. Goodwin would know I had TK at my house and I could avoid kidnapping charges. Then I rummaged through the kitchen cabinets, shoving a canister of powdered formula in the stroller basket. A navy blue diaper bag leaned near the front door, and I crammed the pre-made bottles in it, and some baby food, too, along with the list of emergency numbers stuck to the fridge.

I snatched the rest of the supplies from the bathroom and loaded up the stroller. All I needed now was an extra outfit for him, in case he had another explosive poop before Mr. Goodwin picked him up.

My shoulders slumped as I realized his clothing would be in the nursery with the body.

Before I could change my mind, I dashed toward his room, but my courage failed me and I paused in the doorway. *You can do this. You have to do this.* Holding my breath, I hurried in, jerked open the dresser drawers, and grabbed the baby clothes without looking at Mrs. Goodwin. A tiny pair of socks fell to the floor near her blue feet. I left them there. With shaky legs and a pounding heart, I pushed TK away from his home.

I parked TK's stroller in the middle of our kitchen. He was a beautiful baby, about ten months old, with chunky cheeks and pudgy little arms and legs. When I unpacked his stroller, he eyed the bottles ravenously. But looking healthy was no guarantee he wasn't actually sick. What was I going to do with a potentially infectious baby?

Before feeding him again, I carried him to the garage where Dad stored paper masks for yard work. I wore a mask for about ten seconds before TK grabbed it with his chubby hand and pulled. Then he let go, smacking it against my face. Fascinated, he mask-smacked me four or five more times.

"Epic fail," I said, tossing the mask onto the workbench.

Back in his stroller, TK conked out after a second bottle and a big burp. I washed my hands for several minutes, praying he wasn't contagious. Would the antiviral be enough to protect me?

I had been taking the medicine after dinner each day. With TK in the equation, I decided to forget the precise schedule and take the pill earlier. A tension headache was building, so along with a big glass of water, I also took an ibuprofen.

The least amount of time exposed to TK, the better. Contacting his family became my top priority. I hoped it would only be a few hours until someone came to get him. The pre-filled bottles, the cheerful nursery, even his mother dying nearby showed TK was well-loved. Mrs. Goodwin didn't want to leave her baby, even at the end.

While TK napped, I checked the emergency phone number list I'd snatched from the fridge. I called Mr. Goodwin's cell. It rang and rang until his voice mail message kicked in.

"Um, Mr. Goodwin, this is Lily Snyder, your neighbor. Mrs. Goodwin is . . . is not feeling well so I'm watching TK at my house. I need you to call me as soon as you get this." I left my phone number and address. As for his poor wife, I wasn't about to mention her death in a message.

Next, I tried calling the other numbers on the list, like Mr. Goodwin's work phone, "Aunt Shirley," and "Aunt Rachele," but no one answered.

This was not promising. I bit at a ragged cuticle, then tried all the numbers again. Still no success.

While I waited for someone to call me back, I turned on the TV. Instead of the bad weather-related closures that appeared during the winter, the news reported "business shutdowns" in a scrolling ticker across the bottom of the screen. Newark Airport, the Short Hills Mall, and the Livingston Mall were closed, along with multiple school districts. A "breaking news" banner flashed.

"The water supply in Morris and Union Counties may have been affected by employee absenteeism and work stoppages," a woman in a black suit reported. "There is a Boil Water Advisory in place. Although contamination has not been confirmed, all residents are advised to boil water for a full minute before consumption. Boiling is a precaution to kill any possible bacteria until further pathogen tests can be conducted."

Water contamination? No way. I drank some less than five minutes ago. My stomach churned at the thought.

"Tap water should be boiled before drinking, cooking, washing produce, or brushing teeth," she continued. "Dishwashers should be run on the hottest cycle. Washing machines and showers can be used as normal. Consumers are advised to throw out any ice cubes, food\, or beverages made with tap water in the past twenty-four hours."

Agitated, I turned off the TV and tossed the remote on the coffee table. I made myself a note that said BOIL and taped it to the faucet as a reminder not to drink tap water. As I stared at TK's empty bottle in the sink, dread settled over me. How long ago had Mrs. Goodwin mixed the bottles?

Was TK contaminated? Was I?

I put a pot of water on to boil, deciding to save the jugs stashed under my bed. The nausea came so quickly I convinced myself it had to be hypochondria instead of bacteria. I rested on the couch until the water bubbled.

Queasy, I made my way to the kitchen and turned off the stovetop. While the pot cooled, I checked the water company's website. There were instructions about boiling, but no information about the possible consequences if you didn't get the warning in time.

I couldn't take the chance with TK's last premade bottle. I hated to waste the formula, because the remaining tin was only one-third full, but it was too risky. I made three fresh bottles with the boiled water.

Still nauseated, I called TK's dad again but kept getting his voice mail. I needed to speak to him by dark, because TK wasn't about to spend the night sleeping in a stroller. I called Mr. Goodwin's work number, let it ring three times, and hung up. Then I called back for three rings and hung up, again and again and again. If there was anyone else near his phone, surely I would annoy them into picking up. I was rewarded on the ninth try.

"Hello?" an older woman answered.

"Hi, I'm trying to reach Mr. Goodwin. It's an emergency."

"Mr. Goodwin? I'm sorry, dear. He's no longer with the company."

"Do you have his new number?"

"No . . . what I mean is, they took him to the hospital for that dreadful flu yesterday, but not in time to save him."

"Oh." I closed my eyes for a moment. Poor TK. "Is there any other family? His wife died, too, and someone needs to take care of their son. I've got him with me for now, but—"

"I'm sorry, honey. I didn't know Mr. Goodwin that well. Tragedy has hit a lot of families."

"But his son is only a baby and—"

"Do the best you can, dear. That's what we're all doing."

The pain in my stomach worsened. There was no Mr. Goodwin, no Mrs. Goodwin, no Mom or Dad to help me. For now, it was only me and TK. He whimpered in the stroller next to me.

"Hey, buddy."

He opened his eyes, looked at me, and started to wail.

"I know, I know. I'm not your momma." My practical attitude cracked. Holding TK against my shoulder, I cried into his baby blanket. But I had to compose myself. "We'll find your family soon. Are you hungry again?"

I fed him and shook a few rattles. Right as I convinced myself that babies were a nine out of ten on the boring scale, he started to throw up. Repeatedly.

After changing our clothes and cleaning the mess, I checked his forehead. He didn't feel feverish. A night of endless worry stretched ahead of me. Would he become dangerously ill? Would I?

My stomach rumbled as if it were possessed. I strapped TK in his stroller so he'd be safe, then ran to the bathroom. He screamed but I had no choice. There was nowhere else to put him.

Please let it be the water making us sick. Not the flu. Anything but the flu.

It took forever until I moved again. Our stomachs finally settled and TK rubbed his eyes. I realized there was no place for him to sleep, unless I returned to his house. But Mrs. Goodwin was in the room with the crib. I couldn't face the corpse ever again.

The corpse. I couldn't let it stay there.

When the cop came to the door about Megs, he'd given me his contact info. I carried TK around the house searching for it, finally finding the number in Mom's sweater pocket.

I wasn't sure how to report a dead person. I dialed slowly, hoping for a machine.

"Portico Police Department. Officer Julio speaking."

I paused. The one time today I wanted to leave a message, someone actually answered.

"Um, I'm trying to reach Officer Raitt?"

"He's not here. Can I help you?"

"The woman down the street . . . she passed away and I wanted to let someone know about the, um, her remains."

"Call the hotline." He rattled off a number.

"The hotline?"

"For body removal. They'll get to it as soon as they can. There's quite a backlog right now."

"OK." I tried not to imagine the decaying body, which of course froze the image in my head. "And I have a baby. I mean, I'm watching him because his parents died. Is there a phone number for that?"

"Family Services is inundated, completely over-loaded with cases. You can try contacting them, but quite honestly, with this many deaths, it's chaos. The infant may be better off with you."

"With me?"

"That's my opinion as a father, not as an official member of the Portico Police," he said. "You're not sick are you?"

"Not feverish—"

"You're a responsible girl, with babysitting experience?"

"Yes," I said, "but—"

"Then keep him with you."

I thanked him and hung up. My cuticles were a bloody mess. Gnawing at them was not helping.

TK smiled at me, making little cooing noises. I sniffed the air. Yep. He'd pooped again.

I changed him on a beach towel on the bathroom floor. My hands shook as I fastened the tabs on the disposable diaper. Panic set in. I counted the number of diapers, trying to estimate how many days they would last.

I was not equipped to care for a baby. None of my supplies would be of much use to TK. We needed more diapers, formula, and baby food. I didn't have a crib, or a changing table, or the right mentality to handle this. I desperately wanted to call Megs, to ask her advice. The need to speak with her was like a physical ache.

Megs, what should I do? How can I possibly deal with this?

If I concentrated, I could almost hear her voice. "You're one of the strongest people I know," she'd say. "You have inner strength. Remember that time I broke my wrist? The bone was pushing out of my skin."

Inner strength. Right. I found myself remembering that broken bone fondly, the familiar crisis—one I knew how to deal with.

Holding TK close, I breathed in his baby scent, the smell of powder and innocence. "We're stuck with each other for now. And we definitely need a plan." He relaxed in my arms, content for the moment. I carried him over to the kitchen pantry, surveying the contents. "I'm guessing you don't eat black beans, so there's not much here for you. If I had known about you when I bought food online—"

Online! I ran up the stairs as fast as I could without jostling TK. Holding him on my left side and typing with my right, I logged onto the computer, but the site I usually ordered from had a big yellow banner across the top of the page:

Due to overwhelming demand, we are running low on inventory and need to limit the quantities purchased by individual customers. The number in red next to each item is the maximum quantity that can be ordered at this time. Expedited shipping is available for $50.00.

Damn. But even a limited quantity was better than nothing. I ordered the maximum that I could from that site, even splurging for the shipping. Getting the food faster was worth it. Who knew when they would run out completely or if more delivery drivers would fail to show up for work.

As I submitted the order, Dad called.

"How's the quarantine?" I asked.

"A few people from our group have gotten sick. The doctors were keeping a close eye on us, but now that the bird flu's spreading throughout Delaware, they've been swamped. I spoke to Mom. She's miserable but healthy. How are you holding up?"

"OK." I told him about TK. My voice didn't crack until I got to the part about Mrs. Goodwin.

"You're doing the right thing by caring for him. I'm proud of you. But there will be tough times ahead. After the disease swept through Maryland, there were looters, riots. Not a good situation. I need you to be careful. Don't go outside after dark, even in our yard. And keep the house locked up."

"You're not making me feel any better, Dad."

"You never liked it when I sugar-coated things before."

"True. Do you think we're sick from the water or the flu? TK had to be exposed."

"I don't know. He's not coughing or feverish. . . . If it worsens, Reggie can drive you to the hospital. But if he can get through tomorrow without further symptoms, he's probably in the clear."

"Tomorrow?" My voice quivered. "I need someone to take him sooner than that."

"I wish I could help you."

"Tell me some happy news." I cradled the phone against my chin and rocked TK in my arms.

"The antiviral you took is expected to work fifty percent of the time."

"Um, those aren't great odds."

"It depends on whether you're a glass half-full or half-empty kind of person," he said.

Right. My glass had emptied months ago. But I didn't want to bring that up.

"How's the weather?" I asked, making him laugh.

We talked until his phone battery ran low.

"Dad, don't go—"

"Sorry," he said. And then the line went dead.

Not long after, TK started to fuss.

"Is it your bedtime soon? It looks like you're sleeping here tonight. You need a crib, buddy. Who would have an extra crib?"

I mentally ran through the options. Other neighbors with babies? They would be using their own cribs. Preschools? No. Day care centers?

Of course! Ethan's mother ran a day care center, Portico Pals, on Main Street. She had always treated me kindly. Forget only asking for the crib. Maybe she could take TK! Why didn't I think of that sooner?

Excited, I grabbed my phone. Ethan answered on the second ring.

"Lil, hey. What's up?"

He sounded happy to hear from me, so I launched right in. "I need a favor."

"Oh." His voice deflated. "What is it?"

As if on cue, TK started to cry.

"What's that noise? It sounds like a baby."

"That would be the favor." I patted TK on the back, trying to soothe him as I paced around the house.

"Uh oh."

"Hear me out. The baby's parents died from the flu and I'm taking care of him until I can find his relatives. But this is turning into more than a one-day thing. Do you think your mom could help?"

"I don't know. She had to close down the day care for now. Parents worried their kids would catch the flu there. Then my aunt and uncle got sick, so my four cousins are coming to stay with us."

"But you could ask her about one more, right? Please?"

"It's crazy here. She's not going to take in some stranger's potentially ill baby," he said.

Any chance for help slipped through my fingers. "But I don't have anywhere for TK to even sleep and—"

"Lil, I can't help you. You don't want me as a boyfriend anymore. I get it. You haven't talked to me since you blew off our date. The roses wilted and everything. So now you call because you need something? I'm not going to be your friend, hold your hand when things go wrong, still hope you'll change your mind about me. I'm sorry."

TK wailed. I could barely speak over his cries.

"Please—"

"Good luck."

I stared out at our darkened backyard, straining to spot illuminated windows in the neighborhood. Those I could find seemed as distant as stars, light years away. The crooked tree limbs looked eerie under the moon. I turned on our floodlight to dispel the shadows that slithered across the lawn. Tears came faster than I could wipe them away. There was no one around to help.

CHAPTER 14

"We live for sh*t like this," said one professional looter. "It's really just taking advantage of an opportunity, kind of like finders-keepers. If people leave their valuables behind, their mistake is our profit."
—Blue Flu interview, anonymous criminal

What Ethan had said about us was true. It wasn't like we were actual friends, like he was someone I could count on to help. We hadn't spoken since Megs died. And he mentioned flowers. I felt a tinge of regret, even though it would have taken more than roses to change my mind about our relationship. Mr. B was the catalyst that caused us to drift apart, but truthfully, once it ended, I didn't miss Ethan as much as I should have. There was no pining away for him, no sad reminiscing about what might have been. We were together then suddenly we weren't. Despite the mild jealously when he dated Cassandra, my life continued just fine without him.

I sighed, rocking TK in my arms. Megs had been right. I couldn't turn back time. I could never undo what had happened to me.

"You would have liked Megs," I told TK. "And my mom and dad will adore you. They can be annoying sometimes, but you'll get used to them. Of course, you'll be with your own family soon."

TK blinked his sweet baby eyes.

"Let's check my phone again, OK?"

Finally! Mom had texted.

Mom: hi lily

Mom: it's mom again

Mom: can't get through on the phone

Mom: hope this works

Mom: tell me if you get this

Mom: flights are a mess

Mom: trying to take one to london

Mom: at least i'd be that much closer to home

Mom: portico was profiled on news along with a few other towns

Mom: is it that dangerous there?

Mom: hard to tell how bad the flu is here

Mom: airport workers wear masks

Mom: i've been trying to read to pass the time

Mom: but i am too worried to focus on much

Mom: let me know you are safe

Mom: need to hear from you

Mom: ox

Mom: supposed to be hugs and kisses not farm animal

Cradling TK, I typed:

> Me: I'm not sick but things r bad here. I'm
>   taking care of the Goodwins' baby. Mr &
>   Mrs Goodwin died.
> Me: Feeling anxious. Come home soon!

I rocked TK for awhile, hoping she'd text back right away. But there was no reply.

When I finally checked the news again. Morris County had close to eighteen hundred people ill, with nearly one hundred fatalities.

Damn.

New Jersey's governor compared the devastation to Hurricane Sandy and asked all Western states to send supplies and medical personnel to help with the crisis. One governor replied, "Sandy wasn't contagious. We need to save our resources for the inevitable spread across America."

On a local level, towns debated whether the now limited supply of masks and antiviral medicines should be given to patients or to first responders. Firemen were being asked to remove bodies, but obviously feared becoming infected. "This is a crazy bunch of sh*t," one captain said with his curse bleeped. Then he coughed into the microphone.

Worries circled in my brain like buzzards. The town's infrastructure had clearly crumbled. There were hotlines to report the overwhelming deaths.

Supplies were limited. Mom and Dad were far away, and for all I knew, they could be battling the flu right now. TK could be a baby influenza bomb, poised to detonate in my home.

I knew it would take me a long time to fall asleep.

I made a bed on the floor with couch cushions as barriers so TK couldn't crawl away. Afraid to leave him, and afraid to be alone, I snuggled next to him in a pile of blankets on the rug.

Waking up next to TK in the morning surprised me, as if my sleeping mind had momentarily erased yesterday's drama. But there he was, all cute and needy. I did a quick health inventory. My stomach pains were gone and he seemed fever-free, and hungry.

Baby food moved up on my list of concerns. I realized we needed to visit his house again in search of more supplies. Dad's talk about being careful weighed on me, but I didn't have much choice with TK as my new roommate.

After breakfast, I braced myself for the task ahead. If only Megs was around to keep me brave as I hurried down the silent block past piles of accumulating trash.

TK and I reached the Goodwins' house to find the front door ajar. Despite my call to the hotline, I doubted they took care of Mrs. Goodwin's body that quickly. Had I left it open? Holding the storm door with one arm, I used the other to move the stroller through the doorway.

"Hello?"

I stepped inside and gasped. Their house had been looted.

It looked like a fast and messy job. Cabinets were left open. Tupperware littered the floor. A broken bag of rice was spilled across the kitchen tile.

"It's all right, baby," I whispered in a quivering voice, even though TK hadn't made a sound. I wasn't ready for a confrontation with thieves, especially with a baby to protect.

I took a few cautious steps forward, ready to bolt at the first noise. "Hello? Anyone here?" I listened, glancing around the kitchen. The rice trail went toward the rear door, so the looters were presumably gone, I hoped.

Then a harsh male laugh broke the silence—it was coming from the backyard.

With no time to unstrap TK, I shoved the stroller past his room, past the body. I imagined the decay, the smell, the blueness of her skin. It made my knees rubbery.

I couldn't fall apart now, not without a place to hide.

A bedroom beckoned from the end of the hall and I aimed for the beige carpet, the green walls. Once inside what must have been the master bedroom, I locked the door behind us.

The voices outside were louder now, talking

about meds, food, and "the going rate." Their laughter had a sharp edge to it, like a serrated knife.

I shivered. These men were only a few yards away.

As if sensing trouble, TK squirmed, flailing his arms in what I recognized as the precursor to a meltdown.

I unbuckled, lifted, rocked him in one smooth motion. "Shh, baby. Shh."

He whimpered, reached his arms toward a playpen near the bed.

"OK, but no crying," I whispered, more a wish than an instruction. I plopped him into the playpen with some toys, banging my shin in the process.

"Ow—" Too late, my hand flew to my mouth to muffle the cry.

"Did you hear that?" one of the looters asked in a gruff voice.

"We were just in there. The house is empty."

"I dunno. It sounded like a girl."

"Wishful thinking. You're just lonely."

I gripped the edge of the playpen to steady myself, waiting for the thieves to crash through the door. I was sure my heart thudded loud enough for them to hear.

Finally, the voices drifted farther away, but I was afraid to shift close enough to the window to look. TK fussed until I stacked soft plastic blocks in the

playpen to quiet him. After several towers were created and destroyed, I found the courage to move.
No noise came from outside and a peek through the
window confirmed they were gone.

"Be right back." I piled some cheerios from the
diaper bag into the playpen for TK.

Still afraid, I searched the house as if it were on
fire. A quick scan showed that most of the regular
food was taken, but I grabbed some more baby food
from the floor in the pantry behind extra paper towels. I opened and closed cabinets at lightning speed.
In the bathroom, nothing remained in the medicine
cabinet. I found extra diapers in a drawer and managed to stuff them into the bottom of the stroller
with still-shaky hands.

I needed to get out of there, back to the safety of
home, but the lack of a crib was still a major issue.

Wait. During my rush, I missed the answer right
in front of me. The playpen was portable and would
give TK a place to sleep. I moved him to the stroller.
After three tries, I managed to fold up the playpen.

Transporting it presented a different problem.
It didn't fit under the stroller. After checking that
no one lingered outside, I tried carrying the playpen under my arm while pushing TK. I could only
make it to the street before putting it down again. It
would get ruined if I dragged it. I wanted to stomp
my feet in frustration. Why was this so hard?

Then I remembered a baby carrier by the front door. I brought TK back inside, strapped him into it, then buckled the contraption over my chest, checking to make sure he wouldn't fall out.

Wow, was he heavy. He still had a fistful of cheerios, which he promptly dropped down the front of my shirt.

"Ack!"

TK looked at me. "Ba ba ba."

"Silly boy. Is that baby talk for totally gross?"

He smiled, showing four little teeth.

I propped the playpen on the stroller seat and began pushing his new bed. After the loud voices of the looters, the quiet street seemed even more unnerving. Every scrape meant potential danger, every breeze a warning. I locked the door behind me when we finally made it home.

～

Back in my house, I stayed on high alert, speaking to TK in whispers as I moved from window to window, checking the locks. Outside, the garbage announced that our house was occupied by living, trash-making people. Maybe looters wanted vacant homes, so they could steal without a hassle. But who knew how lawless people actually thought? I'd rather not advertise that I was home.

With TK on my hip, I glanced outside for menacing strangers. The coast was clear. At the curb, I checked the mailbox. A folded piece of loose leaf paper sat alone in the otherwise empty box. So the mail service had stopped as well as the garbage pickup. That wasn't a good sign.

I kept the piece of paper out of TK's grasp as I carried the trash can up the driveway. Normally, a flier in the mailbox meant an upcoming neighborhood block party or announced a new restaurant in town. But this looked like the same paper I'd write my biology notes on. Did someone from school leave me a letter? The anticipation was a splash of color in the grayness of my day. I left the unopened note in the kitchen, waiting for me.

Dad and I texted back and forth several times and there were a few more messages from Mom. I fed TK jarred peas for lunch, then planned our schedule for the rest of the day, as if eating at regular times could stop the world from falling apart. After my brief adventure to the curb, I couldn't get anything else done. TK clung to me, so that even putting him down for my shower became tricky.

His need for constant attention started to wear on me. I considered nicknaming him Leech but pushed the thought out of my head. He wasn't an orphan by choice. None of this was his fault.

Still, I needed my babysitting days to end soon. Contacting his family hadn't turned up any results.

I finally called Family Services. A recorded message told me the office was understaffed and to call the police if I suspected child endangerment. The police had already said TK should stay with me. Day care facilities, like those run by Ethan's mom, had closed. I thought about my parents' friends, my preschool teacher, a lady at the church who ran the family events. I needed someone to help care for TK. But who was healthy enough to help? Then it dawned on me.

The elderly.

The flu skipped most senior citizens. And grandparents loved babies, right? I had to find a way to reach out to the older people in town. There was Reggie. And the Senior Center. Maybe someone there could help us.

That might relieve my immediate situation, but at the back of my mind was a niggling thought that wouldn't go away: what if TK wasn't the only orphaned baby? What if there were hundreds of wailing kids behind the closed doors of Portico? The babies could be healthy, like TK, with no one to care for them. Could the seniors help on a larger scale?

After a crying protest, TK finally napped in the playpen—a huge victory. When Reggie called to check on me, I explained my idea.

"If the flu is affecting the parents, then there are going to be babies who need to be cared for, at least temporarily. Right now it's just TK, but what if there are lots of healthy little kids out there and the parents are hospitalized, or worse? They can't survive alone. And with looters breaking in . . . "

"I see what you mean," he said.

"Maybe we can set up a mini day care at the Senior Center? People could take shifts watching the children so it's not too much of a burden. And if the kids could sleep there, we'd know they're safe. TK could be a trial run."

"I'm going there for dinner," Reggie said. "I'll talk to my friends tonight. In the mean time, keep taking good care of the little fella."

At the prospect of solving my TK dilemma, I felt a familiar stir of excitement for the first time in months. It's what I used to do for the Teen Humanitarian Club at school. Identify a community problem, then try to make a difference. I started making lists. We would need cribs and more baby supplies. We'd need a way to find the children who needed help and a system to track who was where at what time.

Exhilarated, I decided to read the mysterious note from the mailbox while TK continued his nap. I settled on the couch with my legs tucked under me and opened it slowly, savoring the suspense.

My hand flew to my chest. I recognized the scrawled handwriting. It had appeared at the top of my essays in phrases like, "Great metaphor," "Need more detail here," and "Nice descriptive language."

The note was from Mr. B.

> Lilianna,
> I need to see you, to talk to you, soon. Just for a few minutes. You can trust me.

He hadn't bothered to sign it, but he had scribbled his phone number across the bottom, as if I would actually call. I crumpled the paper into a tight ball, squeezing it with my fist before hurling it across the room. *Trust.* What the hell did he know about trust? Absolutely nothing. He represented the antithesis of the word. Evil incarnate dressed as a kind English teacher.

Nervous, I checked each window and door in the house again to ensure everything was locked. It didn't make me feel much better. I thought about tearing the note to bits, but shoved it in a desk drawer in case I needed evidence. Evidence of what, I didn't know. My brain wasn't thinking logically. I desperately wanted to smoke or to run through the streets screaming. The anger whipped around me with no place to go.

By the time TK woke up, serious stir-craziness had set in. It was time for us to venture out again, but we needed some form of protection. The garage yielded a baseball bat and a whistle. I tucked them into his stroller basket, feeling slightly ridiculous but a little safer. My plan was to stay fairly close to home. Pushing TK in the stroller, I sang the alphabet song to him.

"ABCDEFG, HIJKLMNOP, QRS . . . "

Nervous, I stopped singing. Like before, the streets lacked the usual people walking or driving. What if we were the sole human beings left on our block? What if all my neighbors had left town or worse, died?

Out of habit, I started in the direction of Megs's house. I thought about going to her room and smelling her favorite perfume, the one like honeysuckles. But I couldn't face her absence yet. Turning the stroller around, I headed in the opposite direction.

As I approached Jay's, shouts broke the silence. I rushed forward, worrying someone was hurt. TK fidgeted in the stroller. Maybe he was used to the quiet, too. As I reached the gate, a boy bolted across the backyard.

"No!" he yelled over his shoulder. "It's still my turn to hide!"

"OK," Jay said. "I'll give you thirty seconds. One, two, three—"

"Hi. I heard shouting and thought maybe there was trouble."

"It's all good," he said. "Considering the circumstances. I've been trying to keep my brother busy. My aunt's been working nonstop." He smiled, the kind big enough to reach his eyes, and I realized he was happy to see me. Then again, seeing anyone familiar was a special occasion now.

"How can she be working?" I asked. "School's closed."

"Nurses are in demand. She's practically living at the hospital."

A voice came from behind a tree. "Are you going to find me or not?"

"Tyler, come out. We have company."

His brother peeked at me and the baby. "Forget it. Babies are smelly. I'm going inside." The door closed behind him.

"I could use a cigarette right about now," Jay said. "Quitting sucks."

"Yeah, I know. I stopped, too."

He nodded at TK and the baseball bat. "You've been busy. And he's a little young for batting practice."

I gave him a wry smile. "Ha ha." TK started to fuss so I dug some teething toys out of the diaper bag and plopped them on his tray. "His parents died from the flu," I said, trying to sound matter-of-fact, but saying it aloud made it more real somehow. "He was alone in their house, so now I'm caring for him kind of by default. When I went back to get more baby stuff, their home had been looted." I glanced around. "Do you think maybe you should go inside? Or play something quieter, so no one hears you?"

"I was trying to unplug Ty from the video games. But you're right." His eyes were thoughtful. "It's going to be chaos for a long time. I heard the driver of a produce truck was practically mauled the other day."

"Really?"

"The worst part was that the truck was empty," he said. "It was an older one and refrigerated, so it was heading to the morgue for temporary storage."

"Gross."

"The alternative is worse when you consider it."

"I'd rather not think about it." But of course it was too late. Time to change the subject to another worry. "Doesn't the street seem abandoned? It's creepy."

"Do you have any hornet spray?"

"I'm not that worried about bees right now—"

He laughed. "To spray in the face of an intruder."

"Oh. No, but it's a good idea. Do you think we're the only people left on the block?" I asked. "Besides Reggie, of course, but he lives closer to Fairview Road."

"I don't know. It's surreal. The Singh family packed up and took off. They told my aunt that they'd lived through the plague in Surat about twenty years ago. Once was enough, they said. The Dunns left to stay with family in Ohio." He pointed at a huge house across the street with a bright yellow "for sale" sign. "That one's empty, too."

"I doubt anyone will buy a home here right now."

"Yeah, everything's come to a halt. Do you have enough food?"

I nodded, envisioning my closet of supplies. "You?"

"We're doing all right. Mostly trying to fight off the boredom."

"I know what you mean."

"Want to come back later for dinner?" he asked. "Around six? I boil a great pot of pasta."

He looked eager, but I hesitated.

"Don't worry, it's not a date," Jay said. "It's spaghetti with my brother and your baby-friend."

That settled it. "OK. As long as it's still light out." Jay and Tyler didn't seem contagious. They'd been isolated, too. "I'll bring some food for TK."

I walked a few blocks without seeing a single person. I thought I heard a crying baby on Hillside Lane, but when I stopped to listen, there was only silence. Nervous at being so isolated, I hurried home.

Back at our house, I locked the stroller wheels before moving the baby toys from the tray back into the diaper bag. I hoisted TK into my arms with the bag slung over my shoulder. Then I froze.

We'd been looted.

CHAPTER 15

The American justice system has grinded to a halt.
No lawyers, no judges, no jurors would possibly
participate in a trial right now.
—Blue Flu interview, Manhattan judge

I steadied myself with a hand on the kitchen counter. Staring at the disaster in our house was a lot worse than surveying the Goodwins' mess. Cabinet doors had been flung open revealing emptiness where Mom usually kept coffee, sugar, and spices. Shards of glass created a glistening pattern of destruction across the kitchen floor. Why? Why break our plates? Mindlessly, I picked up a fragment of pink rose and placed it near the toaster.

The refrigerator motor kicked in, making me jump. I did not want to stay inside the house, possibly alone with violent thieves. Every creak seemed dangerous. I grabbed TK and the phone and went into the backyard. When I was reasonably sure we were alone, I plopped him onto the grass and called the police.

"We can be there in two to three days," said the cop who answered.

"But I'm home alone *now*. What if the robbers are still in the house?"

"I'm sorry, miss, I really am. But there's a riot at the pharmacy on Main Street where people are attempting to steal medicine. We had two officers called to the Newark morgue this afternoon, and several more are out sick," he said. "You're our twelfth looting report today and there's no one to send. Can you stay someplace else?"

"Never mind." My voice cracked in desperation. If the police couldn't help, Portico was in worse shape than I realized. I hung up without giving him our address. What was the point? I'd contaminate any evidence over the next few days anyway.

I needed a plan. Neither Reggie nor Jay answered his phone. Sitting outside with TK all day wasn't an option either. Plus, my mind was already onto the next worry. If there was a riot at the pharmacy, then medicine was in high demand. Had the looters found our safe?

I got up and took TK with me into the garage to find the hornet spray. Armed with bee killer, I forced myself upstairs with TK on my hip, afraid to leave him alone. My breath came short and shallow as I scrutinized each room. Brandishing the bee spray like a gun, I started with the top floor and methodically worked my way downstairs. Like a robot, I ensured each window was locked, that every possible hiding spot was empty. I inspected all the closets and under the beds. Otherwise, I'd never sleep again.

In Dad's office, I tried to ignore the way the robbers had carelessly swept his research folders onto the floor and knocked his books from the shelves. The linen closet was bare, our sheets toppled in a heap. My desk drawers had been dumped out, creating a pile of schoolwork and unused stationery. I spotted the crumpled note from Mr. B.

Was he behind this somehow? But that didn't make any sense. I had to think rationally. Looters had ransacked our house. It wasn't personal, but it sure felt like it. The scattered papers, the jumble of clothing Mom always folded so neatly, the dirty shoe prints across my bedroom rug. It seemed *very* personal.

Like at the Goodwins' house, the looters had emptied the medicine cabinets, leaving only a few cotton balls and stray hairs behind. My mother's jewelry box was also gone. The bed pillows looked naked without their cases, which the looters had presumably taken in order to carry our belongings away.

The good news: Dad was right. Burglars didn't care about laundry rooms and the safe was untouched. The bottled water remained under my bed and a few cans of food that I hadn't moved downstairs sat on the top shelf of my closet. Dad's computer was also intact. In the hall closet, even though the lanterns and batteries were missing, the emergency hand crank radio had fallen behind several boxes of tampons, hidden from sight.

I saved the kitchen—the worst—for last. Even though I anticipated the bare kitchen pantry, the stark emptiness took my breath away. Someone had stolen my substantial supply of food. It must have been a group of people, because it would have been a lot to carry. All of that planning and buying and stacking.

Gone.

"This is bad, TK. This is very, very bad."

My family meal plan for the next several weeks had fallen to the floor. I left it there. My hands shook as I tried to keep the panic at bay. I'd have to scrape together something to eat. I had TK to think about, too. Thankfully I had some formula and food in the diaper bag, enough to get by until the arrival of the baby stuff I ordered online.

Online! Maybe there was still a chance to refill the pantry. I dragged TK's playpen into Dad's office so he could play while I accessed the grocery site.

Using my previous order, I restocked my virtual grocery cart, ignoring the exorbitant delivery fee. I typed as fast as possible, as if the inventory would evaporate if I moved any slower. Satisfied, I clicked the "purchase now" button. The website froze.

"Damn!"

I rebooted, tried again. My order wouldn't go through. I felt physically ill, as if someone had taken one of my last cans and rammed it into my stomach.

But I couldn't sit and brood. I needed to keep moving.

TK whimpered. I had to ignore him while I went downstairs. Fragments of glass from the back door glistened on the linoleum floor of our small mud room. Cursing, I swept the floor wearing flip-flops to protect my feet. After cleaning that mess, I tackled the broken door. Using a thin piece of wood, a hammer, and nails, I covered the hole. Then, tapping into my rage, I shoved our biggest chair in front of it. No one else would be able to use that entrance.

TK had quieted. Thirsty, I opened the fridge to get a soda, only to be greeted by vacant shelves. They had emptied the freezer, too. Unbelievable.

I was already hungry and my head throbbed. All the pain relievers were stolen, of course, along with the remainder of my antiviral. If I took 40 percent of a medicine that had a 50 percent chance of working, and if my food lasted three to four days, what were my odds of survival?

Not good.

I could open another box of antiviral from the safe, but something held me back. I hadn't gotten sick yet. Mom and Dad might still need the medicine. It seemed like I should save it for them, only opening another pack as a last resort.

A last resort. Could things actually get that bad? What if I became desperate for food? Would I be driven to steal from strangers, too? With empty houses throughout town, there must be uneaten food somewhere. Too many people had died, like Megs and her mom.

No.

I couldn't do it. Could I? Would it be bad to steal from my best friend?

I crawled into bed and the tears came fast. It wasn't a silent weeping, but aching sobs for everything wrong with the world. For Megs, my missing parents, orphaned babies, our violated homes. It was only when TK bawled that I climbed out of bed to hold him.

Resignation settled over me as I fed him. I wasn't calm, exactly. But I couldn't shut down with a baby to care for. I strapped him to my chest in his carrier and started to clean, bending carefully so as not to tilt him too far over. There was no sense waiting, staring at the depressing remains of my emergency food supply and the clothes strewn on the floor. When I finished, I put the hornet spray in my bedroom on top of the book case where TK couldn't reach it but where it would be nearby during the night.

It was nearly six. I was in no mood to go to Jay's and be social. But I wasn't about to pass up a meal. Dinner at his house would stretch my meager food supply that much longer. After splashing cold water on my face, I changed into black pants and a black shirt with ruffles. My nose was red and my eyes were puffy, but I was in no mood to fuss.

"Let's do this, little man," I said, scooping up TK.

When I rang their doorbell, Jay yelled to come in. The kitchen was surprisingly neat for two guys and a frequently working aunt. Jay dumped pasta into a strainer in the sink, the steam rising into the air. His brother hovered nearby. I tried not to stare desperately at the spaghetti.

"Hi," I said. "Is it OK to wheel the stroller in here? I don't have a high chair."

"Sure," he said. "But we might have an old one in the basement. Ty, can you check?"

Ty sniffed the air. "That baby doesn't stink too bad. I guess he can stay."

When he left the kitchen, Jay turned to me. "What's the matter? You look upset."

There was no sense keeping it a secret. "Looters," I said. "Most of my food is gone." I sniffed, willing myself not to cry again.

Jay looked solemn. "Wow."

"Wow what?" Ty asked, returning with a booster seat that attached to the kitchen chair.

"Nothing," Jay said.

"I hate when you do that," he said.

I grabbed some paper towels and wiped the seat off.

"Hate when I do what?"

"Act all secret-ish. Lie about what you were talking about." Ty set the rectangular wooden table, slamming the white bowls in front of each chair.

"Someone stole food from Lil's house," Jay said.

"Oh. What's the big deal about telling me that?"

Jay shrugged. "I don't want you to worry about things."

"I saw stuff like that on TV. We can share our spaghetti, right?"

"Sure."

"Is he your son?" Ty asked.

Jay laughed. "He's been watching too many episodes of *High School Moms*, I think."

"I'm babysitting him," I explained. "His name is TK." I strapped him into his seat and put a bib on him. He banged on the tray with his palms, smiling.

"If you're being his mom, where's your mom?"

"My mom and dad are away," I said.

"Oh. Jay, can I show Lil my video game? He can watch, too."

"After dinner," Jay said.

We ate family style, the pasta in one big bowl, the sauce in another. There was some baked bread, too. Everything was delicious, but I would have eaten it even if it tasted like dirt.

"You have fresh bread? That's amazing." I broke off a small, soft piece for TK to go with his jar of sweet potatoes and chicken.

"Auntie freezes it," Ty said. "She's at work. Sometimes we save her dinner for later."

"Did you make the sauce, Jay? It's really good."

"Yeah." He handed Ty some extra napkins, since most of the sauce ended up on his face. "My mom taught me."

"Jay wants to be a chef when he grows up," Ty said in a tattle-tale voice.

"Be quiet."

"It's true. He watches cooking shows and everything."

Jay's cheeks reddened.

"What do *you* want to be?" I asked Ty.

"A doctor. So I can help sick people." He looked down at his food, suddenly quiet.

During the long pause, I thought about his mother dying, how hard that must be for him. I struggled to find a more neutral topic.

"Are you feeling better?" I finally asked. "Jay said you had strep throat."

"Yeah." His face lit up. "At the doctor's office, they put this swab-thing in my throat, then they dipped it into some chemicals like a science experiment. A few minutes later the plus sign showed."

"That sounds cool."

When Jay offered me seconds, I refilled my bowl, too worried about my next meal to refuse. We spent the rest of dinner talking about anything but looting and the flu. Afterwards, Ty convinced us to leave the dirty dishes and watch him play his game on the TV screen. The brown leather couch in the family room was big enough for the four of us.

"I reached level fifteen since school is closed," he said. The screen pinged a few times. "Did you see that? I got the bonus!"

We watched until TK started to fuss.

"Time for a bottle," I said.

"Let's go in the kitchen," Jay said. "I have to load the dishwasher anyway. Tell us when you get to level sixteen, Ty."

Jay rinsed the plates while I sat at the kitchen table and fed TK.

"I'm sorry your house was robbed. That happened to us once in Arizona. It felt so invasive, knowing people had searched through our stuff."

"I tried to clean up so I can pretend it didn't happen."

"Are you spooked about staying alone?" he asked.

"A little. But they took what they wanted, right? It wouldn't make sense for them to come back. I did put the hornet spray in my room."

"That's good."

"But all my supplies . . . Do you think it would be awful for me to take food," I paused, ready to gauge his reaction. "To take it from Megs's house?"

"I'm sure Megs wouldn't mind. She'd want to help you if she could."

TK whimpered. I adjusted the angle of his bottle, grateful for the distraction.

"You must babysit a lot. Either that or you've got great maternal instincts," Jay teased.

He leaned over to clear the spaghetti, putting his hand on my shoulder. Already tense, I stiffened at his touch.

"Just a joke," he said, carrying the big bowl over to the sink.

Jay had been so generous. Not wanting him to think I was a total jerk, I decided to go with the abbreviated truth. "I, um, I'm not that good with people touching me sometimes. Like when I'm stressed." I leaned TK where Jay's hand had been and patted the baby's back.

"Oh?"

There were a lot of questions in that one syllable. I hadn't meant to start a conversation about my hang-ups. I was comfortable with Jay, but not that comfortable.

"Maybe it's an only child thing." My voice sounded unconvincing, even to me. While I struggled with what to say next, TK saved me. He spit up all over me—thick, yellow baby barf.

"Gross," I said.

Jay handed me a wet towel to clean up. "That smells foul. Do you want to borrow a shirt?"

Big splotches covered my black ruffles. "I guess so."

"I told you babies stink," Ty called from the adjoining room.

Jay came back a few minutes later and handed me a pale blue hoodie with the *Chef Adventure* TV logo across the chest.

"Can you take him?" I held out TK.

I expected him to hesitate, but he seemed to know what to do and the baby snuggled against him. It made me respect Jay a tiny bit more. Of course, he still talked too much. But he had a responsible, take-charge attitude that was endearing. Ethan had stopped by once when I babysat, and he wouldn't even hold the baby so I could take a bathroom break. Jay seemed older, more mature than the other guys in our grade.

Is that what attracted Megs to him? Knowing

how she liked him made me feel more dirty than the spit-up did. Here I was, eating dinner with him while she was dead. It seemed all wrong. And if there was anything between him and Kayla now . . .

"Bathroom's down the hall," he said.

After changing, I rolled up the filthy shirt and stuffed it in the diaper bag. When I came out, TK slept soundly in Jay's arms.

Jay nodded toward my new outfit. "I've never seen you in anything but black."

I raised my eyebrows, not in the mood to discuss my fashion sense. Jay hadn't known me before, when I wore pretty skirts and had two best friends and a sense of optimism.

"I mean, blue looks good on you."

"Thanks," I said with more politeness than gratitude. I sat across from Jay, too weary for small talk, watching TK nestled against him. His compliment had shifted the friendship balance and an awkward tension filled the air. I jiggled my leg under the table.

"You seem nervous. If you're worried about food, you can take some of ours to last you through tomorrow."

"I'm fine for a little while. And you've got Ty to feed. But thank you." I glanced at the microwave clock. "It's late. I should go."

Jay moved TK to the stroller without waking

him. When he tucked the blanket tenderly around him, it made my heart lurch.

No. I could not be falling for this guy, for Megs's guy. She adored him, was so excited to meet him the night she became ill. I couldn't betray her. I couldn't even think about it. Jay wasn't meant to be anything more than a neighbor to me.

"Ty, it's time for me to walk Lil home."

"Me, too!"

Jay pushed the stroller and Ty told jokes on the way to my house. Having Ty there seemed to ease the tension between us.

"Why was six afraid of seven?" he asked. "Because seven ate nine! Get it? Eight sounds like ate, A-T-E."

I laughed. "Good one."

"I have one," Jay said. "What's brown and sticky?"

Ty practically bounced along beside the stroller. "I give up."

"A stick."

Ty giggled. "That's pretty good. Do you know any, Lil?"

I had to dig deep, back into my silly innocent years. "Hmm. What do you call cheese that's not yours?"

"I don't know. What?"

"Nacho cheese."

As we rounded the curve in the street, Ty's happy laughter floated through the air. My house was visible ahead.

I stopped short, breathing in sharply.

A red convertible blocked my driveway: Mr. B's.

CHAPTER 16

*Since the East Coast outbreaks, the Blue Flu is hopscotching
across America with no rhyme or reason. Some towns are hit
hard; others are spared. There's no correlation to geography,
climate, or economic status. While we'd all love an answer, there
doesn't seem to be a scientific one.*
—Blue Flu interview, award-winning scientist

At the sight of Mr. B's car in my driveway,
my stomach dropped like it does on an airplane during turbulence. Jay, Ty, and I stood a few houses away from my own, but I wouldn't move any closer.

"What's the matter?" Jay asked.

I swayed and he reached out to steady me.

"That car . . . I can't go home." I pulled the hood up over my hair and then grabbed the stroller, turning it in the opposite direction. Without another word, I raced TK down the street.

Ty and Jay moved to either side of me, practically jogging to catch up.

He's at my home. He's at my home.

"What's the matter?" Ty asked, and I realized too late that I'd been speaking aloud.

"I can't talk about it."

"We can go back to our house," Jay said.

"Too far. He could spot me any minute."

"I know where to hide," Ty said. He steered me toward one of the neighbor's houses that Jay had said was empty. In the front yard, a short Japanese maple tree fanned out into a dense canopy.

"Here." Ty took my hand and pulled me under the branches. Jay ducked in with the stroller. The hanging boughs blocked the street from sight.

"It's a tree-cave," Ty whispered. "A great hiding spot."

No hiding spot is safe enough, I thought. *Never safe enough.*

We sat quietly until Mr. B's car passed by. I trembled as he drove away.

"Was that a looter?" Ty asked.

"Shh," Jay said.

Hugging my knees to my chest, I tried to slow my breathing. *Rock back and forth, back and forth, inhale. Back and forth, back and forth, exhale.* I breathed in the smell of earth and leaves, my eyes closed, until TK started to fuss. Jay unstrapped him from the stroller and I held my arms out, comforted by the weight of him against me.

"What's green and red and goes 100 miles per hour?" Ty asked.

"Now's not the—" Jay started.

"It's OK," I said. "Tell me, Ty. I give up."

"A frog in a blender!"

I forced a grin. "Good joke." The street was quiet since the car had passed. "I can go home soon. I want to wait a few more minutes to be sure."

"Maybe you shouldn't be alone tonight." Jay blushed. "That doesn't sound right. I mean—"

"It's all right. I know what you mean."

"You won't get any sleep home alone, worrying," he said. "You should stay with us."

Ty jumped up, nearly hitting his head on a branch. "Like a sleepover!"

It felt reassuring to know I wasn't completely isolated, that Jay and Ty would look out for me. But even though it was tempting, staying at their house would never work, not with TK.

"Thanks, but it's hard with the baby." I thought about the long night ahead of me in my empty, just-looted home, clutching the hornet spray, terrified that Mr. B would return. He'd written in the note that he wanted to talk. I guess he meant sooner rather than later.

"Maybe . . . you could stay at my house?" I said. "Both of you. We have a guest room. Would your aunt mind?"

"She'll be fine with it," Jay said. "Let's get Ty's pjs and stuff, and then we'll be all set."

"And my joke book!" Ty said as he bolted from the shelter of the tree's branches.

～

An hour later, we sat in my family room watching *Funniest Family Videos* in our sleepwear: Jay in flannel pants and a navy T-shirt, Ty in dinosaur pajamas, and me in black yoga pants and a charcoal Henley. It was the only suitable outfit I could come up with for a boy-girl sleepover.

When the doorbell rang, Jay, Ty and I sat motionless on the couch. I sucked in my breath, deciding whether to open it.

"I have to see who it is," I finally said. It was better to know if it was Mr. B, if he would return every few hours. Then I could prepare myself for the next time. Reluctantly, I stood, not quite ready to face my nightmare.

"I'll come with you," Jay said.

Easing up to the side window, I peeked out. A delivery truck idled in the driveway.

"It's TK's food! I ordered it online." Relief flowed through me.

We opened the door. The delivery man wore a mask over his nose and mouth. "Sign here," he said, before handing us two large boxes.

I locked the door behind him, then washed my hands after touching his pen. Jay and Ty helped me unload the baby food.

"I can't believe his food actually came. That's one less thing to worry about."

"TK's a lucky little guy."

"Do you think it's safe to store it in the pantry?" I asked. "What if the looters come back?"

"We could set traps!" Ty said. "Like in that movie where the boy gets left home alone!"

"Um, that might get messy," Jay said. "Maybe we should just hide the food."

The jars were small enough to fit under the couch, so we slid them there. I placed the canisters of formula under the kitchen sink.

"At least TK will have enough to eat for now. If I get desperate, I can try his mixed vegetables in a jar," I said, half joking.

"Did you try the online grocery stores?" Jay asked.

"Yeah, but the order wouldn't go through."

"We can check again later."

It was ten o'clock before TK and Ty were both asleep. Jay and I moved upstairs to Dad's office so we could use the computer. Jay sat at the wooden desk, checking stores online. I perched on the arm of a leather chair nearby.

"You know I'm a good listener, right?" he said.

"Um, yeah," I said, confused.

He kept his eyes on the computer screen. "Are you going to talk about the car in the driveway then?"

I averted my eyes. What could I possibly say? My brain fumbled for a plausible story, something believable that wouldn't give me away. I stared at the ceiling, waiting for inspiration to hit.

Tell the truth, the voice in my head whispered.

Could I actually tell Jay about Mr. B? I considered it. Jay seemed nonjudgmental. But was he completely trustworthy? I had trusted Kayla, too, and she couldn't understand after being my friend for years. How would Jay react?

I took a deep breath, trying to form the first sentence. But when I tried to speak, my chest tightened, the familiar band of tension compressing my insides. Suddenly describing what happened, finding the words . . . it was too much.

"I . . . um. . . ."

Jay paused from typing, looked at me with sincere eyes.

"I can't."

"OK then."

The room was silent except for his typing. Regret seeped through me. Jay had been honest about his mother's death, which couldn't have been easy for him. Now I had thrown this barrier between us by not telling him about Mr. B.

I sighed. "Principal Fryman would use the cliché, 'honesty's the best policy,'" I said. "But it's not always that easy."

Jay smiled and I relaxed a little. Maybe we were still good.

"We can talk another time if you want," he said. "So, this site has limited supplies and there's a seventy dollar delivery fee."

"Order the max. I'll charge it to my dad's card. Aren't you worried about food, too?"

"A little. I have restaurant friends from writing reviews, but the businesses have all closed, so that's not much help. The hospital's been good about feeding my aunt, so she brings home what she can for me and Ty. Plus she's been able to get stuff on the black market."

"There's a black market?" I was shocked.

He nodded. "The people who robbed you probably weren't hungry. It's more likely they were looking to make a profit. Portico will be a different place for a while. Do you want to check this before I submit the order?"

I read the screen over his shoulder, trying not to get my hopes up that it would work this time.

"Looks fine to me."

He clicked the "confirm order" button. The website froze.

My shoulders slumped. Empty grocery stores, closed restaurants, inundated websites. All my careful planning was thwarted. I didn't even have that much cash to buy food on the black market, wherever that was. And anything worth selling, the looters had taken with them.

Except the medicine. I could get a lot of money for that. But not yet. Selling that would be like giving up on Mom and Dad's return.

"Don't worry," Jay said. "We'll figure something out. Let's try a different site."

The next one didn't work either.

"Maybe if we wait, it will be less busy later," he said. "Mind if I check my blog?"

"Sure." After grabbing a pen and paper, I curled up in the chair to make a new meal chart with my dwindling supplies.

"Holy Jesus," Jay said.

"What?"

"Look at all these postings!"

I stood to peer over his shoulder. He scrolled through the comments section.

Please add James Mass to your memorial page. 7:14 pm

David Pymann is sick. Say a prayer! 8:21 pm

Karen Krozynski died today. 9:34 pm

The list went on for several pages.

"What if we're the only ones left?" I asked.

"We can't be. Someone from school typed the names on my blog. So there have to be others still alive," Jay said.

I imagined other kids isolated in their homes like me, each grieving the death of a friend alone.

Jay must have been thinking the same thing. "Maybe we should try to get the survivors together," he said.

"Sure, if we weren't in the middle of a contagious epidemic. Getting together with a germy group of people doesn't sound appealing."

"But we might be able to help each other. Maybe they have food to share and you have something, like blankets, to give them."

"All I have is a giant headache."

Jay crossed his arms over his chest. "I'm surprised, Lil. You seem like the kind of person who would worry about the greater good."

"Yeah, until my house got looted and all my food was stolen. And . . ." I thought about the note, the visit from Mr. B. "And I have all kinds of stuff to worry about."

He raised his eyebrows. "Really?"

"I did have an idea about helping orphans in the neighborhood, but now . . . everything feels too hard."

"What was your orphan idea?"

Reluctantly, I told him.

"That's a decent plan. Maybe we should get the other high school kids together, canvass the neighborhood for babies in trouble."

"I don't know."

"You wouldn't help? Didn't you used to be the Community Service Queen? I seem to remember Ethan bragging about an award you won."

Yeah, and look what that got me. Nothing but trouble and an emotional crisis.

"Maybe the town's already doing something," I said. "We can't be the first ones to think of this."

"Maybe not." Jay typed something on the computer, then pulled up an article criticizing the town for its lack of action. "This article says, 'Portico's using a triage system to deal with the ill but the town's overwhelmed by the number of deaths. Healthy people are expected to care for themselves until officials can organize an outreach effort to help the living.'"

"Really?"

"That's what it says. So it looks like we could do something useful. I'm going to post something on my blog."

"Like what?"

"I'll set up a meeting for tomorrow. We can sit outside in my backyard, with fresh air and hand sanitizer."

"What about Ty? You'd risk exposing him?"

Jay glowered at me.

I ignored him and checked my phone. There were three brief messages from Dad and one from Mom, saying the airport situation was crazy but that she should know her travel schedule tomorrow. When I finished responding, I realized that Jay was uncharacteristically quiet.

"Sorry," I said. "I didn't mean to upset you about Ty."

"It's OK. It's just that when my mom was sick, she begged me to always take care of him. She asked me, not my sisters. Ty's the youngest, the baby, and I promised her he'd be safe." He twisted side to side in my dad's swivel chair. "He can stay in the house. I would never put him at risk."

"I know you'll be careful. I was being mean. You made me feel bad because I don't want to help."

"During Mom's illness, we would have fallen apart if so many people didn't help us—neighbors, friends, even strangers."

"Cancer isn't contagious, though. Those people could be involved without any personal risk."

"It's good karma, Lil. What goes around comes around."

"You sound like Fryman. And I don't believe in karma."

"Anyway, I've made some changes to the site. I'm waiting for them to upload," he said.

The computer dinged.

"It's finished." He twisted the screen so I could see. "I posted a note saying healthy kids from school should contact me. We'll meet at three o'clock tomorrow outside at my house. Got plans?"

His eyes had a soft pleading look. Anxiety welled up inside of me, making it hard to breathe. The looters, Mr. B, the germs—danger hovered everywhere. I couldn't do it. Jay had good intentions, but I needed to protect myself.

"Sorry," I said. "I just can't."

Chapter 17

Pandemic phases 1 to 3 are like the pre-ignition of a fire. Phase 4 is like combustion—you've got dangerous flames. In phases 5 and 6, wind spreads the embers and the fire grows uncontrollably. So the official upgrade to phase 6 means major trouble.
—Blue Flu interview, Colorado Emergency Medical Technician

TK was still in blissful baby sleep and there was no sign of Jay and Ty being up when I awoke. My stomach grumbled for breakfast. Ignoring it, I showered and braided my hair in a loose plait, then surveyed my clothes. I reached for a striped black T-shirt and hesitated. Jay had complimented me on wearing blue. Did I care, though? Sighing, I pulled the striped one off the hanger.

For breakfast, Jay and Ty ate dried Captain Crunch cereal that Jay had brought over. TK gobbled pureed pears and baby rice cereal. I opened and closed the pantry, trying to overlook my hunger. I needed to stretch my food supply as long as possible.

"What's the matter?" Jay asked.

Was I that transparent? It was almost scary how well he could read me.

"Um, I'm figuring out how long I can feed TK with the food delivered yesterday."

"He should be all right for a few weeks, right? And you need to eat, too." He poured a bowl of cereal and slid it toward me.

I took slow, grateful bites.

"We brought you some lunch. Nothing exciting. Tuna, soup, and some crackers. I'll put it in the cabinet."

"Thank you." I could make that last two days if I had to.

"Hey," Ty said. "We could take some of Priati's jars of mush. She won't mind."

"Priati?"

"One of the families that left town," Jay explained. "They had a kid about TK's age. Ty's right. They don't plan on coming back any time soon. Maybe we could check their cabinets for extra baby food. And supplies for you, too."

"Is that OK? It's not stealing?" Ty asked.

"We can pay them back when they come home."

"All right." Ty smiled, his cheeks full of cereal.

"That would be great," I said.

Once we got TK playing in his portable crib and Ty watching cartoons, Jay and I attempted to order food from the grocery site again. Still no luck. I clenched my hands in frustration. In between tries, Jay pulled up his blog.

I scanned the memorial page over his shoulder. "Am I imagining things, or did the list double overnight? There must be eighty people now."

"How is that possible?" he asked.

"Either the flu is spreading fast or people are catching up, adding names from the past few days. Not really a good situation either way."

Jay clicked on the "Want to help?" section he created the night before. Besides Ethan and Derek, about seven or eight girls had signed up to meet today. Kayla's name was at the top of the list.

I rolled my eyes. "Either girls are surviving better than boys, or they're all looking to hang out with you."

"Don't be ridiculous," he said. "You're sure you don't want to come and see old friends?"

"Huh?"

"Kayla said you used to be best buds."

I flinched. "Not anymore." So they had been talking about me. That was awkward. And annoying.

Jay changed the subject. "If you were in charge of the meeting at my house, what would you do?"

I sat cross-legged in the chair near the desk. "You really want my advice?"

He nodded.

"I don't know. Maybe you could come up with a plan to find kids left alone or people who need help or families without food. You can't take a bunch of kids from their homes, though, even if the parents are . . . deceased. You'll have to leave some type of notice so other relatives can find them and keep track of who you're caring for and where they live. So when things are back to normal, you'll have some type of record."

"Good point. I'll ask my aunt to help me draft a letter. We can leave it with our contact info. I'll print a bunch of copies before we get together."

"While you're meeting, I could follow up with Reggie and see if the seniors can help with the childcare."

"That would be great."

I shrugged my shoulders. My self-preservationist attitude was selfish, but at least I could assist in the background. It wasn't much, but it was something.

While Jay posted on his blog, I checked on the kids. We were watching mindless TV when Jay came downstairs carrying their duffle bags. "Time to head home," he said.

"I don't want to go," Ty said. "I want to stay here."

"We need to see if the Singhs have any baby food for TK, remember?"

Once they left, the house felt too quiet. I wished they hadn't gone. I left a message for Reggie, then carried TK from room to room, hoping to calm my nerves.

If I ignored the chair against the door, I could almost trick myself into thinking we hadn't been robbed, that strangers hadn't sorted through our belongings and walked off with pillowcases of food. But the feeling of comfort didn't last long.

Mr. B had been at my door. Why? What could he possibly want? If he knew I was alone, the situation could be even more dangerous.

When I texted Mom and Dad last night, I hadn't mentioned any of my fears. It would make them worry even more. They would agree that I shouldn't meet with other kids today. It was too risky and helping other people was overrated. Wasn't it?

I was feeding TK his bottle when the phone rang. I tried to juggle the receiver without clonking him on the head.

"Hello, Miss Lil."

"Hi Reggie." TK whimpered until I got him repositioned with the bottle.

"Is that your little baby I hear?"

"Yes and your future best buddy. Did you talk to your friends at the Senior Center?"

He sighed. "It didn't go over well."

"It didn't?" Disappointment hit me like when I unexpectedly failed a test.

"People are worried about the germs, the logistics, the time commitment."

"Don't retired people generally have a lot of time?"

"It's mostly the germs, Miss Lil."

"I totally understand the fear of germs, believe me, but babies are the least likely to get sick and TK has been symptom-free for days."

"I tried to tell them that. But Hazel, well, she has her own opinion."

"Hazel Templeton?"

"That's the one."

"I know Mrs. Templeton. She helped me set up a pen pal program between the seniors and elementary school kids last year. It started out as a reading program, but she was a total control freak and changed everything around. 'A fabulous project' she called it in the end."

"Well, she said this one wasn't so fabulous."

"She knows it was me asking?"

"Yep. It didn't seem to make a difference."

"But why does she get to decide?" I asked.

"She's still the president of the Senior Center. As the former mayor, she's compelled to run something. Last week, she kicked out Mr. Eckhart for cheating at cards. No one even tried to argue."

TK drained the last of his formula as I let out a sigh.

Reggie cleared his throat. "If it helps, I can watch the baby for a bit this afternoon. Maybe take him to the Center for a visit. It'll give you a break at least."

"That would be great. Except I don't have a car seat for him." I dreaded having to return to the Goodwins' house to search for one.

"I can ask around. I'm sure one of the grandmas here has one we can borrow."

"All right."

I hung up after making plans for me to drop TK off at Reggie's later. But that didn't solve the larger problem. TK couldn't live with me forever. I probably wouldn't survive another week. And what about other babies in the community who needed help?

Maybe I was being silly. TK could be an anomaly . . . although it seemed unlikely.

"What do you think, buddy? Are you the only orphan?"

He smiled at me, kicking his little legs while I washed him and got him dressed in his last clean outfit, a pale green jumper with yellow ducks on it. I did a load of laundry while we played peek-a-boo, then we had lunch. I ate half the tuna with one of the crackers Jay left me.

I turned the TV on while eating. In an attempt to screen for illness, several airports had installed "thermal imaging devices" to detect feverish travelers. A siren sounded if anyone passed through with a higher than normal temperature.

The news segment showed masked officials in the Hong Kong airport escorting a businessman away. People practically trampled each other to distance themselves from the infected passenger. One woman trying to avoid getting crushed looked like Mom. She even carried a reusable green canvas bag like my mother's. But Mom couldn't still be in Asia, could she?

While TK napped, I got my answer by text.

> Mom: still in hong kong
> Mom: but next on list for london flight
> Mom: trying but not much i can do to speed things up
> Mom: this place is crazy but i'm close to getting out
> Mom: hope you are well
> Mom: hanger there
> Mom: i mean, hang in there

Ugh. My heart sank. If she became ill in the airport, she would never make it home. She would die there and her body would probably never be returned to us and—

Stop. I had to make those thoughts stop.

> Me: I miss you so much.

I didn't want to sound desperate.

> Me: But doing OK.

I sat holding my phone. On impulse, I scrolled back through the texts Megs and I had sent each other. I found our last ones.

> Megs: if something happens 2 me
> Me: shut up!
> Megs: i mean it. if something happens ur the best bff. 4 the record i'm pissed 2 die a virgin.
> Me: ur not dying. or i will kill u!!!
> Megs: lol. seriously, u can have my necklace. the 1 with blue pearl dad gave me.
> Me: ur scaring me. u will be fine.
> Megs: where r u?
> Me: @ coffee shop. with ur mystery guy.
> Megs: !!!! we r @ hospital. have 2 go. I <3 u.

I re-read her words a dozen times, wishing I could tell her what a great friend she was, how much she helped me through the crisis with Mr. B. If she were here now, what would she tell me? Probably to take a risk, to do something crazy, even as I feared leaving the safety of home.

Then it registered: It was time to visit her house.

CHAPTER 18

Social distancing measures can be helpful in curbing the spread of influenza. But the Blue Flu is hitting US teens hard, and how many of them will stay isolated with school cancelled?
—Blue Flu interview, public health official

I dropped off TK at Reggie's house with a diaper bag of supplies and my cell phone number, making sure my phone was charged in case Reggie needed to reach me. Then I walked to Megs's with a backpack filled with shopping bags and a can of hornet spray, just in case. I moved quickly, glancing around me every few seconds, always aware of my surroundings. Several houses had broken windows like ours. I didn't have any real weapons to defend myself, but so far, no one else was out.

Before entering the Salernos' house, I checked for signs of looters, but everything seemed locked up. I took the spare key from under the fake rock where Megs had hidden it without telling her mother. As a cop, Mrs. Salerno hadn't approved of keeping a key four feet from the front door.

Stepping through the doorway was the hardest thing I'd had to do. Being at the empty house made reality impossible to ignore. I hovered in the doorway before finally going in, locking the door behind me.

I stood in the kitchen for a long time. Megs and her mom were dead. Not away on vacation, like I tried to imagine. For a crazy moment, I smelled popcorn, but it was only my longing that Megs would push the bowl in my direction like she had a thousand times before.

I had come to say good-bye, but I had to take care of business first. The germs in the house would be gone by now. Jay was right: Megs and Mrs. Salerno would want to help me, would want me to survive. They wouldn't mind if I took food and medicine that I needed.

Still, it somehow felt intrusive looking through their bathroom cabinets. I mumbled, "Sorry," as I opened the doors. I found a bunch of over-the-counter meds, which went into my bag, and some unknown prescriptions for Mrs. Salerno, which I left. Then I checked the pantry. No baby food, of course, but lots of soup and canned goods I could eat. When the backpack overflowed, I filled three shopping bags, too.

I thought about leaving the food by the stairs, but I didn't want to let it out of my sight. Panting from the burden, I trudged up to Megs's room and put the bags down outside her door.

Stopping at the threshold, I breathed in the honeysuckle smell. There was a finished history assignment about the *Titanic* on her desk, next to a half-empty glass of water. Clothes she had been trying on for her mystery date covered the floor.

Her life, cut short.

Memories of us together flashed through my mind: Megs laughing so hard on the last day of freshman year that orange soda came out her nose; Megs letting me sign her cast first when she broke her wrist; pinky swearing that we wouldn't pick ugly maid-of-honor gowns for each other's wedding.

My legs started shaking so hard that I couldn't stand. I sank onto her bed, burying my face in her pillow.

Oh, Megs. How can you be gone? This can't be real. It can't be.

When the sobbing finally slowed, I grabbed a tissue from her nightstand, knocking a flash of blue to the floor. I leaned over, grasping the necklace she'd mentioned in her last message to me. My sorrow for Megs seemed to have settled on my chest like a hundred necklaces. I slipped the silver chain around my neck, the teal blue pearl cool against my skin. It wasn't enough to heal my hurt but it did make me feel a fraction better. "I hope you're watching out for me, Megs," I whispered.

If she hadn't gotten sick, she would have met Jay

that Friday night. Maybe they would be going out now. Megs and I would've had a good laugh over that. Her mystery guy had been in our school all along. She would have chided me for fretting about her safety. I could almost hear her voice: "See? I told you not to worry."

Now her life was over. And how could the world measure the value of a time so brief? What was the point? Did her existence even matter?

Of course it did. Megs made a huge impact on me, acting as a lifeline over the past year. High school post-Mr. B would have been unbearable without her support.

That made me wonder. If I died next week, would my life count for anything? This was our very own *Titanic*, our history in the making. It was an opportunity for heroism and greatness and yet I was an anxious ball of nerves, crying in my dead friend's bed.

Leaving everything else in Megs's room untouched, I grabbed the backpack and bags of food, locked up, then rushed home as fast as I could under the weight. If I hurried, I could still make it to Jay's meeting.

⌒

There's safety in numbers, I tried to convince myself as I surveyed the group assembled in Jay's backyard. I knew Beth and Elsa by sight. And then there was Kayla, overdressed for a charity mission. She raised her eyebrows at me but didn't bother to say hello.

"You made it," Jay said, looking pleased as he approached me.

Ethan arrived with Derek shortly after. We gave each other a cautious greeting. Then Derek sat with the girls and Ethan pulled me aside.

"Where's your baby?" he asked.

"My neighbor's watching him for me."

He looked sheepish. "Sorry about our last conversation. Things got stressful when family moved in with us. Then Aunt Lori died—"

"The one who liked to crochet?"

He nodded. "And my cousin, Barry, too, the one who lived alone in New Providence. If someone would have checked on him, maybe . . . well, that's why I'm here."

"I'm really sorry," I said.

"Everyone will lose somebody before this is over."

Somebody like Megs. I toyed with her necklace. *I'm doing the best thing by being here, right? I'm acting strong and brave, trying to help other people because it needs to be done.*

Ethan and I joined the others. Elsa shimmied over to make room for him at the picnic table. Jay sat next to me on the other side, while Ty presumably played video games in the house. Kayla and Beth lounged on mismatched chairs.

Once everyone was settled, Jay explained the general plan: by banding together, we could help people in the immediate area. Then I explained about finding TK uncared for at a neighbor's house.

"There could be others," I said.

"And besides the memorials," Jay said, "there were two new posts on my blog. Scott McGraw asked for pain reliever, and Jenna Fuentes needed food."

"Yo, I know Scott and Jenna," Derek said.

"How many people are listed on the memorial page?" Kayla asked.

"One hundred and eight." Which included Megs, although Kayla hadn't said a word about her to me.

"The disease is international now," Elsa said. "The World Health Organization upgraded it from a phase five to a phase six. The virus is spreading among the general population, not just in localized clusters."

No one spoke for a few minutes.

Beth, the school's theater diva, enunciated as if speaking to an auditorium full of people. "Look, I feel bad," she said, raising her hand palm up for effect. "But why should we help anyone else? It's a big town. What are we going to do, knock on doors and see who's still alive? My parents would kill me if they knew I was involved with that."

"I'm not sure that's safe," I said. "There have been lootings and . . ." Fears of Mr. B rushed my mind. I thought of someone like him answering a door, grabbing me, and pulling me inside. I doubted 911 had a quick response time these days.

"What if we focus on other high school students?" Ethan said. "We could check on our friends."

"I think it needs to be wider than that," Jay said.

"Who put you in charge?" Ethan argued.

Whoa. Since when was there so much tension between those guys?

"Chill out," Derek said. "Does anyone have a map?"

"We must have one somewhere," Jay said.

"Don't they give school employees a master student directory?" Kayla asked. "If we use your aunt's directory to mark where the kids live, we could begin with those families."

"What about pets?" Elsa asked. "There might be animals trapped in the houses, too. We should bring some dog and cat food along, just in case. My mom's a vet. I can get her to drop some off for us."

I remembered the cat that had scurried out of the Goodwins' house, suddenly feeling guilty that I didn't try to help it.

"Animal food. OK," Derek said.

"What I want to know is why the town isn't organizing anything like this?" Beth asked.

"*Portico Press* reported that half the volunteers they counted on are too sick to help," Jay said. "They're caring for the ill people first."

"And what if we become fatally infected?" she asked.

"I have some masks from my aunt you could wear," Jay said. "I can't drag Ty around, so we'll serve as home base here. You can call me with any updates and I can track which houses you visit. If people are nervous about the first round, they can stay here with me."

"I could stay with Jay," Kayla piped up. "I mean, I could keep an eye on his brother while he works on the computer."

"Right." Her motive became as obvious as her shiny red lip gloss.

"I could stay with Jay, too," Beth said.

"Do you like animals?" Elsa asked Derek.

"Love 'em."

"We can visit houses together then."

Ethan looked at me. "Lil?" he said. "Partners?"

Not seeing a way out, I nodded. Apparently the pandemic made everyone want to hook up—some type of hormonal-survival thing.

"It's too bad we can't bring soup or something with us, in case people are desperate," Derek said.

"Does anyone have extra food?" Beth asked. "I know we don't."

I thought about the bags I'd taken from Megs's house. Did I have enough to share? Even with my improved attitude, the idea of giving my food away made me panicked.

"You're Miss Community Service," Kayla said with a cold stare. "At least you used to be, remember? Too bad you can't whip up a food drive."

Next, she'll be inviting Mr. B himself to help us, too. I pushed him out of my mind. We needed extra food. I looked away from Kayla. Then I smacked the table. "That's it! A food drive! The school held a spring collection, remember? The donations must still be there. There were boxes and boxes in the hallway. We could each take some home to our families and still have enough to share."

"If you could find a way into the school," Ethan said. "Do you think anyone's working in the building?"

"I doubt it," Jay said. "Could we get someone to unlock the doors?"

"Even if we could, I don't think they'll simply hand over the food," Beth said.

I thought about completely restocking my shelves and almost started to salivate. "We need to take it. If someone hasn't already, that is."

"You want to break into the school?" Elsa asked.

Derek smiled. "Cool! I'm in."

"I'm not stealing anything," Jay said.

I glanced at him. His mouth was set in a determined line. Why was he so reluctant about this? "But all those donations, sitting there, unused," I said. "If people contributed the food, it's not steal—"

"No." He crossed his arms, looking away. "I'm not doing anything illegal."

I followed his gaze to where Ty waited safely inside.

"I need to go check on my brother. I'll look for maps while I'm in there."

"OK then," Ethan said when Jay was gone. "Someone's a chicken."

I glared at him. "Shut up."

"Just because your new boyfriend—"

"He's *not* my boyfriend."

Kayla smiled like when she won class president in eighth grade. "Really?" she asked. "So, should you leave for the school soon?"

"My bro's got a pickup truck I can borrow," Derek said.

Jay returned to the group, calmer, and soon we had outlined a plan. Kayla would stay to watch Ty and plot the student directory homes on the map. Elsa would call her mom to make arrangements for the pet food. I'd ride my bike to the school and meet Derek, Beth, and Ethan there. The less time I spent with Ethan, the better.

"I'll ride part way with you," Jay said. "It might not be safe."

Ethan frowned. "Come on, Jay. Everyone who's helping can squeeze into the truck."

"Where are we going to put Lil?" Derek asked. "In the way back, holding onto the tailgate?"

"I don't think so," I said. "Besides, we'll need that room for the food on the way back. I'm hoping there's a lot. Can you get a wagon to pull it out of the school? And some tools to get us in?"

Derek nodded. "Worse case we hurl a rock through the window, stick our hand in, and unlatch the door."

Which was exactly what we did. The broken glass made me pause—that's what the looters had done to my house. But this was to help other people I reminded myself. And when we saw the huge amount of food collected inside, it was worth it.

"There must be ten boxes here," Ethan said. "And another twenty bags."

"Let's start moving them," Derek said. "Where are we going to take all this?"

"We can store it at my house." I promised myself not to hoard all the food, as tempting as it was.

"It smells like bleach," Beth said.

I sniffed. "Maybe they disinfected the school?"

By the time we almost finished moving the food, our mood turned giddy. The boys shouted rock song lyrics and even Beth seemed surprisingly cheerful, turning cartwheels in the hallway. Derek kept the beat by banging on the lockers.

Then we passed the entrance to Mr. B's old class-room.

I stopped in the doorway as if in a trance.

Miss Scher had taken over his teaching position and there were no signs that he had ever taught there. But the memories couldn't be erased as easily as a whiteboard.

⌒

I'd worked with Mr. B before. He helped coach me before my speech when I won the town's Teen Humanitarian Award. He was an affectionate guy, and even though I felt uncomfortable around him a few times, I doubted myself. I mean, students adored him. Mr. B was handsome in a rugged kind of way and he exuded positive energy that even the guys responded to. Sometimes you could almost see the passion for a project in his eyes. So when he asked me to help organize a Thanksgiving food drive, I couldn't say no.

"You're perfect for this project, Lilianna," he said, his brown eyes intense as we discussed it in his classroom after school. "We can coordinate a great drive together. I've talked to all the English teachers. They'll give a homework pass to each student who brings in at least three cans or boxes of food."

Throughout November, the donations piled up. Right before Thanksgiving break, we drove together to drop the food off at the pantry. The coordinators there were thrilled about what we had donated. They said it would be one of their best Thanksgivings because they wouldn't have to turn away anyone in need. I left feeling giving, generous, proud. Mr. B drove me home, singing to Top 40 radio in his tenor voice. He asked if we could stop by his house on the way.

Should I have known then what he was about to do?

We stood inside his kitchen, drinking a soda. "What a great event. And you were fabulous. Your energy, enthusiasm. I've worked with a lot of students, but none quite like you."

I blushed. "Thank you."

"Are you tired? It's been a long day."

"A little."

He moved behind me, resting his hands lightly on my shoulders.

There is no reason to be afraid.

"I should be getting home," I said.

"I give great massages."

With my back to him, I couldn't see his face. The way he brushed against me was unsettling, though. His breath in my ear set off a subtle internal warning signal.

"It's getting kind of late," I said.

He rubbed my neck. "You're so tense. We're both so tense."

Before I could say anything else, his hands left my shoulders. They crept down the sides of my breasts until he stopped at my hips.

This cannot be happening.

"I need to go." I tried to move forward but he pulled me back against him.

"You want to spend time with your favorite teacher, right? Lilianna, I work with beautiful girls all the time. So many beautiful girls. And I chose you. Do you know how special that is?"

My throat felt like it was closing. I could barely breathe.

"Let me help you relax." He forced me around to face him. I tried to step back, but he held me tight, one hand sliding under my skirt. He kissed me roughly.

I jerked my face away, struggling to push my arms against him.

"No," I said, but the word came out strangled in fear.

"No!" I shouted, louder this time.

He released my arm. I had to move, had to put distance between us. I took a step back. But he grabbed me again with one hand, the other fumbling with his zipper.

"No!" I screamed and this time the volume startled us both. I jerked away and crashed into the counter. The safety of the doorway was within reach. I ran out without looking back.

～

"Lil!" Beth yelled.

I jumped at the sound of my name.

"We have to leave! The janitor's here."

Everyone sprinted past the English room toward the exit, doors banging closed behind them. I couldn't move at first, still trapped in the horror of the memories.

The janitor, Mr. Finley, loomed large at the end of the hallway, holding a jug of bleach. "What the hell are you kids doing?"

Uh oh. I bolted through the door in time to see Derek's pickup pull away.

CHAPTER 19

I'm trying to focus on the Who, What, When, Where, and Why of this horrible disease. But I'm worried for the safety of my family and concerned we won't all survive.
—Blue Flu interview, quarantined journalist

I pedaled quickly, only glancing back toward the school once. Mr. Finley, fast for a big man, wasn't far behind me. After turning the corner, I spotted Jay on his bike.

"What are you doing here?"

"Waiting for you," he said. "It's not safe to be—"

"The janitor's after us! Go!"

We sped down the street next to each other, passing driveways with old newspapers. Jay's face was pale. I could tell he wanted no part in this.

If Finley caught us stealing, he probably couldn't even get the police to come arrest us. But he'd certainly tell the principal. Would theft become part of our permanent record? Someday the flu would end and I'd be applying to college. Wouldn't I?

"This way," Jay said.

I couldn't keep the pace much longer. Jay turned onto the street behind ours. No time to question. He raced up a driveway, jumped off his bike near the side of the house. No kickstands. Our bikes toppled. We left them behind and ran through the connecting backyard. I followed him to the front of the next house.

The red maple beckoned with its familiar canopy. He ducked under, grabbed my hand, pulled me with him.

Under the tree branches, it was quiet except for our breathing. We didn't talk for a long time. I didn't want to jinx our successful escape. Jay still held my hand. It was sweaty where our skin touched.

Jay had waited to make sure I stayed safe. He sat close enough now that I could feel the heat from his body. Holding his hand made me feel happy. Almost at peace. And slightly guilty, too.

What would Megs think of this? Would she blame me? Encourage me? Hate me? And now Kayla was involved. Not that I felt any loyalty to her. But Megs . . . I closed my eyes, letting myself feel the warmth from Jay's hand one last moment before I eased mine away, brushing the hair from my eyes as an excuse.

A motor rumbled past us and we peered out. Derek drove by, heading toward my house. Part of me wanted to stay under the safety of the branches with Jay. But I couldn't hide forever.

"I have to go meet them. Thank you . . . for riding with me." We locked eyes. I looked away first. When we retrieved the bikes, there was no sign of the janitor.

"See you soon?" Jay asked.

"Yes."

When I reached home, Derek and Ethan fist-pumped about a hundred times. Ethan grinned. "That was awesome!

"You made it OK?" I asked.

"We didn't see that dude again once we left the parking lot," Derek said.

"Pull into the garage just in case."

Once inside, I closed the garage door behind us. The four of us unloaded the boxes of food. I couldn't wait to see what was in each box.

"Where are your folks?" Derek asked.

"Away," I said. "Here. Take some of the canned soup over to Jay's to hand out this afternoon." I pulled some paper shopping bags out of the recycling basket. "Everyone should bring some home. We can move the rest of it into the house. It will be too easy to steal if we leave the food in the garage."

"Where do you want it, the kitchen?" Derek asked.

I shook my head. "Looters robbed us. But they

missed things upstairs in my closet and under my bed."

"You want us to drag this all up?" Beth asked. "You know, I better get home before my parents start worrying."

Derek offered to drive her, so that left Ethan and me to deal with the food.

Ethan and I carried the items upstairs without saying much. It took several trips and we were both out of breath as we made room on my closet shelves.

"It won't all fit," he said.

Despite the exertion, I grinned. It was nice to see food packed in there. Even if it wasn't all mine to keep, the sheer quantity made me feel much better.

"What?" Ethan asked.

I shook my head, not wanting to explain. "We can slide the rest under my bed."

Ethan paused in the center of my room. "It's been a long time since I've been in here." He nodded toward the playpen TK slept in each night. "Nice addition."

"Ha ha. Help me slide this under."

We knelt on the floor, pushing the food back by the bottled water I had hidden beneath my bed.

"So," he said.

The phone rang. I jumped at the excuse to move away from him.

"Hello?"

Cough, cough.

The line went dead. I checked the caller ID.

Dad.

I tried to dial his number, but pushed the wrong keys. I hung up, tried again. Busy signal.

"Who was it?" Ethan asked.

"My father. He's quarantined in Delaware. He sounded awful."

I paced around my room, straightening the pillows, aligning the book spines on my shelf.

Ethan sat on the floor with his back against the bed. "Do you want to sit a minute?" He motioned next to him. "We should talk."

I knew him well enough to see where this was going. "About what?" I stalled.

"Look, it's hard to start over. You already know everything about me—my annoying mother, my lunatic brother. You've had Sunday dinner with my grandma. And I know all about you, too," he said. "In crazy times like these, there's comfort in that, don't you think?"

"I'm not sure you can ever know everything about a person. There's always something left unsaid." In cases like ours, that something was significant.

"Look, I realize what happened, why we ended."

"Really?" I frowned. Had Kayla gossiped about me? Because Megs and I hadn't told a soul.

"After this flu, school will never be the same for

us. I see that now. We should ignore the past and move on."

"What do you mean, ignore the past?" I pressed my palm to my forehead, confused.

"If you cheated on me and that's why we broke up, I'd be willing to forgive you. Just tell me the truth. Even if it's someone I hang out with."

"I didn't cheat on you."

"What about Jay?"

"What about him? We're friends."

"There's nothing going on between you two?"

So that's why Ethan had been so tense around Jay during the backyard meeting. But it was a complicated question. There was how I felt about Jay while dating Ethan, which amounted to nothing. Then there was the thrill when he held my hand under the tree less than an hour ago.

Ethan waited for an answer.

"No, there's nothing going on," I said.

"OK." He relaxed his frown.

The phone rang again.

"Dad?"

"Lily," he answered in a gruff voice. "I'm glad I reached you."

Leaving Ethan in my room, I moved to Dad's office and plunked into his chair. "You sound terrible."

"I'm a little under the weather."

I hadn't noticed the absence of his messages. When did they stop? I got used to them, took them for granted, the same way I'd taken for granted the school bell ringing, the stores stocking food, people not dropping over dead.

Dad coughed—a wet, hacking sound.

"You've got the flu, don't you?" I stayed perfectly still.

"Afraid so."

"No," I whispered.

"They're checking for hospital beds, but even if there is one available, I'm not sure there's much more they can do. I haven't been able to reach Mom." More coughing. "I wanted to tell you how much I love you. You're the best daughter a father could ever ask for."

"Dad, you have to get better!"

"Be strong," he said before the coughing overcame him and the phone went dead.

I tried calling him back, but there was no answer, so I stayed in Dad's office, looking at the folders I had restacked after the looting, some notes he'd jotted in his neat penmanship. He couldn't be dying. He couldn't be. Instead, I imagined him growing stronger, getting healthier, slowly recovering. I didn't move until Ethan finally roused me from my stupor.

He stood in the doorway. "Did you hear me?"

"What? No, I didn't."

"Do you want to come back to your room and talk for awhile?"

"Um, my dad . . . he has the flu." I sat with my head in my hands.

"That sucks." Ethan leaned against the doorjamb. "I wanted to talk some more."

"Are you crazy? I can't think about anything else. My father is *dying*."

"Well, we should go then. They'll be waiting for us. Unless you want to stay here?"

But sitting in Dad's office alone was depressing and didn't help anyone. Reluctantly, I followed Ethan outside. We walked most of the way to Jay's in silence. I thought about my father, replayed the sound of his cough in my mind.

"I'm sorry," Ethan said when we reached Jay's door.

"What?" I asked. Ethan had always been a snail about apologizing.

"I'm sorry," he repeated. "I know you're worried about your dad. I shouldn't be such an insensitive jerk."

Wow. I paused with my hand on the doorknob.

"But I can't help feeling that we're letting something great slip away. Maybe . . ." He looked down, as if he were afraid to meet my eyes. "Never mind."

"What is it?"

He took a step closer, put his hands on my arms. "I thought that if we kissed one last time, maybe it would help you see how special this is. If you don't feel anything, anything at all, I'd be willing to move on."

"I'm not—"

Ethan was already leaning toward me, his face tilted at an angle that used to fit perfectly with mine.

I shut my eyes, resigned to the kiss that followed. I wanted to feel something, to prove to myself that I was normal again. His lips felt familiar, but wrong somehow. I did feel longing, but not for Ethan. What I felt was a longing for my life before. Before Mr. B. Before the flu.

We were kissing when the door swung open. I pulled away in time to catch Jay's expression, to see him mistake our embrace for something it wasn't.

"You didn't need to ring the bell," Jay said. "You can just walk in. That's what friends do." He rushed back inside before I could say anything.

Ethan smirked, clearly pleased with himself.

"You are such a jerk." I shoved Ethan hard with both hands. "You actually rang the doorbell during our kiss? So you staged that little scene for Jay's benefit?"

"What difference does it make?" Ethan said. "You told me there's nothing going on with him."

Furious, I marched into Jay's house, stopping

near the others gathered in the family room. Ty played video games while the group studied a map. Everyone glanced at me except Jay.

Ethan shuffled in. I moved next to Ty on the couch.

"You'll start on the nearest roads and fan outward," Kayla said. "Ethan, Lil, you can go toward River Street, then loop back."

"All right," Ethan said.

I quietly gritted my teeth.

"What about Scott and Jenna?" Jay said. "They needed supplies."

"Derek and Elsa, you can stop by their houses on your route," Kayla said. "Then you can circle out to the surrounding roads."

While we were gone, the others had filled four large backpacks with water, canned soup, pain reliever, crackers, and baggies of pet food Elsa had assembled. Everyone was ready.

Except me. I wanted to clear the air with Jay, but he still wouldn't look at me, not even when he handed out the masks to everyone. Kayla hovered near him like a predator stalking its prey.

"Keep a lookout for looters," he said. "Everyone has my number in their phones?"

We nodded.

"OK. See you later."

"Let's do this," Ethan said to me.

Clenching my fists, I reluctantly fell in step beside him.

We made our way down the first streets quickly, falling into an awkwardly quiet routine. I kept the map, pointing out the houses from the school directory. Ethan did the talking at each door, handing out supplies if needed. We kept our conversation to a minimum. I reported the results back to Jay as we walked to the next house.

"No one home at twenty-four Barngate," I said.

"Got it."

"Four sick people at twenty-eight. We gave them soup and pain reliever."

"OK."

"We fed a dog through the mail slot at number thirty-two."

"Great."

Four whole words from Jay. Should I care? He was my neighbor, Megs's mystery guy, Kayla's next conquest. His abruptness shouldn't sting as much as it did, should it?

The backpacks got lighter as we made our way along the route Kayla had plotted. I had managed to avoid face-to-face contact with any sick people. Ethan had kept his distance, too, stepping back when people came to the door. After a few hours, we had twenty-seven no answers, two families who were fine, nine who gushed their thanks when we offered supplies, and the one dog we managed to help. Our conversations remained matter-of-fact and I stayed busy enough to avoid obsessing over Dad, worrying if he had his own soup and pain reliever to keep him going.

We approached a gray house on River Street. I had some things to say to Ethan and we were almost done with our visits. I didn't plan on talking to him again any time soon, so it was now or never. I took a deep breath and skipped the preamble.

"Don't ever touch me again," I said.

"You're still upset about that?" He sounded cavalier but avoided my eyes.

"I want to make sure I'm perfectly clear."

"Why? Was the kiss that awful?"

"That's not the point. You manipulated me."

"So? It was a kiss, Lil. It's not like I tried to rape you or anything."

As he rang the doorbell, the volcanic rage rose inside me with no place to go.

"Come in, come in," a screechy old woman called.

Filled with anger, I wasn't thinking about what I was doing. I wasn't thinking at all. Moving past him, I shoved the front door open and entered the house.

Chapter 20

In 1918, they used orphan trains to find homes for the children left parentless by the flu. What will we have today? Orphan blogs? Welfare services are completely overrun. We can't possibly deal with the magnitude of children left without families.
—Blue Flu interview, New Jersey social worker

Hello?" I called inside the house.

"Hello!" someone answered.

I stepped forward. Ethan followed, moving in beside me. I was about to yell at him when the smell hit me like a smack in the face. I gagged. "What is—"

"Don't look!" Ethan said.

Too late. Three bodies sprawled across the family room couch—two boys and a younger girl. A man with brown hair like Dad's lay on the floor. Their dark blue skin seemed surreal, as if they were part of a sci-fi movie.

"Oh my God." I walked backward toward the door, bumping into a wire cage.

A large green parrot squawked and ruffled his feathers.

"Oh my God," it mimicked. "Oh my God."

We bolted outside. Ethan kept going when we reached the street but my stomach heaved. I bent over, ripping the mask off right before I threw up on the curb. "I can still smell it. Death. Can you smell it?"

I leaned over, gasping. I wanted to run home, take a shower, and never leave my house again. I could shutter myself away with the donated food, stay inside forever while waiting for Mom and Dad. Helping other people was a stupid idea. Stupid, scary, and dangerous.

"Let's get away from here," Ethan said, breaking my train of thought.

We trudged to Jay's house without speaking. Once inside, I bee-lined to the bathroom to splash my face with cold water and rinse the gross taste from my mouth. Lowering the toilet lid, I sat there, waiting for the shakiness to pass.

But it didn't. My legs trembled no matter how long I rested. I couldn't get the smell of decay out of my nose, the image of death out of my mind. When I could finally stand, I found Ethan whispering to Jay in the kitchen. I tried to listen but Ty practically jumped up and down in front of me.

"I'm at level twenty-four!" he said. "It's my all time high! Come see."

He took my hand and led me to the TV, jabbering on about his game. Grateful for the distraction, I followed. Kayla lazed on the couch, looking relaxed. Ty's cheeriness helped push away my annoyance at Kayla, my worries about my father, and thoughts of death.

"See, Lil? That's my score." He pointed. "I'm only five thousand points away from the next level!"

"That's great, Ty."

"Will you watch me? She got bored." He motioned at Kayla.

"Of course." Anything to forget the dead family.

Sitting next to Ty, I let his continuous narration soothe me. "Now I have to jump to the next cave, see? Look! I got the speed bonus." I watched him for about ten minutes until he took a bathroom break. By then, my heartbeat had finally returned to normal.

Ethan and Jay moved to the backyard, leaving Kayla and me alone. I glanced at her.

"So," I said.

"Sew buttons," she answered, a stupid joke we'd shared for years.

I smiled, considered apologizing for the slap, but then Kayla cleared her throat.

She angled her body toward me. "I loved Mr. B, you know. A lot of us did. But you . . . you had to practically ruin his life."

I bit the inside of my mouth, any desire to apologize gone. "Actually, he brought it upon himself."

She shrugged. "I was angry at you for a long time. But Jay could help me recover."

The thought of Kayla with Jay disturbed me more than I wanted to admit. "But—"

"I'd hate for you to mess this up for me, too. So please don't interfere. Or I might slip and tell him all about you."

It took me a minute to understand what she meant. She was threatening to tell Jay about what happened with Mr. B. She knew how important it was for me to keep that a secret. And now, in the midst of the flu pandemic, she threatened to expose my hurtful past.

Does it even matter anymore? That family on River Street was dead. Megs was dead. The odds of my own family making it through this alive were bad. Jay wasn't speaking to me and Kayla still wanted to cause drama.

I had bigger things to worry about.

I never answered her. I rose slowly from the couch, walked outside, then sunk onto Jay's front stoop, wishing for the millionth time that I could call Megs. Or Dad. Or Mom. Did she even know how sick Dad was?

Scanning through old emails on my phone, I found the itinerary Dad had sent me. It included the number of the hotel he'd been staying at. Since he wasn't answering his cell, I hoped to reach the people taking care of him or at least find out where he was being treated.

Someone answered on the twelfth ring.

"This is Rick at Salina Hotel. How may I direct your call?"

"I'm trying to find my father, Keith Snyder. He was part of the hotel quarantine. He called me earlier. They were trying to move him, I think."

"I'm sorry to hear that, miss. Unfortunately, we don't have access to any of the quarantine records. You'd need to talk to the Salina Health Department. They've been in charge of the victims."

"Victims?"

"I mean, um, the patients. They're in charge of the patients. If you need more information, call the Health Department directly." He rattled off the number.

I hated getting the runaround but called anyway. The line was busy. I programmed the number into my phone and tried a few more times.

Of course when I got through, I was stuck in automated menu hell. After pressing zero, the system put me on hold for ten minutes before the woman who answered told me to call Patient Services.

"But I'm not a patient. I'm trying to find someone who is ill."

"That's the department you want, sweetheart."

Right. After nearly endless phone prompts, a re-corded voice told me that due to high volume, no one at Patient Services was available to answer my call and to try again later.

As I tucked my phone away, the sound of voices startled me. Derek and Elsa approached the house followed by three little girls with suitcases. So they had found orphans in town. My heart ached for the kids with no one to care for them.

The last girl trailed behind, her blonde head down.

Oh no. I knew that blonde head.

"Cam," I said softly.

She looked at me, her eyes lighting with recog-nition, then she ran into my arms.

CHAPTER 21

This pandemic has placed a tremendous burden on our net-work and communication systems. We apologize for any lapses in service but can't be held accountable during these unusual times.
—Blue Flu interview, president of telecommunications company

Cam's presence could only mean bad news about her mother. The moment she reached me, she started sobbing in my arms. I tried to be strong, to hold it together, but her crying made me weep, too. She was an orphan. For all I knew, I was an orphan as well. She hugged me for a long time after everyone else went inside.

"You're not sick at all?" I asked. "Achy? Coughing?"

"My heart hurts. And my chest feels sad," she said.

I held her on my lap. Her stomach rumbled.

"Is your belly sad, too?" I asked.

"No, silly. That's me being hungry."

We rose and joined the rest of the group inside. The two other girls were sisters who lived down the street from Cam. No one spoke about what happened to their families. Frankly, I was relieved. None of us could play the grief counselor role well enough for these poor kids.

"Are you girls hungry, too?" I asked them. They nodded.

Inside the fridge, Jay found leftover pasta from our dinner that seemed like a lifetime ago. He heated it while Ty set the table and I poured everyone boiled water to drink. Ty amused the girls with knock-knock jokes while they ate. Jay, Derek, Ethan, Elsa, and I crowded with Kayla in the family room to figure out what to do next.

"What are we going to do with them?" I whispered to the group. "I have to pick up TK soon from Reggie. Then we'll have four orphans." Unease settled over me. I hadn't thought this through. We had taken the kids out of their homes presumably to help them, but now what? We couldn't handle taking care of them and the seniors weren't willing to babysit at the center.

"Should we contact the police?" Elsa suggested.

"I'll have my aunt try the next time she's home," Jay said. "Maybe if a nurse calls, we'll get a different response. But we need someplace for them to sleep tonight."

Kayla studied her fingernails. Ethan shook his head. "My parents don't even know I'm doing this."

"Puppies, yes. Children, no," Elsa said.

Derek, Jay, and I looked at each other.

"Dude, my parents will kill me if I bring home some random kids," Derek said, shaking his head.

"The sisters can sleep here for a night," Jay said.

"And Cam can stay with me and TK. They all seem healthy, right?"

"Yeah," Derek said. "They seem all right. We left the letter you gave us," he told Jay. "But the parents . . ."

He didn't have to say it.

"There may be other relatives we can contact," Elsa said. "But it seemed wrong to leave them to fend for themselves now. Anyway, I need to get home soon."

Derek agreed to drop me and Cam at the Senior Center, then return to Jay's to take Ethan and Elsa home. I wasn't sure what Kayla's plans were.

"Lil," Jay said as I was preparing to leave.

I turned to him, eager to resolve the awkwardness between us since the Ethan kiss. I wanted our easy friendship back. And who else could I tell about Dad getting sick?

"I stopped by the Singh's house for baby supplies," he said. "There wasn't any food. Either they packed the cupboards when they left or they were looted, too."

"Thanks for checking," I said, knowing now wasn't the time to discuss anything else. I tried to ignore my disappointment as he turned back to help the others.

I summoned my strength for Cam, taking her hand as we walked to Derek's truck. "You can stay with me, OK? I'm taking care of a baby, too. His name is TK. We're going to pick him up now, then we'll go to my house for tonight."

"OK," she said. "Can we watch some dance shows later?"

"Sure."

We found Reggie at the Senior Center, sitting in a large room set up with round tables and chairs. He bounced TK on his knee while making conversation with three women across from him.

I waved as we walked over, trying to squelch my nervousness at being around so many people. Old folks weren't likely to be contagious, though.

"Hello, Miss Lil. Are your ears burning? I was telling the ladies here what a nice job you're doing with the baby. And who's this new friend?"

"This is Cam. She's going to help me with TK for a while."

A lady with wispy gray hair reached for TK, cooing at him. Reggie handed him to her, then stood, motioning for Cam to take his seat. "They have cookies," he said. "I'll get you some."

Cam sat, dangling her feet. The lady handed her a rattle and she shook it for TK.

"Let's talk over here," Reggie said, "away from little ears. What's going on?"

"It's bad," I said. "Jay has two other orphaned girls at his house. We can't take care of all these kids."

A woman heh-hemmed behind me. "Well, if it isn't Miss Teen Humanitarian," the voice said.

I turned to see a small wrinkled woman with curly white hair. She looked like a tiny Mrs. Claus, but I knew better than to underestimate Mrs. Templeton based on her appearance. She had a big personality inside that little body.

"Hi Mrs. Templeton. How are you?"

"I'm fine," she said. "Unlike you."

She'd had a gruff attitude even when we worked on the elementary school project together. The months hadn't mellowed her any.

"Unlike me?" I asked, taking the bait.

"Since you won your damn award, Lilianna, I've only seen you on a few occasions. And once you had a cigarette in your hand. Tsk, tsk."

I don't know what was more shocking: that she had seen me smoking or that she was actually tsk-ing at me.

She gave me the once-over. "You've certainly changed your appearance. Since when do you want to help orphans?"

"Since their parents dropped dead from the flu." I wasn't about to back down, not even to the former mayor.

"Tell me more about these kids," she said.

Using an eyebrow raise, I asked Reggie if she was reconsidering. He nodded, so I explained to her what we had accomplished in one afternoon. I hit the highlights: the number of houses we visited, the families we helped, the unfortunate circumstances of TK and the three girls who were left in their homes. I ended with a simple "please."

"I can't officially condone using the Senior Center as a day care. And you'd have to make your own arrangements for the evenings. We can't have children sleeping here, orphans or not," she said. "But I suppose if Reggie brings a few kids here of his own accord and some of the others happen to help out, well, I wouldn't stop it."

"That's great," I said. "Even a few hours a day would help." Having Reggie and the other seniors involved would make a big difference. If Mrs. Templeton had been a sweet old woman, I would have hugged her in gratitude.

Reggie grinned. "It's the right thing to do, Hazel."

"Now, don't go making me change my mind," she said.

ᐤ

Later that night, Cam watched me try to scrub TK with a damp washcloth as he wriggled on his changing pad.

"Don't you have a bathtub?" she asked.

"Yes, down the hall. But it's too big for a baby."

"I could sit and hold him in the tub while you wash him. He would get cleaner."

"You're right. That would be a big help."

"I love bubble baths," she said.

"Let's wash TK first, then you can have bubbles. He might try to eat them."

She giggled.

Once TK was clean, I offered her a choice of bubble bath scents. "Tangerine or strawberry?"

"Ooh. Strawberry is my favorite."

I poured some under the running water.

"It's turning the water pink!" she said. "My favorite color."

Cam stayed in the tub until her fingers wrinkled. I found a fuchsia T-shirt in the back of my closet for her to sleep in.

"Where's my bed?"

Carrying TK, I led her to the guest room where she would sleep.

"Where's your bed?" she asked.

"Down the hall."

She sniffled.

"This is a pretty bed, don't you think?"

More sniffling.

"What's the matter?" I asked.

"It's *beige*. And it's too lonely in here. I'm all by myself."

I sighed. Of course she didn't want to be alone. The poor kid had been through a lot. I should have realized that. "Let's go in my room and think about it," I said. "TK needs his bottle."

She sat on my bed next to me, swinging her legs while I fed the baby.

"Where does TK sleep?"

I pointed at his nearby playpen, sensing where she was going with this.

"The baby gets to sleep in here. It's not fair."

"You're right." Once TK was comfortable in his playpen, I dragged a small loveseat from my parent's room into mine. It made long scrapes in the wooden planks, but the condition of the hallway floor didn't matter much these days. I tucked sheets on the mini-couch the best I could and found a soft blanket in the closet.

"Better?"

"Yes." She held her hands behind her back. "And guess who's here?"

"Who?"

"Milkshake!" She displayed the stuffed cow proudly. "I packed him with my clothes."

"Good thinking." I tucked her in. "The bathroom's down the hall if you need it, remember?"

"Uh huh."

"I'll leave the hall light on in case you wake up."

"OK."

"Goodnight, Cam. Goodnight, Milkshake."

"Goodnight." Her voice was thick with sleep.

I waited until her breathing was steady before tiptoeing to Dad's office. I called Dad's cell, then Mom's. No answer from either of them. I crawled into bed a few minutes later, wide awake.

Spring rain pattered against my window, a comforting sound, and finally weariness set in. I peeked at TK and Cam sleeping soundly nearby. We were nice and cozy in my room, like a nest of mismatched birds. I tried not to think about how many predators attacked defenseless chicks or about how vulnerable we were on our own.

Had it only been a day since Jay slept over? I wondered if Kayla had finally gone home, and if he was awake and alone now, afraid like me. I drifted into an uneasy sleep with thunder rumbling in the distance.

An hour later, a loud boom jolted me awake. The electricity flickered once, twice, then died completely.

CHAPTER 22

Whether in 1918 or today, I have to believe the main worry
during a pandemic is the same: concern for our loved ones.
We may have cell phones, email, and texting now, but
in the end, we just want our children to survive.
—Blue Flu interview, a Delaware mother

I was too old to be afraid of the dark, but the sudden blackness took my breath away. I rummaged around blindly in my nightstand drawer the looters had skipped. Ever since the Mr. B incident, I'd been sleeping with a flashlight in there. Fear had its benefits for once.

Somehow TK and Cam didn't wake during the storm. I made my way by flashlight to the hall closet to retrieve the big battery-powered lantern. In my sleepiness, it took a full minute to process the empty shelves, to remember that the light had been stolen.

Worried and annoyed, I climbed back into bed. If I turned the flashlight off, the utter darkness disconcerted me, but I didn't want to waste the batteries. Finally, I raised the window shade a little, letting some moonlight peak through.

When a grayish sunlight filtered through the house on Saturday morning, the power was still out. After several minutes of searching, I found an old utilities bill in Dad's desk and used my cell phone to call the number listed. Once I navigated through the automated menu to report the outage, I received prerecorded bad news: "Due to the high rate of employee absenteeism, we are experiencing longer than usual delays in handling power outage problems. We appreciate your patience during this difficult time. Press one if you would like a courtesy call when power to your area is restored."

Shit.

I did not press one. Instead, I tried calling Mom, then Dad. How many hours had passed since our last conversations? Neither answered. I stood there, immobilized, until TK woke up crying, which woke up Cam, who couldn't figure out where she was. She screamed when I came into the room. TK cried even louder.

"You slept here last night, remember?" I rocked TK, sitting on the edge of Cam's makeshift bed and rubbing her back. "You helped give the baby a bath."

Her bottom lip jutted out and she inhaled a shaky breath. "I want to go home," she said. "I want my mom." Saying the words released a floodgate of tears.

I patted her back, trying not to cry again, too. Parents were hard to come by these days. Finally, her sobs settled into a few last sniffles.

Reggie called my cell phone while Cam ate dry cereal and TK slurped down his bottle.

"We have electric at the Senior Center," he said. "Do you want me to bring the kids over after breakfast?"

"Absolutely," I said. "Can you pick them up around eleven?"

"Can do, Miss Lil. See you later."

"What are we doing today?" Cam asked after I'd hung up the phone.

"You're going to visit the place where we picked up TK yesterday. Lots of grandmas and grandpas stay there. They can't wait to see you."

She stirred her cereal with her spoon. "Will there be more cookies?"

"If you eat breakfast," I said, feeling about forty years old. It was an effort to act mature, but I had to hold it together for TK and Cam. It made me proud and weary at the same time.

After TK was fed, burped, and changed, Cam got dressed. She put on an orange T-shirt, purple leggings, yellow socks, and finished off the look with a wide red hair tie.

"You look like a rainbow," I said as she preened. Her smile disappeared.

"What's the matter?" I asked, holding TK in my arms.

"I'm missing green and blue. I can't be a rainbow without green and blue."

"Right." I read once that patience was like a muscle you could strengthen over time. Mine was definitely getting a workout.

It took fifteen minutes, but after more searching in my closet by flashlight, we found some colored bangle bracelets that made her happy.

"I'll do a rainbow dance!" Twirling around, she chanted, "Rainbow, rainbow, rainbow." She stopped, surveying my black outfit with her critical six-year-old eye. "You," she said, "are missing the rainbow feeling."

I slipped on Megs's silver necklace with the pearl. "Better?"

She sighed. "One rainbow will be enough."

When Reggie knocked on the door, I checked out the side window before opening it. I doubted looters would knock first, but I wasn't taking any chances.

"I rang the bell a few times before I realized it needed electricity," he said.

"Yeah, I keep flipping light switches out of habit. Let's hope the power outage doesn't last long."

"Everything will work out," Reggie said with his usual optimism.

Reggie pulled out of the driveway with Cam and TK, passing Jay as he walked toward my house. I sat on my front step and waited for him, trying not to stare as he approached. He wore a brown T-shirt and jeans—very casual—but somehow he still looked good.

"Hey," he said.

"No kids in tow?"

"My aunt's off for the morning. And good news," he said. "I tracked down the girls' grandfather before losing the computer. He's coming to get them."

"That's great." If he could pretend everything was fine, I could, too.

"I would search for Cam and TK's family but my phone's about to die. That's why I thought I'd walk over instead of calling."

"Oh. I have an emergency hand crank radio that also charges cell phones. It's one of the few useful things that the looters missed. You can borrow it if you want."

He followed me into the house. I handed him the small box from its new hiding spot.

"I figured the looters wouldn't look inside the microwave." I gave him the list of TK's phone numbers. "I tried calling, but I haven't been able to reach anyone. Later we can ask Cam about her family. Maybe she knows some names. She has at least one uncle—that much I know."

"I can use a reverse directory with TK's phone numbers, things like that. What's TK's full name?"

"Tobias Kutchner Goodwin."

"That's some name."

"I know."

"You'll have to show me how to use this," he said, pointing at the charger.

I lit a few candles so we could see better in the dim kitchen. We hooked the charger up to his phone and took turns with the crank. The kitchen was quiet except for the cranking, which took longer than I expected. Our silence dragged. There were so many things to talk about, yet no easy way to start in on any of them.

"Do you think it's a good sign that we haven't gotten sick yet?" he asked after a while.

"Maybe. I did use some medicine. My dad had antiviral stuff, and after Megs . . . well, he told me to take it. I finished about half before the looters took the opened box. So that may have helped."

"You're lucky," he said as his phone finished charging.

I shrugged, not feeling so fortunate. "My dad's sick. I better check on him. I'll use the phone upstairs."

Jay shot me a concerned look, but I left the kitchen before he could say anything. I sat in Dad's office with our old phone, the one with the cord that didn't need electricity. I had the phone, a candle, and the hope that I'd make progress on where he was being treated. I tried Patient Services several times but kept getting a busy signal.

Next I tracked down a hospital near the hotel. There was no one available to answer my call there either. I thumped the desk in frustration, unsure about what to do next.

From downstairs, Jay let out a whoop.

"I think I found someone!"

"Really?" I blew out the candle and hurried to the kitchen.

"A woman in Connecticut. Do you want to call?"

"No, I'm too nervous." I'd taken good care of TK, but what if they had been desperate to find him and were outraged that I took him from his home? Or what if they didn't want him at all? "You call."

"OK." Someone answered and I hovered as he explained the situation. "Not me. My friend Lil has been caring for him 24/7. Here she is."

I shook my head no, but he handed me the phone. "It's TK's grandmother," he whispered.

"Is this Lil?" a woman asked.

"Yes."

"Thank you." Her voice cracked. "Thank you. We've lost so many people. To know that Tobias is thriving, it gives us hope. God bless you."

My eyes started to tear. I turned from Jay so he wouldn't see. "You're welcome," I said. "It's nice to know he still has family around."

Jay handed me a napkin. *So much for hiding my emotions.* I dabbed at my eyes.

"Can I come get him today?"

"Of course." I hung up after we worked out the details.

"She's coming to pick him up later," I told Jay. "I should probably pack his things. I think I'll actually miss the little guy."

"You still have Cam."

"True. Do you think she could stay with you when TK's grandma arrives? I don't want her to feel bad when his family comes."

"Sure," Jay said. "We can have Reggie drop her at my house. That'll give me a chance to ask her about other relatives and search for her family, too."

"I can't believe you actually found TK's grand-mother. That's the best thing that's happened in days."

We stood in the kitchen among the flickering candles, smiling at each other. I fought the urge to hug him. He stood close enough for me to reach out my arms to touch him. He moved closer, narrowing the space between us, and I wondered if he thought about holding me, too.

I shook it off. How could I be thinking about this in the middle of the awfulness? With Mr. B stopping by my house and my parents missing and all the deaths. I needed to get a grip.

And I needed to clear the air.

"About Ethan . . ." I started.

Jay's posture stiffened.

"I didn't want him to kiss me."

"It's not really any of my business. But why did you let him?"

"I couldn't stop him. Everything happened so fast. I—"

With horror, I realized I could be describing Ethan or Mr. B. I clutched and unclutched my hands. They were raw from washing them so much lately.

"You don't owe me an explanation," he said.

"I think he did it to try to make you angry. I mean, not that you care, but—"

"How did it make you feel?"

I thought about it. "Uncomfortable. And sad."

He nodded. "Kayla said you were complicated."

"Oh?" I fought back the urge to find her and claw her eyes out.

"She said I should stay away from you. Romantically."

"That's funny, because she pretty much told me the same thing about you."

"Will you?" he asked. "Stay away?"

I looked at the floor. "It . . . it feels like a betrayal to Megs."

"You must miss her."

I nodded, not trusting my voice.

"I did like chatting with her even if I thought it was you. But Megs and I never spoke in person, never really connected on that level."

"Can I ask you a personal question?"

"Boxers," he said.

I smiled. "Underwear preference aside, why were you using that chat site to meet someone? I mean, Megs has been around the same Portico guys since kindergarten, so going online gave her a chance to talk to new people. But you haven't lived here that long. If you were looking to hook up—"

"I wasn't looking for a quick hook up. You should know me better than that."

"Should I?" I asked. "No deep dark secrets?"

"Only one," he said.

CHAPTER 23

In 1918, the Spanish Flu may have been transmitted from town to town by the mail carrier. Today, air travel accelerates the spread of highly contagious diseases. Any pathogen could travel to almost any country in two to three days. No place is safe.
—Blue Flu interview, renowned epidemiologist

Jay went home without answering my questions, without explaining what his secret might be. He seemed sheepish after bringing it up, looking at the ground, changing the subject.

We'd spent so much time together lately and talked about so many random things that it seemed like I knew him even better than Ethan. But maybe our closeness was only an illusion. After all, I hadn't been exactly forthcoming about Mr. B with him. I couldn't demand that he open up and bare his soul to me. I decided to put it out of my mind.

Once Jay left, I organized TK's food, clothes, and baby stuff, making a pile by the front door. As we planned, Reggie dropped Cam off at Jay's, then brought TK to me.

"Thanks for all your help," I said. "Chauffeuring, babysitting, dealing with Mrs. Templeton, all of it."

"No problem," Reggie said. "Mrs. Templeton's like a baked potato. Crispy on the outside, but mushy in the middle."

I laughed. "Tell her I said thanks, too. I'll probably keep Cam with me for the next few days. It'll be lonely once TK's gone."

Reggie left quickly, so I could have a few moments with TK. His grandmother arrived too soon. She was a slightly hunched, thin woman, but she seemed healthy. She held TK close as we talked about the baby's family and I explained how I found him. Then we moved on to more pleasant topics, like how well he was doing. Soon it was time to say good-bye.

I tearfully loaded the car with his baby gear. Giving TK one last kiss, I handed him over. His grandma took my information and promised to stay in touch.

"Thank you, Lil. For everything." She gave me a cheerful wave good-bye.

After TK was gone, the afternoon had an unsettled air about it, like I'd forgotten something important. Maybe it was the lack of electricity or the loss of my routine. In my old life, I would have been studying. Maybe. Or I might have been watching TV or texting Megs. Now I needed to track down my parents. My texts still went unanswered.

I couldn't exactly call the airport looking for Mom, so I decided to focus on Dad. Holed up in the office, I called Patient Services again. The line was still busy.

Next, I used my cell phone to find the number for the Delaware police department near where Dad had been staying. I explained the situation to the officer who answered.

"You need to call Patient Services."

I sighed. "I tried that a bunch of times and haven't been able to get through. Can I file a missing person report?"

"He was part of the quarantine." His voice sounded doubtful. "So he's not really missing."

"I haven't heard from him in twenty-four hours. Doesn't that count?"

"With spotty phone service, that's not unusual. He might be hard to track down. Any living quarantine patients were divided between two different hospitals and those hospitals are using additional overflow areas."

"Please," I said. "Can you tell me the hospital names and how to reach the overflow areas?"

"If Patient Services can confirm he's alive, call me back. But you need the confirmation first."

"Thank you."

It took eighteen more tries, but I finally got through.

"I'm trying to find information about my father,

Keith Snyder. He was part of the Salina Hotel quarantine, but I don't know where he is now."

"Spell the name," the woman said in a weary voice.

As I spelled it, I heard the click-clack of typing.

"How old are you, honey?"

"Sixteen," I said.

"I'm sorry, but we can't give any information out to a minor."

"What?"

"I'm sorry, but—"

"Don't hang up! My mom was resting, but I'll wake her."

I partially covered the phone.

"Mom, I know you don't feel well, but can you talk to this lady?" I said to the empty room, feeling ridiculous but desperate. "It's about Dad."

Then I put my Mom-self on the phone and tried to make my voice different.

"Hello? Do you have information about my husband, Keith Snyder?"

"Can you confirm the spelling of the name?"

"It's K-E-I-T-H S-N-Y-D-E-R."

"Middle name?"

"Frederick."

Silence. A small cough. "I'm sorry, ma'am, to give you this news over the phone. Keith Frederick Snyder is dead."

"No!" I cried.

"I'm so sorry," she said. "We can mail a death certificate to the address on his driver's license. You'll need it for insurance purposes."

"And his body?" I whispered.

"Everyone from the quarantine was cremated. A mandatory safety precaution. You can retrieve his ashes and personal belongings after processing in—" I heard her flipping through some papers—"five more days."

I held it together long enough to carefully write down the address and other information she gave me. But when I hung up, I couldn't contain my sobs any longer. Megs had lost her dad. Now I had lost mine. I rested my head on his desk, not even bothering to cradle it in my hands.

Grief overwhelmed me. If Megs's death was like losing part of myself, with news of Dad's death the very ground beneath me vanished. Life seemed suddenly impossible without him.

How could it be that he'd never hug me again, never share our secret eye roll over Mom's cooking, never give me advice I didn't want to hear? Dad planned to take me for my road test, to walk me down the aisle on my wedding day. He needed to explain infectious diseases and other scary things in his clear, factual manner.

I ached for his physical presence, his sturdiness, his inner calm. My world was disintegrating bit by bit, with each person I loved being taken from me. Heaviness settled in my chest, as if boulders piled on top of my center. No matter how I shifted, the weight remained.

I stayed in his office, hoping it was all a big mistake, praying for a miracle. If only Mom was home.

And what if she was gone, too? I'd be totally alone—an orphan like Cam.

She was still at Jay's, probably missing me. I blew my nose, washed my face, and tried to summon strength from the little actions before leaving to get her.

Poor Cam. The only person she had right now was me, which wasn't much. I promised myself then and there that I would take care of her. She had no one. And Dad would want me to. It would have made him proud.

I trudged to Jay's under a somber sky. Animals had knocked over several garbage cans, chewing through the bags and leaving a trail of trash in the street. The air smelled rotten.

An animal squeaked nearby. Rats could carry parasites, plague, and other diseases. Dad would be able to name them all. I wiped at my eyes as I kept going.

When I arrived at Jay's house, no one answered my knock. I let myself in, greeted by silence. "Jay?"

"In here," he said.

His tone sounded odd. It sounded afraid.

Trembling, I moved as if I were treading water with heavy boots on. I followed his voice, slogging my way toward the bathroom.

Jay kneeled over two small bodies in the bathroom as if he were praying. They both lay on towels, pale and sweating.

Ty and Cam had the flu.

CHAPTER 24

*How the **** can we fix the ****ing power outages if
everyone's too sick to show up for work? What the ****
do I look like, a ****ing magician?"*
—Blue Flu interview, senior manager, Jersey United Power

N^{o.}

I stared in shock at Ty and Cam, lying on the bathroom floor. First Megs, then Dad. What if Ty and Cam didn't make it? I couldn't take any more death. I just couldn't.

Jay moved to make room for me, kneeling next to the kids with his head in his hands.

"Why didn't you call me?" I asked.

"I was afraid to leave them. It came on fast."

I wanted to tell him about Dad, but I couldn't break down again. I needed to stay calm, to hold it together.

"Lil?" Cam said, trying to sit up.

I squatted next to her. "Lie down and rest. I'll stay right here with you." I pushed a sweaty lock of hair from her eyes, trying not to panic.

"Did you give them any medicine?" I asked Jay.

"Children's ibuprofen an hour ago. But they're still feverish."

"Should we get them to the hospital?" I whispered.

"I called my aunt. It's impossible. The rooms are full. They set up tents, 'surge capacity,' she called it, and those are overflowing, too. She said she'd come home soon."

"She can't get them in?"

"If we could get them into the damn hospital don't you think I would have done it already? What are you, stupid?!"

I retreated as much as I could from him in the crowded bathroom. "Stupid enough to put up with you!"

"Sorry, I'm sorry." He put his hands to his temples as if he had a tremendous headache. "I can't let anything happen to Ty. I promised her. I promised."

"It's OK," I said softly. "Where are the washcloths?"

"The hall closet."

I retrieved two, rinsed them with cold water, rung them out, then placed them gently on Ty's and Cam's foreheads.

"Mmmm," Ty mumbled.

"Why don't you take a break," I told Jay. "I'll sit with them. Maybe you could call Reggie? We should warn the people at the Senior Center that they may have been exposed. TK's family, too."

"At this point everyone's been exposed."

"Please?"

"All right," he said.

I rolled towels to put under the kids' heads. Without electricity for a fan, the bathroom felt stuffy. I knelt by them, stroking their arms, first Cam, then Ty, then Cam again. They both seemed on the verge of sleep. That could be their bodies resting to repair themselves. Or it could be their systems shutting down.

Ty moaned. "It hurts. It really hurts."

"What hurts?"

"All of me." He moaned again. "Can you take me to the prison?"

"What?"

Ty's eyes were glassy, his face flushed with fever. "I need to go there. I need to go to the prison."

"Um, OK. After you get better we'll go," I said. That calmed his babbling.

Cam coughed, a hacking sound. It reminded me of Dad on the phone. But I couldn't think about him now, couldn't worry that everyone I loved would soon be gone.

Logic told me to keep replacing the cool cloths on their foreheads. But my emotions were like a broken merry-go-round, spinning in frantic circles, unable to stop. *Don't let them die. Don't let them die.*

Cam stirred. "Mommy?"

"It's Lil. Jay and I are taking care of you."

But if the hospital couldn't save Megs or Dad, how could Jay and I save the kids?

She closed her eyes again. I adjusted the washcloths, rubbed their cheeks, did everything I could to feel helpful. *Don't let them die.*

Jay checked on us every few minutes.

"We should move them," he said a little later. "There's not enough air in here. The family room couch opens into a bed. I'll put on sheets and pillows. And my aunt said to make a rehydration solution."

I barely heard what he was saying. *Don't let them die.* I was so focused on Ty and Cam that it took me awhile to realize that he didn't return.

"Jay?" I called softly, afraid to wake them.

He didn't answer.

I knew he was right, that the kids would be better in a room with windows. Cam felt frail and weightless in my arms as I carried her to the family room.

And there was Jay, pale and lifeless, sprawled across the pullout bed.

I would have screamed if it wasn't for Cam. *This can't be happening! It can't be!*

After gently placing Cam next to him, I ran to get Ty. I hovered over the three of them, rearranging pillows, replacing washcloths. I opened the window hoping the breeze would clear my head. All three of them were sick. Their survival depended on me now.

Once I found the instructions for the rehydration solution on the kitchen counter, I measured a triple dose: twelve cups of boiled water, six tablespoons of sugar, and one-and-half teaspoons of salt. I stirred everything together, then tried to get each of them to drink it. Cam and Ty got about half of it down, but Jay would barely raise his head. I rummaged through the kitchen, found a crazy straw, and finally got him to drink. It didn't feel like enough, though. If only I had stronger medicine—

The antiviral! Why didn't I think of it sooner? It was my best chance to save them.

I hated to leave them alone, but getting the medicine for them would be worth it. "I'll be back soon," I said to the dozing bodies.

I sprinted the whole way. Thankfully, I didn't see anyone. Back at home, my hand shook as I quickly opened the safe. The two boxes were still there. One for Mom, one for Dad. I grabbed them, realizing bleakly that it was too late for Dad. Should I save a box for Mom? But who knew when Mom would make it back. Jay, Ty, and Cam were sick right now. My parents would want me to help them.

Two boxes. Three sick people. If I had to

choose . . . but no. I would divide the two boxes evenly. They would take less medicine each, but it had to be better than nothing.

I shoved the medicine in my backpack, along with some extra soup and bottled water. At the doorway, I caught my breath, trying to calm my many fears: getting sick, witnessing their deaths, dying myself.

Then it occurred to me that I didn't have to leave the security of home; I didn't have to immerse myself in the contagious flu; I didn't have to run down the street alone. I could stay right where I was, safe from the virus, safe from death. Jay's aunt would be home soon enough to care for them.

Stalling, I weighed the choices. Security or danger?

It was tempting to choose the cautious option. I had spent the last months trying to protect myself from every possible threat that I could think of, real or imagined. Self-preservation had become a way of life for me since the Mr. B incident.

But I finally thought of something worse than dying from the flu: living through it by being selfish. Yes, I wanted to survive, but at what price? My heart thudded, ready for fight or flight. But I was not ready to sit at home. I pictured Jay, Ty, and Cam waiting for me. I imagined them turning blue.

I threw the backpack over my shoulder, locked

the door, started to run. Sweat dripped down my face from the exertion. I was harried, careless. And when I rounded the bend, I ran right into a pair of looters.

CHAPTER 25

The funeral parlors have a waitlist. Coffins are impossible to obtain and the cemetery workers can't keep up with the grave digging. Death is a business for some of us, and right now the demand for services far exceeds the supply.
—Blue Flu interview, funeral home director

Two men in their twenties left the house closest to me with bulky pillowcases slung over their shoulders, like a pair of evil Santa Clauses. Before I could react, one dropped his haul and rushed to block my path. He had slicked-back hair and stood close enough for me to smell his hair gel.

"Hey," he said.

Danger crackled in the air between us. I couldn't let him take the medicine. I glanced around for someone or something to help me. Already winded, I couldn't outrun them. There was nowhere to go. No weapon to fight with. My mind raced to come up with a plan.

I was totally screwed.

His friend picked up the second pillow case and stood by his side. He leered at me, revealing perfectly white teeth.

"Where are you going in such a hurry?" Perfect Teeth asked.

I clutched the straps on my pack with shaky hands. If I opened my mouth to speak, I might puke.

"The quiet type, huh? You should hang with us for awhile," Hair Gel said. "Talking is overrated. And you look fun."

He said this to my chest, leaving no doubt what kind of fun he meant. With Mr. B, the fear crept up on me before I knew why. But now, the terror slammed into me head on.

Perfect Teeth took a step closer. "And she's pretty, too."

I thought about screaming. Who would possibly come to my rescue? Pins and needles invaded my hands. Sweat dripped into my eyes. I couldn't move, afraid to let go of my backpack to wipe the drops away. I thought of Jay, Ty, and Cam waiting helplessly for me, dying.

I had to get away. I breathed in, prepared to scream, but my throat was too dry and all I managed was a loud cough. It gave me an idea. I coughed again, doing my best to make it sound flulike. Summoning the courage to move, I wiped my forehead in a dramatic motion and found my voice.

"Been sick for three days. I don't have much time."

Perfect Teeth backed away first, then Hair Gel.

I forced myself to cough again, doubled over from the nausea. That part didn't need faking, and I clutched my stomach and moaned.

They moved away, quickly, leaving me alone.

"Good luck, girl," Hair Gel called over his shoulder.

I lumbered toward Jay's, still pretending to be sick, willing myself not to look back. Finally, I was safely inside.

Jay, Ty, and Cam hadn't moved in my absence. It took me a good ten minutes to calm down enough to decipher the antiviral dosage instructions. The capsules were meant for adults and I could only guess what Cam and Ty weighed. Finally, I took one capsule and broke it open, giving each kid half of it mixed with some apple sauce. Jay seemed delirious but managed to swallow a pill with water.

Jay's aunt called. She had become sick, too, and could barely speak. She couldn't help me. When night came, I thought about changing the sheets on her bed and sleeping there. But each time I left to go upstairs, fear gripped my heart, and I returned five minutes later, terrified that Jay, Cam, or Ty would die during the night. I finally moved a kitchen chair across from the most comfortable seat near the pullout couch and propped up my feet. I didn't sleep much in my pseudo-bed. Jay, Cam, and Ty took turns groaning and whimpering throughout the night. In the morning, they didn't seem any better.

I tended to the three of them all day with medicine, rehydration solution, and cool wash cloths. *Please get better*, I whisper-prayed about a thousand times. If Ty died, Jay would never forgive me. If Cam died, I would never forgive myself. If Jay died . . .

I couldn't imagine it. Jay wasn't the guy from the smoking corner anymore or Megs's mystery date or the object of Kayla's desire. He was Jay who adored his brother, who talked a lot but not too much, who stood by me during the past horrific days. I couldn't pinpoint the exact moment when I memorized the sound of his sigh, the glint of a silver filling when he laughed, the details of his hands.

Megs, I'm sorry. I like Jay. I really like him. He's a good person, and if he feels the same way we could make each other happy.

If we managed to survive the pandemic.

At least I was there with him. I wondered if Dad had died alone. The thought made me weepy. His death still felt surreal, as if it were a bad dream and hadn't really happened.

But it had. I knew at some point I would have to retrieve his ashes, but the logistics seemed impossible now. How could I get to Delaware? How could I be strong enough to face that trip without Mom?

And where was she? I checked my phone again, but there was no word from her.

There was, instead, one text from Kayla. I hesitated before reading it. Her nastiness was the last thing I needed. Finally, I gave in and opened it.

> Kayla: I just heard about Megs. So sorry. We had good times together, didn't we?

I sucked in my breath. That might be the closest we had come to making peace with each other. Was it possible she hadn't known about Megs earlier? In all the craziness, I guess it was. I thought about replying, but what I could possibly say after she threatened to tell Jay about Mr. B?

Then Jay moaned in pain and nothing else mattered.

I stayed with him until he fell back into a restless sleep. I needed something cold to drink but the refrigerator was the same gross temperature as the rest of the house. We didn't need food poisoning on top of everything else so I emptied the contents into garbage bags, then carried the trash to the garage. The thought of going outside alone was too much for me.

I tried to keep busy in other ways, too, when they didn't need me, changing the sheets, replacing the towels, trying to disinfect the house. Upstairs, I opened Jay's window, feeling like an intruder in his bedroom. It was messier than I expected, with cookbooks randomly piled around. A framed photo of a woman I assumed to be his mom leaned on his desk. She had kind eyes, like Jay's. There were no other photos displayed.

So what was the secret he alluded to? A thought kept rattling around in my brain, like a fly tapping against a window trying to get outside. When Jay refused to break into the school, at first I thought it was his way of avoiding trouble so he could take care of Ty. But then Ty had mumbled about visiting prison in his delirium. What if Jay had done something illegal in Arizona? Would that matter to me? How much of his past would I be willing to forgive?

I was holding the photo in my hand when Jay coughed from the doorway. He leaned against the doorjamb, still weak, but the color in his face was less sickly looking.

Was he healthy enough to be furious at me for snooping in his room? "I thought the air would help." I put the frame down with one hand, gesturing toward the opened window with the other.

Jay moved forward slowly, then wrapped both arms around me in a huge hug. "Thank you," he whispered into my hair before pulling away too soon.

"Your fever seems to be gone. Do you feel better?"

"Still weak, but better."

We moved slowly downstairs. I got Jay comfortable in the chair I'd been sleeping in so he could rest near Ty. The kids still slept while Jay checked his phone.

"There's a message from my sisters. They're staying together with my cousin. They haven't gotten sick yet."

"That's good."

"Have you heard anything from your parents?"

I sat on the edge of the pullout couch and finally told him about Dad. Then I broke down. "And his ashes . . ."

Jay held my hand, silent, comforting.

"We'll get through this," he said. "Somehow, we'll get through this."

Ty and Cam lay almost lifeless on the bed. I wanted to believe Jay. I really did. But feeling optimistic seemed like another setup for a giant wallop of pain.

⌒

On Sunday, Jay seemed stronger. He rested near Ty and Cam, searching online for her family on his phone. During her brief periods awake, we asked her questions about aunts, uncles, and cousins. We didn't get far with her mother's side of the family. After tracking down her uncle Robbie's information, a phone call revealed that he had died from the flu, too.

"What about your dad?" I asked her. "Do you ever see him?"

"No. Mom said he went to find himself and got lost on the way."

"Oh." Jay and I glanced at each other. Another roadblock.

We stayed up late talking about strategies to find her family.

"They could be divorced," I said. "Or the father could be dead. Or in jail."

Jay flinched a little.

"Maybe if he wasn't in Cam's life before, he's not the one we should be looking for now."

"True. But there has to be someone to take care of her."

"She's got you," he said. "She seems really attached."

Of course I would take care of her if there was no one else. But I'd barely been able to keep myself safe this past year. I thought of all the bad things that could happen to Cam. The world seemed fraught with danger. There had to be someone better than me to protect her.

I didn't sleep well that night. In one dream I was

trapped in a prison cell while Mr. B stood free out-side the bars. "Is this what you were looking for?" He dangled the key. Each time I reached for it he pulled his hand away. I woke to the sound of his chuckle in my head. It took a long time to fall back asleep.

Monday morning Jay's aunt called to say she was feeling better and hoped to get home soon. We spent the day hovering over Cam and Ty, giving them the antiviral medicine, lots of water to drink, and an occasional cracker.

My cell phone died. It had been days since I'd heard from Mom. I sent a text from Jay's phone but heard nothing in return. The crankable phone char-ger had suddenly stopped working.

"Maybe it needs to rest," Jay said. "We've cranked that thing like crazy."

While the kids slept, we passed the time play-ing endless games of Rummy. Over multiple hands, Jay was winning, 2,210 to 1,845. He recounted the highs and lows of this season's cooking shows and I retold Edgar Allan Poe stories. We avoided all the important subjects: Dad's death, Mom's absence, Ty and Cam taking so long to recover.

The evening should have brought cooler air but didn't. The house remained stifling, even with the windows open.

"Want to sit in the backyard?" Jay asked. "We'll

hear them if they wake up and it might be nice to get fresh air."

I agreed and we moved outside to a gliding bench. I sat at one end, my feet tucked under me, leaving some space between us. There were a few things I needed to know, if only I had the courage to ask. But "were you ever in trouble with the law?" wasn't exactly a good conversation starter. Neither was "I think I really like you. Is it too late for that? Have we already moved too far into the friendship zone?" I struggled to find something neutral to talk about.

Jay finally broke our silence. "I can't wait for the power to come back."

"At least it's not cold and snowing," I said.

"That's one nice thing."

"Do you miss Arizona?"

"No. It wasn't the same after my mom died. It was a relief, in a way, to get a fresh start here. I could leave behind the labels. You know, like 'the boy with tragic circumstances.' My old friends kind of drifted away, and strangers thought once they heard my story, they knew me better than they did. It was frustrating."

Is that when he had broken the law? Right after his mother died?

"What are you thinking about?" he asked. "Your mouth is scrunched into a serious scowl."

"Hmm. Maybe there were other reasons you were happy to leave the past behind?"

He sighed and glanced away. I didn't know whether to feel thrilled that I'd guessed right or terrified about what he might tell me.

"It's OK if you don't want to talk," I said.

I could read the deliberation in his face as he looked out over the yard, still not answering. A wall began going up between us, brick by brick, layer by layer. That's how the not-telling shuts people out.

As I waited for him to decide, I tried to come up with all the honorable reasons he could have gotten into trouble. Maybe he hurt another kid in school while defending someone. He could have stepped in to help a girl. Or maybe he was in the wrong place at the wrong time, or wouldn't tell on a friend.

Jay looked at me intently.

"What is it?" I asked.

"Moral decisions aren't always black and white," he began.

Oh no.

"Sometimes people do the wrong things."

Jay had broken the law and now I would learn why. Did I really want to know?

"Illegal things, for what seems like the right reasons."

It was too late to stop him now. I reminded myself to breathe.

"You know me and my dad . . . we don't keep in touch."

I frowned, confused. "I thought maybe your dad had passed away, too. You never mention him."

"He's dead in a sense. Dead to me and Ty." Jay's face was hard, unhappy. "My father's in jail."

"Oh." It made sense now: Jay's concern with ethics, staying out of trouble, Ty's feverish mumblings about visiting prison. I wasn't sure what to say next. "What . . . what was he arrested for?"

"A financial scam," he said. "I've been meaning to tell you. It never felt like the right time." He took out his phone and pulled up an article he'd bookmarked.

"Mexican Robin Hood" Denied Parole

Jose Martinez, 48, was denied parole at a hearing in Phoenix today. Five years ago, Martinez was convicted of eight counts of security fraud in a Ponzi scheme that targeted mostly high-income investors. Dubbed the "Mexican Robin Hood" by the press, Martinez funneled earnings from his phony investment scheme to help poverty-stricken families in rural areas across the US border. Martinez and his trial dominated the local news for several months. At least 400 investors were defrauded of approximately $100 million, making it one of Arizona's largest Ponzi schemes.

I handed him back the phone. "He was trying to help the poor?"

"At the expense of hundreds of innocent people. And my mom was diagnosed right after his arrest. There were problems with the insurance coverage, getting her the right care. She died four months later."

"That's terrible. Have you been in touch with your dad recently?"

"No. There's nothing to talk to him about. My aunt is our legal guardian now. We're lucky to have her."

"Yes, you are. And you and Ty have each other."

"We do." He paused. "And I have you . . ."

Would he kiss me?

". . . as a friend, I mean."

Right.

He shifted closer, not touching me. "I think Megs would be happy that we ended up friends."

"Yes, she would."

So we were friends now and nothing more. Disappointment tasted bitter, like Mom's weird organic lettuce. I had waited too long to decide I liked him. Emotions evolve and his had clearly gone in the opposite direction.

We sat without speaking. He was mere inches from me and if I closed my eyes, I could feel the world: Jay's breathing, the spring breeze caressing his hair, the very air that filled the narrow space between us. Something fluttered in my chest, softly, like a trapped butterfly.

~~

Tuesday morning, Jay and I sat in his kitchen talking quietly.

"I heard from some of the other volunteers," he said.

"Is everyone OK?"

"Ethan is fine. Derek was under the weather, but it didn't seem like full-blown flu. No news from Beth. Elsa sent me animal-by-animal updates. She's upset there wasn't much they could do for tropical fish with the power outage, but she worked with her mother to rescue thirty-two dogs, fifteen cats, and four hamsters so far, plus that parrot."

Remembering the house with the screeching bird made my knees wobbly.

"And Kayla called me," he said.

"Oh?"

"Her brother died."

I felt a pang of sadness. I'd known Justin for years. His acceptance to UVA had come in March. And now . . .

"She sounded sick. I felt like maybe she was calling to say good-bye."

With my head in my hands, I started to quietly weep. Was it ever going to end? What if I couldn't take any more death? I could just give up, lie down between Cam and Ty and never move again.

Someone rustled behind me, then a hand patted my back.

"Are you OK, Lil?" Ty asked.

"Oh, thank God," I said, squeezing him in a tight hug.

"Can we be done with the hugging? I'm starving."

"Let's get you some breakfast, then." I caught Jay's eye. He looked away, but not before I saw him tear up.

By lunch time, Cam was awake, too. It was the best they had looked in days. And then, as if the universe was feeling super bountiful, the electricity flickered on.

We all whooped with happiness.

"Video games!" Ty said. "Cam, let's go!"

"We should shower and do laundry," I told Jay.

"Not as much fun as video games, but you're right. I'd like to get online, too, and email my sisters that Ty is better."

"I can take some of the dirty clothes to my house," I said, eager for even an hour by myself. I grabbed a bundle of wash and stuffed it into a large green garbage bag.

But then I hesitated by the front door. Going home meant walking outside alone. I hadn't told Jay about escaping the looters and I couldn't ask him to leave the kids and walk with me.

"What's the matter?" he asked.

"Could you watch me from your doorway?"

"Sure," he said, as if it was the most natural request in the world. "Call me when you're on your way back. I'll keep an eye out for you."

Back home, my father's presence filled our house. His *#1 Dad* mug waited next to the empty coffee pot. His sneakers waited by the garage door. His favorite flannel shirt was slung over the doorknob to his closet. I put it on, wrapping it around me, breathing in his dad-ness.

With the comfort of his shirt, I opened the windows, then started the laundry. The hum of the washing machine and the clean scent of detergent boosted my spirits a little. I turned off the random lights that had been on when we lost power and started resetting the clocks, saving Dad's office for last.

The phone rang. I froze. That could be exceptionally good or monumentally bad.

After a small hesitation, I answered.

"Lil, hon, is that you?" The connection wasn't great and Mom faded a little as she spoke. Just the sound of her voice made me cry.

"Yes, it's me," I choked out. "Oh, Mom, where are you? Are you almost home?"

"I'm in London . . . wait-listed for a flight. I couldn't get through to you. Phone battery's going. . . . Are you healthy?"

"Yes. But Dad—"

Her voice was garbled.

"Mom?"

The phone filled with static, then silence.

"No, wait!"

Yelling at the receiver got me nowhere. We'd lost the connection.

But she was alive.

Focusing on that happy thought, I listened to the radio while emptying the fridge and freezer. The top forty hits seemed to be the same now as they were before the crisis, so not everything in the world had changed. A block of mozzarella cheese, however, had turned a color I'd never seen on food before, and I had to leave the fridge doors open for awhile to get rid of the smell. I held my nose as I added the bags to the pile in the garage.

With that chore behind me, I showered, lathered-rinsed-repeated, and in a moment of good cheer, decided to wear a lavender-colored blouse with pale blue jeans. Although I generally hated blow-drying my hair, I felt compelled to use every electrical appliance possible and only clicked it off after every strand was dry.

Mom and I would finally be together again. I dared to imagine it, the sweetness of a reunion with Mom crying and hugging me. We'd figure out how to survive the rest of the pandemic together, somehow. And we'd find a way to honor Dad.

But she would hate to come home to a messy house, so I made the beds, wiped the counters, and folded the laundry, putting Dad's clean clothes in the dresser where they belonged.

I was stacking some of Ty's washed T-shirts by the front door when the doorbell rang. Maybe it was my good mood. Maybe it was the normalcy of having the electric back and doing ordinary chores. I forgot about the danger for a moment. Without thinking, I pulled the door open. It was a stupid thing to do.

Mr. B loomed in the doorway.

Chapter 26

*The need for antiviral medicine and other supplies has well
exceeded the state's Strategic Stockpile.*
—Blue Flu interview, New Jersey governor's office

I tried to slam the door, but Mr. B put out his hand and held it open.

"Lilianna."

My body trembled with fear. Where was the hornet spray? Not by the door where I needed it. I checked outside for anyone who might be able to help me. Even the looters could cause a distraction. But the street was deserted.

"Please, can I come in?" he asked.

"No." I tried to sound strong, authoritative, but the shaking reached my voice. He wasn't holding any obvious weapons, but there was a white shopping bag at his feet. He hadn't even needed a weapon to overpower me the last time. He seemed taller than I remembered. Had he always towered over me like that?

"I need to speak with you," he said, eyes pleading.

I didn't trust those eyes. Why was Mr. B here? Of all the people who had died, somehow he had managed to stay alive. Like a cockroach. And now he was at my house, refusing to leave.

If I couldn't get back inside alone, the safest tactic was to stay outside, where someone might see us. Being out in daylight felt more secure somehow.

"We can talk here." I stepped tentatively onto the front stoop, crossing my arms over my chest. I kept my eyes focused on his Adam's apple. It would make a good target if I had to punch him.

Mr. B cleared his throat. "I came to say I'm sorry."

The words washed over me, but I had a hard time comprehending them. "What?"

"I'm sorry that my actions . . . that I may have upset you," he said.

I let this sink in. Being sorry for upsetting me was not the same thing as being sorry for what he actually *did*. His words sounded hollow. Every part of me stayed rigid, unyielding. "Did you get a court order from another victim or something? Why are you suddenly apologizing now?"

"It's time to make amends."

"Why? It's been months since . . ."

Ignoring my question, he picked up the shopping bag and held it out to me like a peace offering. I braced myself, not sure what to expect. Taking my eyes off him only long enough to glance inside the bag, I gasped. It was filled with boxes of antiviral.

"Here," he said. "It's medicine."

"I know exactly what it is." I took the bag by the handles, careful not to brush his hand with my fingers. I was torn between curiosity about the drugs and the need to get away from him.

"You didn't just buy these off the shelf. Where did you get them?"

"The source isn't important."

"That's not what you said when we didn't use correct attributions in class essays. And for all I know you're trying to poison me."

He sighed. "The boxes are sealed, brand new. My brother worked at Portico Pharmacy. He had access to various medications after the outbreak."

"I don't understand."

"Lilianna, we made certain items available, for a price. But I'm not interested in the money any longer."

"How does your brother feel about this donation?" I frowned, not bothering to hide my mistrust.

"He's dead," he said matter-of-factly. "You've always been effective at community service. If anyone can distribute medicine to those in need, it's you."

He coughed then, and I noticed the beads of sweat on his forehead.

"Oh," I said, backing away. "You're sick."

"Yes. In my defense, I called before the symptoms appeared. When my brother died, I had a feeling this was inevitable. The antiviral might have slowed the illness down, but it's not enough. I thought if I could make things right before—"

"You need to leave. Now."

"Of course." He started down the front stoop, pausing after two steps so that we were eye to eye. "Lilianna . . . can you forgive me?"

I thought of my life before, of the emotional wreckage he'd caused. Part of me wanted to rise above the anger, to feel empathy and compassion.

But I couldn't. My heart was a block of ice, frozen inside my chest.

"No," I said. "And my forgiveness wouldn't be enough to save you."

I slammed the door and locked it. Then I took the shopping bag and hurled it as far as I could. The blue boxes skittered across the floor.

My adrenaline and fear left me shaken. But giddiness bubbled inside, too. I had faced him, my worst nightmare, and I was safe. The confrontation hadn't killed me. He was gone.

My parents would be so proud. And wait until Megs heard about this!

No. I slumped against the door, overwhelmed as the grief battered me all over again. Would I ever get used to her absence or Dad's death?

I needed to talk to someone before the emotion consumed me, someone who understood my history. When the shaking finally stopped, I dialed my therapist. On the third ring, her answering machine kicked in. "This is Dr. Gwen," she said in a strained voice. "Due to illness, I'm not currently returning calls. You can leave non-urgent messages after the beep."

I hung up, then crashed onto the couch. I didn't want to think that Dr. Gwen was dead, too. I stared at the blank TV screen for a long time before finally switching on the news. New Jersey was in the spotlight and things had gone from bad to worse while we'd been without electricity. The death count was now in the tens of thousands. There was an urgent need for more refrigerated trucks to hold dead bodies until the morgues could catch up. Vaccine production, while further along, was still months away. I flicked channels through various dire reports until I found a debate about antivirals. They were at a premium and it was unclear how the existing supply would be distributed.

"All citizens between fifteen and fifty are at risk," one expert announced. "So, who gets it first? Pregnant women? People with preexisting conditions, like asthma? But we can't expect the emergency system to work if those on the front lines aren't protected. Not only doctors and nurses but EMT volunteers, police, and firefighters are expected to help the ill. With the flu so easily transmitted, is it fair to ask them to do so without some kind of protective measures?"

Two other experts weighed in with their conflicting opinions until a shouting match erupted and I turned the TV off.

I had medicine now. Lots of it. Some to save, others to give away. Boxes that people would die for littered my floor. Somehow it needed to be distributed safely.

Were those voices outside? I quickly gathered the antiviral and crammed it into the safe. I took the long way back to Jay's house, feeling more secure the closer I got. I couldn't risk running into the looters again.

I used the time walking to think about the antiviral. The obvious answer was to hand the medicine over to the police. But as I played the scenario out in my mind, it wasn't that simple. The police were sure to question where it came from. Mentioning Mr. B would create a whirlwind that I didn't want to be caught up in. Reporting what happened between us once had been enough. I wouldn't be forced to share those memories with strangers yet again.

So I couldn't mention Mr. B and his pharma-cy-stealing brother. I wasn't an accomplished enough liar to convince the cops that the stuff had just appeared on my doorstep, and I'm sure they wouldn't let such a vague answer slide. If only Mrs. Salerno were alive.

Turning the boxes over to the police was out.

As I walked down the street, an ambulance drove by with no sirens on, a black ribbon tied to the antennae to indicate the emergency squad was transporting dead bodies. The EMTs needed the an-tiviral. So did a lot of other people. It was a compli-cated issue.

As I neared Jay's house, I realized that the anti-viral needed to go to someone respected in Portico, someone who could make the best decision about passing the medicine along to those who needed it most.

I knew who to ask. But I needed Cam and Ty to be completely better first.

When I arrived at Jay's house, he met me in the yard. "Where are the kids?"

Goosebumps prickled my arms. "What do you mean? They're here with you."

"No, I sent them to you," he said, holding open the front door. Even from the entrance, I could see that his house was trashed worse than my own. "Looters. I saw them coming, a big rowdy group of them. I sent the kids to your house to keep them safe."

His mouth was in a tight line, his fear quiet but contagious.

"They never . . ." I whispered, almost unable to finish the thought. "They never made it to my house."

CHAPTER 27

Life insurance companies are too understaffed to deal with the substantial number of fatalities. "We try to process a claim for, say, a dead wife, but often when we call back for further information, the husband has died, too. It's a logistical nightmare."
—Blue Flu interview, Global Insurance agent

You were supposed to let me know when you were on your way back," Jay said.

"I forgot. My mother called and . . ." I didn't want to mention Mr. B.

"But I told them to run to you," he said, shaking his head. "I was still inside getting my mom's jewelry when the looters began trashing the place. I waited in the attic until they left. Where could Ty and Cam be?"

Panic coursed through me. How could they be missing? Did the looters kidnap them? When Jay exploded into action, I followed right behind.

"Ty! Where are you?" he shouted, rushing into the empty street.

"Cam!" I joined in. "Cam!"

"You didn't see them on the way here?" he asked, glancing frantically around. "You should have passed each other."

"I took the long way around the block. I had to think—"

"What if the looters found them?"

"Cam! Ty!" My voice shook as I called louder. "They have to be safe," I said. "They have to be. They would run away or hide."

"But what if—"

"Wait." A half-formed thought nagged at my consciousness. "A hiding spot—"

"You're right," Jay interrupted. "Let's go." He grabbed my hand and we ran to the overgrown maple in silence, too anxious to speak.

When we reached the cave-tree, I expected to hear voices. The silence shattered my courage. I couldn't bear it if we were wrong and the kids were gone.

"You go first," I said.

Jay ducked under the branches.

I held my breath.

Right when I thought my knees would buckle, that I would collapse from the panic, Cam squealed and Ty yelped. And then I was there with them, hugging and crying. We were together, safe under the leafy branches.

For once it felt like enough.

~

After salvaging what supplies they could from their damaged house, Jay, Ty, Mrs. Hernandez, and Cam all moved in with me. It was weird to see Jay's aunt outside of school. But everyone agreed that it would be safer if we stayed together. Ty and Jay moved into the guest room, and Mrs. Hernandez slept on the couch on the nights she wasn't working. All of us had taken the antiviral now, and I saved a few packs, just in case.

Reggie managed to get his own prescription from a retired doctor friend. We asked him to move in with us, but he wasn't interested. "I've got a gun," he said. "And I'm not afraid to use it. Let those looters try me." So he stayed at his home but checked in often with us.

On Wednesday morning, he stopped by and offered to take Cam and Ty for a few hours. Cam, who wasn't sleeping well at night, wanted to know if the Senior Center was safe.

"It will be OK," Reggie assured her. "Ty will come with us."

"Maybe we should stay home," she said.

But Ty had heard all about the cookies. "Let's go for a little while," he said. "I'm hungry. And I bet they have something fun for you to do there, too. Do old people like to dance?"

"As a matter of fact, they do," Reggie said. "The ladies love line dancing. They stand in a row and do the same steps together."

"I bet I can teach them some moves!" Cam said, grabbing her sneakers.

"Maybe I'll come along, too," I said, swinging my backpack over my shoulder.

"Sure thing, Miss Lil."

Once Cam and Ty were occupied with a group of seniors, it didn't take me long to find Mrs. Templeton, who was settling a dispute over the TV channel.

"Take turns," she scolded two elderly men. "You each get half an hour."

"I need to speak with you." I glanced around. "Is there someplace quiet we can talk?"

"Is there a problem?"

"An opportunity."

"This way, then."

I followed her down the hall to a private office. My hands were sweating, which was ridiculous. I had dealt with a lot worse people than Mrs. Templeton.

"Is it more orphans?" she asked. "They're forming a formal disaster committee soon, you know. The town officials can probably handle it now. Some of the seniors here weren't thrilled about being exposed to germy little kids."

I answered by opening my backpack and dumping a pile of antiviral boxes onto her desk.

"Good Lord," she said. "How did you—"

"I can't say how these came to me, but I promise I didn't do anything illegal."

"You could sell them for a lot of money. Enough to help with your college tuition in a few years."

"I wouldn't do that," I said. "Someone needs to handle their distribution or else get the medicine to the police."

"Not you?"

"It's beyond me. You're the former mayor. You have the clout to handle this, and you'll make sure the right thing gets done."

"Yes," she said. "I will." Her face was solemn.

"Thank you." I took my empty backpack and turned to go.

"Thank *you*, Lilianna. Now let's hope the kids aren't eating all the damn cookies."

⌒

We generally tried to stay inside as much as possible. But when I got home from the Senior Center, Jay agreed to come with me on an errand. We decided riding our bikes was safer than walking and we kept watch for looters along the way.

"Turn left here?" he asked at Maple Street.

I nodded. We slowed down by Cam's house, but it looked deserted. Then we were at our destination: Kayla's.

I might have chickened out if I were alone. What did Kayla and I have to say to each other after all that had happened between us? Jay waited on the street a few houses away as I rang the bell. When I glanced back at him nervously, he gave me a thumbs-up.

Kayla's mother answered the door. She had always been tiny but seemed to have shrunk even more. "Hi, Lil. This is a surprise. We don't get many visitors these days."

"I'm sorry about Justin."

"After we lost him . . . Kayla's taking it hard."

"Can I see her?"

"She's too sick to come to the door, but you can go to her if you want."

I made my way to the second room on the left. I knocked lightly before entering. Kayla lay in bed but didn't roll over when I entered the room.

"Kayla," I whispered.

She moved slowly onto her side to face me. Her long black hair was matted against her head and her eyes were puffy.

"Hey," she said.

"Hi."

"You'll catch it from me."

"I've been exposed before, but I'll stand over here," I said, keeping my distance. I rocked back and forth on my heels, not sure how to begin. "I'm, um, sorry for slapping you. I needed to tell you that."

"And I should have been a better friend. None of that really matters now, does it?" She tried to raise herself, then gave up and rested her head on the pillow. "I'm sorry, too. You didn't answer my text about Megs, but I've thought about calling you a hundred times."

I thought I was done with crying, but Kayla was the only other person who really understood about Megs. I couldn't help myself. I looked away, swiping at my eyes. When I faced her again, she was teary, too.

"And your brother—"

"Things are messed up, huh?"

"Yeah." Without a big speech, I took out one of the extra antivirals I'd saved and handed it to her. "Here."

She eyed the medicine like it was a glitzy diamond. "But this is impossible to buy. My parents have been desperate to get it for me. How did you—"

"It's a long story. But I wanted to help."

"Thank you."

"I should go. I hope you feel better, Kayla. I really do."

With the day's good deeds behind me, I should have slept great that night. But I didn't. Cam tossed and turned nearby as I tried to stop the thoughts from swirling in my head. Megs and my father—dead. Jay's father in jail and his willingness to tell me about him. The lost opportunity to be more than a friend to Jay. Mr. B's appearance at my door. All of these images whipped around like debris in a tornado until my head pounded and I wanted to scream.

Weariness suddenly overcame me. Then I decided.

I would tell him.

I would tell Jay about Mr. B.

CHAPTER 28

A well-known movie exec is reportedly planning an influenza-based love story titled Swoon. *"It's* Titanic *meets* Contagion," *he said. But several actors he contacted to play the lead roles were too sick to consider any projects in the near future.*
—Blue Flu interview, Hollywood insider

The next morning, I woke up tired but resolute. Being honest with Jay about Mr. B was the right thing to do. The tricky part was finding a way to talk to him privately. I thought I got my chance when Mrs. Hernandez took the kids to the playground, but then Jay distracted me.

"I've been thinking about expanding my blog," he said. "I thought I'd add a section for good deeds, so we could describe how we've helped people. I'll link it to the thank-you messages. And I heard from Elsa again. She's continued her animal crusade. With all the depressing news, it might be nice for people to read something positive. We've had tons of hits from all over the US."

"That's a great idea. But don't mention where we got the original food that we distributed." Although much of the school's food drive items were gone, we were finally able to place an order through an online grocery site and Jay's aunt had brought home supplies, so the pantry stayed full.

Just as I was working up the courage to tell Jay my secret, Cam and Ty tore through the house, crashing up the stairs and running into the office. They practically glowed with good health.

"I won!" Ty said. "I got here first!"

Cam followed on his heels. "You cheated."

"How was the park?" Jay asked.

"Fun, but now Auntie has to go to work," Ty said.

"We're bored," Cam said. "Can you play with us?"

There went my opportunity to speak to Jay alone. The rest of the afternoon was a combination of video games, Hangman, and a dance contest with Jay, Ty, and me as judges. Cam performed as the sole contestant and won first place.

It wasn't until the kids were asleep that Jay and I had some uninterrupted time. I waited on the family room couch, ready, until he turned on the TV.

"My favorite show is on tonight," he said. "*Chef Adventure.*"

I huddled under a throw blanket.

"You have to see this. It's a cooking show under extreme conditions. One time the chefs had to find bugs as their main ingredient before cooking them as part of a gourmet jungle meal."

"That's beyond gross." Suddenly tired, I struggled to stay awake during the program, waiting for a chance to talk with Jay. I had delayed it too long. Now I needed to get it over with.

The show lasted an hour. The episode took place on a mountain and the aerial shots made me dizzy. I breathed a sigh of relief when it finally ended.

Jay trailed behind me as I carried our water glasses to the sink. This was finally my chance to tell him about Mr. B. My cheeks flushed as I turned to face him. If only he wasn't standing close enough for me to see the different shades of brown specks in his eyes. It would be so easy to step forward, put my arms around him. Maybe words were overrated.

But I had to try.

"I wanted to tell you . . ."

"What?" he asked.

But my courage seemed to evaporate into the air. "Um, I wanted to tell you that I'm really worried about my mom. I wish I knew for sure that she's all right."

"The waiting sucks," he agreed.

"What if she doesn't make it home?"

"I don't know, Lil." He lifted his hand as if to caress me, then seemed to think better of it. "Sorry," he said, dropping his arm to his side. "I forgot you don't like to be touched."

"It's not that, it's . . ." I hesitated, torn between wanting to close the physical space between us and needing to wait—to tell him everything first.

"If you ever want to talk, I can handle it," he said.

The silence stretched between us like a rubber band.

"Want to sit in the office?" I stalled. As we made our way upstairs, I composed myself. By the time we were in the room with the door closed behind us, I was determined.

"I'm glad you could be honest with me about your dad," I said. "There's something I've wanted to tell you about, too. The secret I've been keeping about, um, something bad that happened. It was November . . . right after you moved here."

The stress of the confession made my head spin. "It's painful to explain. The man in that car at my house that day, when you were walking me home with Ty . . ." I lost my train of thought, tried to start over. "You see, there was this teacher. I want you to understand what happened, but . . ."

How to find the opening, the loose piece of yarn I could pull to unravel the knot of my past? I checked Jay's expression. He waited, watching me intently.

"Would it make it any easier if I already knew your situation?" he asked.

"What? How is that possible?" My voice was louder than I intended. "Did Kayla—"

"No, not Kayla." He sighed. "But I shouldn't say."

"You're trying to trick me into telling!"

"Lil, you're already telling me. It's not a trick."

The thought made my temples throb. "There isn't any way you could know, unless . . . did Megs tell you what happened?"

"That's not it." He hesitated. "I don't want to get my aunt in trouble. But as a school nurse, she hears things."

I leaned against the desk, grateful for the solid wood beneath my hands. "What kinds of things?"

"Like when a teacher hurts a student." He looked away, his expression pained.

"You've known all along."

"No. She told me about it without revealing the student's name. Mr. B stopped teaching suddenly, right around the time she told me the story, so I figured he was the man involved. And every guy at school knows his Corvette convertible. When you got so upset about his car in your driveway, I put the pieces together."

"So you felt sorry for me?"

"No. I feel connected to you because I . . . I realized what it cost you to keep that secret. To be on the edge of telling, but to step back and bury it. The fear is there. Always. I feel that way about my father. You're the first person here who I've told about him."

Jay had been honest about his past with only me. He was right. There was a connection between us. It was safe for me to confide in him. My body shook too hard for my mind to focus. To stop the trembling, I concentrated on my breathing. Breathe. Life. Death. So much death. If I died, I didn't want Mr. B to be the last person who touched me. Who was Megs's final kiss? She hadn't been ready to stop living. Megs would have the guts to kiss Jay if she were me, in this moment.

I moved forward until we were inches apart. Images of Mr. B and Megs and death mixed in my brain, and I felt the wet on my face before I realized I was crying. I leaned into Jay, my hair brushing against his shoulder. He smelled like soap and his body felt solid, safe, against mine.

He put his arms around me, softly, as if he were holding a glass mannequin instead of a girl. His chest rose and fell. I nuzzled against him, feeling desire, and uncertainty. I hesitated, my emotions battling.

I lifted my face and kissed him.

"I've thought about this moment so many times," he said. "But I wasn't sure. . . . Is this what you want?"

I wanted it so much that my whole body ached, but the words wouldn't come, so I pulled him closer. We kissed again and I melted into him, until there was only the taste of his mouth and the sound of his heart.

I let the gentle weight of his arms erase every embrace that had come before. There was no more fear. Only that very moment. Only Jay.

It was amazing. So amazing, in fact, that the room started to spin.

Wow. No one ever made the world move with a kiss before.

I blinked, trying to get my bearings. My vision blurred around the edges. Then everything went dark.

CHAPTER 29

This recent influenza strain has shown some resistance to popular neuraminidase inhibitors. In laymen's terms, antivirals don't always work.
—Blue Flu interview, major medical association

Sobs. I heard sobs, the kind where someone's chest breaks open with each cry. A girl, distraught.

Then a male voice. "Shh. She'll be all right. Let her rest."

Jay. There was something I wanted to say to him. If only I could remember, if only the pounding in my head would go away so I could think.

Time passed.

Minutes, hours, days—I wasn't sure. Cool water trickled down my temple but my arms wouldn't budge. I was too weary to wipe the drops away.

"Am I doing it right?" the girl asked.

I recognized the voice now: Cam.

"You're doing it fine," Jay said.

"I wanna help, too," I heard Ty say.

"Hold her hand. Tell her she's going to make it."

Jay's voice cracked. Cracked into darkness.

They visited me between the stabbing agony—the razors in my stomach. Why were razors shredding my insides? I needed the hurting to stop, but no matter how I twisted and turned, the pain moved too, a permanent part of me. A distant voice moaned in misery. I realized it was my own.

The line between sleep and consciousness blurred, like a smoke ring fading in the air. Then someone leaned on top of me, making it hard to breathe.

Mr. B.

His face, blue with cyanosis, hovered close to mine. My arms flailed, my legs kicked, but I couldn't move his weight off me. Then his skin dissolved until only his skull remained. I could peer into the holes where his eyes used to be. He grinned, skeleton teeth inches from my face. My screams stopped only when the coughing took over, wracking my body.

A woman spoke. "It's the fever. I'll stay with her."

I tried to lift my head but couldn't. The razors inside multiplied.

Someone gently fixed the pillows beneath me. "Rest, sweetie. Try to rest. The pain will pass soon."

But it didn't. The torture continued, on and on, and it wouldn't stop until I died. Dad's face floated through my mind, then Mom's too. Was she dead, like Dad? I missed Dad so much. I wanted to see him, to have one more conversation. Would we be together again in death? Someplace filled with light. And Megs would be there, ready to welcome me.

Then Megs glimmered before me in a strapless silver dress. She teetered in high heels, laughing. "Maybe the stilettos are too much?" She wobbled by the edge of the bed. "It's time to get ready for the Spring Formal. They've hired the most amazing DJ and the school is decorated with fresh flowers. Mr. Fryman says, 'April showers bring May flowers.'"

"Really?" I tried to imagine our gym as a garden but it made my head ache.

"You're not wearing black, are you? It's so morbid. Like death."

"Megs—"

She twirled, the silver sparkling as it flared at her knees. "Spin with me!"

I tried to move, but my dress constricted my center until it was excruciatingly tight. Megs glided away but I couldn't catch her. I tried to call out to her but my voice stayed trapped in my throat. Then she was gone and the pain throbbed in time with my breathing. If I stopped breathing would the pain finally end?

Mrs. Hernandez's voice drifted in from the other room. "There hasn't been any improvement," she said. "I don't want to alarm you, but you should hurry."

Improve. Alarm. Hurry. I understood the words individually, but couldn't combine them to make sense. I turned them over and over. *Hurry. Alarm.* It was like another language, like the tiny bits of space between my suffering.

Then her voice came closer. "Hold on, Lil."

That I understood. But the only thing holding on was the internal agony. It had snaked into me with its poisonous fangs and refused to let go.

Somewhere in the house, Cam sang "Ring Around the Rosy." Her voice, sweet and gentle, faded until I finished the rhyme on my own.

Ashes, ashes, we all fall down.

I slid into the weariness, my eyes closing against my will.

CHAPTER 30

Throughout this pandemic, there have been numerous reports of random acts of kindness. Even widespread disease can't dampen the American spirit.
—Blue Flu interview, television newscaster

I woke up, alone. Someone had left a big plastic cup filled with liquid and a pink straw on my nightstand. I tried to reach it. Moving my arms was harder than I expected. I tried again, lifted the cup, brought the straw to my mouth. Victory.

The water soothed my ravaged throat. *Best. Water. Ever.*

Noises came from outside my room. A cabinet door opened. Pans clanked. Little feet climbed the stairs.

"Lil! You're awake!" Cam said.

Then silky hair on my face, the smell of strawberry soap. More footsteps pounded. Jay, Ty, and Mrs. Hernandez soon surrounded my bed.

Ty peered at me. "Is she better now? She seems better."

"I think she's through the worst of it." Mrs. Hernandez's hand was cool on my forehead. "She doesn't feel feverish."

Jay's expression was grim. "Are you sure?" he asked. "She's still so pale."

"I can hear you," I said. "I'm right here."

He broke into a big smile.

His aunt nudged the kids out the door. "Let's heat some soup. Would you like some broth, Lil?"

I nodded.

"I get to use the can opener." Cam skipped out of the room.

Jay sat gingerly on the edge of the bed. He obviously wanted to talk, but all I could think about was using the bathroom.

"Be right back." I tried to stand, but my legs felt like cooked spaghetti. He held my elbow until I stopped swaying.

In the bathroom, I gasped at my reflection: greasy hair, raccoon eyes, and a gaunt face, as if I were going to a costume party dressed as a ghoul. Leaning against the sink for support, I brushed my teeth and wiped away the leftover mascara flakes. Putting my hair in a ponytail required too much energy so I left it tangled and hanging loose.

Jay tucked the sheet around me after I climbed back into bed. His hands on my waist felt familiar. Had our kiss been a hallucination or real? Tentatively, I put my hand on his cheek, and he brought it to his mouth, kissed my palm.

Definitely not a hallucination.

"You were holding me and then . . ."

"The flu," he said. "You had us all worried."

"How long have I been sick?"

He counted the days off on my fingers. "Five days. It's Monday."

"But . . . how can that be?"

"You've had a rough time. The flu made you much sicker than we were."

I shook my head. "That doesn't make sense."

"What's important is that you're getting better."

"I'm not sure I feel that much better."

"Maybe some good news will help," he said. "Your mom's on her way home."

"What?" I tried to sit up too fast and nearly toppled over. "She is? How do you know?"

"She called after she got a flight into St. Louis and rented a car. She's driving to New Jersey. She should be here by dinnertime tomorrow."

"Is she healthy?"

He repositioned the pillow behind my back. "Yes. My aunt spoke to her."

Mrs. Hernandez bustled into the room and placed a tray on my lap. "This will do you good."

I lacked coordination, but managed to get some broth into my mouth. Jay looked away politely while I wiped the misses from my face. Mrs. Hernandez busied herself by straightening the covers and opening the curtains. The bright sunlight made me squint.

"You talked to my mom?" I asked her between spoonfuls.

"Yes, for a long time. She can't wait to see you."

"Did you tell her about . . . about Dad?" I dreaded being the one to break the news.

"I told her, honey."

Cam sauntered in. "Lil's eating! She's eating soup!" She wiggled her butt and stomped her feet. "This is my happy soup dance. Soon you'll do the dance, too! I'll teach it to you."

"That would be fun." I tried to smile but even my face felt weary.

After the soup, I desperately wanted to wash up. But no matter how many times I tried to stand, I couldn't control my wobbly legs for long. A shower would be impossible without asking for help.

"You should take a bubble bath instead," Cam suggested.

"That's a good idea," I said.

Once I managed to get into the tub, I scooted under the faucet and let the water run over my stringy hair. I stayed in the water until my fingertips were as wrinkled as Mrs. Templeton's face.

It took forever to get black yoga pants and Jay's

blue "Chef" sweatshirt on, because I had to balance myself with one hand while maneuvering the clothes with another. The whole experience wore me out.

Jay came to check on me when I finished.

"Is it possible for me to be exhausted from getting dressed?" I asked, climbing back into bed.

"You'll get stronger each day."

"I hope so. Tell me what's new with the world. Have they created a vaccine yet?"

"Sadly, no. But they lifted the Boil Water Advisory. And the county finally formed an official disaster relief team that's working with the Red Cross. They're offering supplies to people who need them and checking houses for survivors and those in need. I passed along the info to them about what we've done."

"That's good news," I said, snuggling under the quilt.

"They were so impressed that I took a risk and mentioned the school break-in as the source of our supplies."

"Really? Are we in trouble?"

"Since we used the food to help people, we're in the clear with the police and the school. They repaired the door and explained the circumstances to Mr. Fryman. He said, 'Desperate times call for desperate measures.'"

"You made that up."

Jay put his hand on his heart. "I swear."

"Well, that's a relief." I stifled a yawn.

"Get some rest," he said.

"Will you stay with me a little longer? I had some really bad dreams while I was sick."

He kissed me softly on the forehead. "Sure."

With Jay by my side, I soon fell into a soothing sleep.

⌒

I woke up thinking about my phone. It was six in the morning and the rest of the house was quiet. Standing up slowly, I found it on my desk, then took it into bed.

There was no word from Mom, but Kayla had texted:

> Kayla: Feeling good. How r u? Hope 2 c u soon.

I wrote her back, telling her about being sick but that I was getting better. If we could become friends again, maybe all kinds of things were possible.

After hobbling to the bathroom, I got dressed and ready for the day. Going downstairs would be nice, but my legs still couldn't handle it. A few rounds of solitaire on my phone helped pass the time. Recuperating was incredibly dull. By the time Jay brought in breakfast, I practically pounced on him.

"You definitely seem better," he said.

"My body feels weak, but my brain is bored beyond belief."

"Would it help to have visitors?"

"Yes!" I tried to think of who might come over. Kayla? Elsa? Ethan?

"This woman, Mrs. Tempertown—"

"Templeton? She's the crabbiest old lady in the world."

"She's been in touch with my aunt a few times. I guess Reggie mentioned it to her after I told him about your dad dying and you getting sick. She asked if she could visit you. Only if you're up to it, of course."

"Anything to break the monotony."

After another nap, Jay, Ty, and Cam brought me a picnic lunch in bed and they all piled on and ate with me. Ty had taught Cam how to play his video game and although she was still twenty levels behind him, they were having fun.

"It would be better if you could watch us," Ty said.

I got out of bed and teetered to the stairs.

"Do you need help?" Jay asked.

I shook my head. My legs wouldn't make it to the family room. The only way was to slide down the stairs on my butt like when I was little. Peals of laughter followed me all the way down.

"Glad you can have fun at my expense," I said, looking up at them and smiling.

"I want to do that, too!" Cam said, sliding along.

I sat on the couch, watching Ty and Cam play video games until Mrs. Templeton arrived.

"Hello, Lilianna. You look awful."

She didn't hug me. Somehow it was nice knowing some things had remained completely unchanged by the pandemic.

"Thanks for visiting."

She sat across from me at the kitchen table with a large tote bag by her legs.

"How's the Senior Center?" I asked.

"Fine," she said. "Very few people have become ill. And I passed your supplies along. Half went to the Police Department and half to the Health Department."

"Thanks for helping with that."

"I'm sorry to hear about your father's passing."

"Thank you." Tears welled, but I blinked them back.

She reached into her bag, took out a small gray box, and placed it on the table between us. "One of the things I've learned in my life is the importance of closure, especially in traumatic times like these. So I thought the wisest thing to do was to retrieve your father's ashes for you."

I gasped. "How did you—"

"I have some connections in Delaware," she said. "Here are his personal belongings, too." She put another box on the table. "And your father left some papers as well."

She handed me a pile of manila folders grouped together by several large rubber bands. They were neatly labeled in his handwriting with titles like "History," "Personal," and "Interviews."

"Thank you. This is an unbelievable gift."

I held the box of ashes for a moment, then placed it carefully on the table. He wasn't in that box. He was in his notes, his articles, his words. That was what I needed most, to hear my father one last time.

I clutched the folders to my chest and cried.

CHAPTER 31

Keith Snyder, final interview: "It is with great sadness that I realize my chronicle of the Blue Flu must end. I had wanted to survive this illness, but with each passing hour hope fades. To my darling wife: know that our marriage was my greatest source of joy. To my dear daughter, this is what I wish for you: love, happiness, and the resiliency to survive these difficult times. You'll need a tender heart and a tough soul, but you will heal."

That night, I closed my bedroom door and hunched over my desk with Dad's folders. I read every single word of his interviews through my tears. By the time I reached his last note to me, my sobs became uncontrollable. But it was what I needed. Closure. A final, loving good-bye.

I read them all again the next morning. I had just finished when the house rumbled. It took me a minute to recognize that the unfamiliar sound was the garage door opening.

Mom was home!

As I wobbled downstairs toward the front door,

Mom burst in and embraced me. Everything was in that hug. Desperation, grief, and love.

"Thank God you're better," she said. "When I called and Mrs. Hernandez told me how sick you were . . ."

"I thought you'd never get here."

"We have so much catching up to do," she said.

I stumbled a bit, so she helped me up the stairs and tucked me in bed. Then she sat by my side, holding my hand. We cried over Dad together, sharing bits of our last conversations with him. I told her about Mrs. Templeton and Dad's ashes. I had moved them to my dresser and she picked the box up, cradling it in her arms.

"You should decide where to put them," I told her.

She nodded, tearful.

"She brought back his wallet, too, and some work papers. He wrote something to us." I handed her the folded paper I'd already memorized.

"I'll read this later."

I nodded. "Would you mind if . . . could I hold onto the rest of his notes for awhile?"

"Of course, honey."

After more tears, we filled each other in on the past weeks. I told her about the looters and she described living at the airport.

"It took forever to get a flight from Hong Kong

to London," she explained. "Then I caught the first flight I could to the US. I didn't care what city it was, as long as I got back. So I ended up in St. Louis."

"You didn't get sick?"

She shook her head.

"When you stopped calling—"

"The battery died and somewhere along the way, my charger disappeared. Stolen, I think. It's a crazy world. I never want to eat vending machine food again. After taking the max out of a working ATM, I paid extra for whatever I needed, like the rental car."

"You bribed people?"

"I prefer to think of it as a pandemic premium. It was worth it to get home. It took so long. I'm glad you weren't alone this whole time."

After Mrs. Hernandez came home from work, the six of us squished around the table for dinner. Jay created a meal from rice, beans, dried spices, and canned tomatoes. He called it "pantry cuisine." It smelled tasty but I stuck with canned noodle soup.

Cam and Ty seemed to be on extra good behavior for Mom. Without their chatter, the dinner conversation lagged a bit. Mom's business trip had become irrelevant, there was no school day to discuss, and not much to talk about in general. Finally, we began to speculate about when Portico might return to normal.

"The incoming cases at the hospital have leveled off," Mrs. Hernandez said. "But the beds are still pretty full."

"The flu is picking up steam in other areas of the world," Mom said. "I listened to the news for hours on the ride here."

Mrs. Hernandez nodded. "They've been discussing possible patterns at the hospital, too. And the threat of a second wave. I'm working again tonight, but tomorrow we'll finish cleaning our house so we can move back home."

"I want to stay here," Ty said. When Jay caught my eye, I knew he agreed.

"There's no hurry to leave," Mom said. "It's probably better for the kids if we stay together."

Cam pushed her food around on her plate. I could guess she was thinking that she had nowhere else to go. But I had no intention of abandoning her.

After dinner, Jay taught Ty and Cam to play War with cards while Mom and I talked in the kitchen.

"Cam doesn't have anyone else to care for her," I whispered. "Mrs. Schiffer died and we haven't been able to track down a father. I think . . . I think she has to stay with us."

"It's not that simple," Mom said. "We should contact her family first. There's an uncle I can call."

"Dead. Jay already tried to reach him."

"Look, we can't take her in permanently. We've

had such a disturbing year. I'm not sure adding another member to our family, even temporarily, would be best for you."

My shoulders set in their old defensive posture. Could Mom and I be fighting already? I had missed her so much but within a few hours of being back, she was already questioning my ability to cope.

"I'm emotionally stronger than when you left, Mom." I tried to keep my voice even. "I've thought this through. It makes sense for us to take care of her. The world has changed. I'm pretty sure we can decide what's best for now. Cam needs us. Can you imagine how many kids will be in foster care? She'd end up with strangers. At least we can offer her a safe home with people she trusts."

"But legally—"

"With all the deaths and wills and backlog of lawyer crap, I'm sure Cam will be in high school before they even realize she's an orphan. If she's happy here, she should live with us."

Mom sighed. "OK," she agreed. "She can stay for now. But don't complain when she touches your stuff."

I squeezed Mom tight.

"We need to paint the guest room pink," I said. "It's her favorite color."

"I have some rose-colored throw pillows in the attic she can have."

"Cam would like that."

"Like what?" she said, popping into the kitchen.

"We thought you'd like pink pillows. Mom said the guest room can be your new room when Ty and Jay move home. You can stay with us, and I'll be your big sister."

"Oh," she said, pouting in front of the refrigerator.

Uh oh. "I know you're sad—"

"I miss my own mom."

I braced myself for her tears. Was this the wrong solution after all? I could already hear Mom's I-told-you-so. But Cam took a juice box from the fridge and seemed to pull herself together.

"Besides," she said, "why do you get to be the big sister? I know I'm smaller, but I'm extremely mature for my age."

"Yes," Mom said. "You certainly are."

"Maybe we can just be sisters then," she said, "with no big or little. Equal sisters."

"OK." I poked the straw into the juice box for her.

"Good," she said. "But I'll have to make up a new dance for that. Maybe Ty will help." She grabbed her drink and scurried out of the room.

"He's going to love that," I said.

⌣

At dusk, Jay and I sat on a bench in the back-yard, enjoying the quiet.

"I read through all my dad's papers," I final-ly said. "It was like hearing his voice in my head again. He wrote me a note, saying good-bye. It helped somehow. And he documented his time in Delaware, with history and interviews woven in. He knew toward the end that . . . his time was lim-ited. So he compiled everything, like a final article. I want to try to get it published for him."

"I bet he would like that."

I nodded.

"Speaking of fathers, while you were sick, I called mine," Jay said. "He was surprised to hear from me. It's the first time we've spoken since . . . well, in a long time. It wasn't as awkward as I ex-pected. It was the right thing to do, reaching out to him."

"He must've been happy to hear from you."

"He was."

"So. . . ." I said.

"Yeah?"

"We don't need to talk about Mr. B anymore, right?"

"Not unless you want to."

"I don't. Not in the near future, anyway."

"It's your choice." Jay tilted my chin with his hand. "No more secrets, right?"

"Agreed," I whispered.

Kissing Jay the second time was even better. He clutched me against him as if we needed to make up for lost time. Maybe we did.

We stayed outside for hours. I curled against him, watching daylight fade into night. A few stars twinkled like distant promises.

"I'd like to take you on a real date," he said. "Maybe dinner and a movie? A funny comedy."

"That would be nice. You can walk me home from school, too, if we ever go back."

"There was an email from Mr. Fryman today," Jay said. "They want to do a virtual roll call, see which students and teachers will return when the school reopens."

"Really?"

"Yes. He said he's been 'sick as a dog,' and 'only time will tell' how we'll make up the schoolwork. 'Rome wasn't built in a day,' you know."

I held my stomach, laughing. "It hurts. The clichés hurt."

"He also mentioned that this weekend would have been the Spring Formal. The school is going to replace it with a Survivor's Ball sometime in the future. Instead of a dance, it will be kind of a group memorial."

I tried to imagine it. "The concept's a little morbid, don't you think?"

"Not if we can pay our respects to the dead. It's a way to say good-bye, right?"

"True," I said. "I guess that's better than expecting us to act as if none of this ever happened."

"Fryman said there would be grief specialists on hand to counsel us at the event, too."

"It really will be a Survivor's Ball."

"Well, I'm a survivor. So are you." He rested his arm gently around my shoulder, where it belonged.

"Yes," I said. "Yes, I am."

RESOURCES

To get help for a victim of sexual assault:

- Rape, Abuse & Incest National Network (RAINN). National Sexual Assault Hotline: 800-656-HOPE (free, confidential advice 24/7). Help online at www.rainn.org/get-help/national-sexual-assault-online-hotline (secure and anonymous through an instant-messaging format).

- A list of links for international organizations is available through the RAINN website at www.rainn.org/get-help/sexual-assault-and-rape-international-resources.

- The National Center for Victims of Crime. Helpline: 1-800-FYI-CALL or 1-800-211-7996. Website: www.victimsofcrime.org. Help finding local assistance online at http://victimsofcrime.org/help-for-crime-victims/find-local-assistance---connect-directory.

- National Sexual Violence Resource Center. Phone: 877-739-3895 (TTY Hotline: 717-909-0715). Website: www.nsvrc.org. Does not provide crisis counseling but can provide referrals.

- The Office for Victims of Crime (US Department of Justice) provides a list of national toll-free numbers for various organizations that may be of help (http://www.ojp.usdoj.gov/ovc/help/tollfree.html) and an online database of local organizations (http://ovc.ncjrs.gov/findvictim-services).

To learn more about preparing for emergencies:

In the United States:

- Information about making a plan, creating an emergency kit, and knowing the facts from the Department of Homeland Security (DHS) and the Federal Emergency Management Agency (FEMA). www.ready.gov/kids/make-a-plan.

- Frequently asked questions and preparedness information from the American Red Cross and the Centers for Disease Control and Prevention (CDC). www.bt.cdc.gov/preparedness.

- Flu-specific information about seasonal influenza, pandemic awareness, and emergency preparedness. www.flu.gov.

- Planning for pet care in a disaster. www.humanesociety.org/issues/animal_rescue/tips/pets-disaster.html and www.aspca.org/petcare/disaster-preparedness.

- At the state and county level: Various states may provide information from their Department of Health. For example, New Jersey offers information about Emergency Preparedness at www.nj.gov/health/er/index.shtml. Morris County's Office of Emergency Management website is www.morrisoem.org. To find other states and counties, search on the state or county name along with phrases like "emergency preparedness" or "office of emergency management."

In Canada:

- Canadian Red Cross. www.redcross.ca/what-we-do/emergencies-and-disasters-in-canada/for-home-and-family/get-a-kit. Get Prepared, Government of Canada: www.getprepared.gc.ca/index-eng.aspx.

In the United Kingdom:

- British Red Cross. www.redcross.org.uk/What-we-do/Preparing-for-disasters/How-to-pre-pare-for-emergencies.

In Australia:

- Australian Emergency Management Knowledge Hub. www.emknowledge.gov.au.

In New Zealand:

- New Zealand Ministry of Civil Defence & Emergency Management. www.civildefence.govt.nz.

ACKNOWLEDGMENTS

The first thank you goes to my brother, Kenneth Hein. One childhood vacation as he suffered inside with a horrible sunburn, he eagerly listened to me summarize my favorite novel chapter by chapter. His love of a good story reinforced the desire to create my own. He's been a great source of advice and wisdom on my journey to publication.

Thank you to Sky Pony Press and especially Julie Matysik who took great care to edit my manuscript in a thorough and kind way. She's what every debut author dreams about in an editor.

Special thanks to my critique group, C. Lee McKenzie, Melissa Higgins, Heather Strum, and in memory of LK Madigan, who is missed so often and so much. I'm also grateful to Wendy Whittingham and Janine Camm, two of my first and longest critique partners. Thanks to Sharon Sorokin James for offering helpful plot advice on an early version of the story and to Susan Brody for her moral support.

I've shared lunch (and laughter) many times with Natalie Zaman and Charlotte Bennardo. Natalie has been incredibly supportive during times of uncertainty. And I finally get to sign books next to Charlotte, who's been encouraging me for years. Their friendship may have saved me from changing careers once or twice.

To some of my oldest friends: Katie Orphanos listened to the hard parts. Sometimes that's the very best thing a friend can do. A big thank you to Catherine Brennan for decades of memories. And thanks to Joy Adams, for lending me Nancy Drews and for making me want to read as many books as she did.

Claudia Whiteley has served as an inspiration in Isshinryu Karate and beyond. The Chatham Karate Academy and Mendham Karate Academy dojos are filled with amazing people.

The Society of Children's Book Writers and Illustrators has offered wonderful chances to learn and improve. Kathy Temean, the former New Jersey Regional Advisor, helped provide the opportunities every writer needs.

Thanks to Rebecca Grose of SoCal Public Relations for helping to get the word out.

Thank you to Alex Palmer for helping to connect the industry dots at just the right time.

As I researched this book, Jennifer Bronsnick, Licensed Clinical Social Worker of Jennifer Bronsnick Counseling, offered insight into the psychology of traumatized teens. Dr. George Van Orden, Health

Officer/Environmental Specialist at the Township of Hanover Health Department, spoke to me about pandemics and possible public health responses. They were both incredibly helpful in these matters.

Thank you to Marcy Posner for her early support.

In the in-law lottery, I hit the jackpot. I'm grateful to Rachele and Julio Ventresca for their love and support. "It doesn't hurt to ask" has served me well. Thank you to Doreen, John, and Julianna Sullivan for their encouragement. Thanks to JC Sullivan for always being willing to talk books with me, and to Ryan Sullivan, who loves a good disaster story as much as I do.

A loving thanks to Liza Hein (a kindred creative spirit), William Hein (hugs!), and Amanda Hein (love you lots!).

My parents, Peter and Shirley Hein, have been proud of all of my writing, even my really bad poems in seventh grade. My dear mom is the best free proofreader ever. I'm thankful for many things they've done for me, but most of all, for raising me in such a loving environment and for showing me the power of persistence.

The best comes last: my children, Lauren and David, have listened to me talk about writing every step of the way. I appreciate the spinning hugs (Lauren) and the funny jokes (David). Thank you both for the tremendous joy you've given me.

Sometimes even a writer doesn't have enough words, so I'm grateful to my husband, Chris, for *everything,* and especially for believing this was possible from the beginning.

ABOUT THE AUTHOR

Before becoming a children's author, Yvonne Ventresca wrote computer programs and taught others how to use technology. Now she happily spends her days creating stories instead of computer code. In addition to *Pandemic*, Yvonne has written two nonfiction books for kids: *Avril Lavigne* (a biography of the singer) and *Publishing* (about careers in the field). When she's not working or worrying about deadly disasters, Yvonne spends time learning Isshinryu Karate and recently earned the rank of second degree black belt. She lives in New Jersey with her husband, two children, and two dogs. For more information, visit www.YvonneVentresca.com.